THE COMPLETE CASES OF THE
ACME INDEMNITY OP, VOLUME 2

THE COMPLETE CASES OF THE

ACME INDEMNITY OP ™

VOLUME 2

BY JOHN LAWRENCE
WRITING AS

JAN DANA

ILLUSTRATIONS BY

JOHN FLEMING GOULD

POPULAR PUBLICATIONS • 2024

TABLE OF CONTENTS

MOVABLE ALIBI

WHEN THE LITTLE RED-
HEAD PLAYING THE WHEEL
ACROSS FROM ME RAKED IN
THE DOUBLE SAWBUCK ON
WHICH MY FAVORITE STOOLIE
HAD WRITTEN HIS MURDER
MESSAGE, I KNEW I HAD TO GET
IT BACK—OR ELSE. I NEVER
GUESSED THAT GREENBACK
WOULD LEAD ME INTO THREE
MURDERS, THOUGH, OR THAT
THE PREACHER'S NIECE
WHO'D WON MY BILL WAS
THE MOVABLE ALIBI FOR THE
CAGIEST SHREWDSTER IN THE
TOMBS—AND THE WEAK LINK
IN DAISY CHAIN'S SWINDLE
SET-UP, INSTEAD OF THE
STRONGEST.

CHAPTER ONE
DEATH ON A DOUBLE
SAWBUCK

IT WAS a man's death warrant—beyond all argument. A death warrant for as decent a little Frenchman as ever kept his ears open while working on a dice table. If you want to call him a stoolpigeon, it's all right with me. The point is, he had slipped me this little item half an hour earlier. I should have—and would have sworn that I had—tucked it in some pocket away from the rest of my money. Instead, by a disastrous miracle, it had somehow slipped in among my other bills. My first inkling of this was when it floated out of my hand, down the blazing, green roulette table, to cover a bet at the opposite end of the board. My hair stood on end.

It was only a twenty-dollar bill, but scribbled on its face, in green ink, was a message. As nearly as I could recall, from my hasty glimpse in the lavatory where I'd gone after the Frenchman had slipped it to me, it had read—*Try Big Joe on H. emeralds. Maybe mobbed up with Harry P. and the Biscuit. Rooms somewhere on Bowery. Fence named Ike.* And it had been signed *Andre.*

It was absolutely damning to the little Frenchman if it reached the eyes of even one of the hundreds of New York grifters who could spot its significance at a glance. It concerned a little matter on which Acme Insurance had me working and the thugs mentioned were big-time. If word of the message reached one of them, the best Andre could expect was to have his bullet-riddled little body dumped in a Jersey marsh within twenty-four hours. I had betrayed him—if ever a man was betrayed.

I almost went fuzzy with panic. I simply had to get that bill back and the wheel was spinning busily, already. I tried to throw a hex on my bet—to *make* it win.

It didn't.

I won't say I wasn't sweating a little as I saw the croupier's rake sweep it in, saw it piled in the little stack against the cushion. I threw a sidelong glance down toward the far end of the jam-packed, vast red-crystal-and-gold gambling salon, and caught a glimpse of the back of the little Frenchman's neck through the crowd as he functioned placidly at his dice table.

Then I cut out all thoughts except that I absolutely *had* to win that bill back.

MY EYES should have bored a hole through the croupier's stack of twenties, the way I concentrated on it. I played, but don't ask me what, continually watching that pile, waiting till my double sawbuck should again come to the top. In the back of my mind I was reviling myself, damning the carelessness that had let me mix the contents of my pockets. What I should have done was leave the joint immediately after I had collected the bill at the Frenchman's table.

As a matter of fact, I would have been long gone, the bill a charred little heap in some gutter, if it were not for a certain headquarters detective whom ill luck had placed on the premises. I've known some shady cops in my time, but this Herman Cullen was dynamite. A lieutenant, with powerful political pull, he was almost openly crooked. He looked like the old cartoon character of Foxy Grandpa—little mild blue eyes behind half-spectacles, powdery tufts of orange hair, beaming, carefully tailored. But I wouldn't have put it past him to cut a man's throat with his own

I pounded the bulbs to pieces as the clock chimed twelve.

hands—if there was enough cold cash involved. He had been practically at my elbow at the moment the Frenchman had tossed me the bill and, whereas I did not actually think he had seen us, nevertheless I was afraid to mark the incident by breaking away too quickly. If there could be degrees in disaster, Cullen's knowing that the Frenchman did a little work for me had as dire possibilities as any that might accrue from the thieves on whom he had squealed. Hence my idling around from dice table to chuck-a-luck, from chuck-a-luck to roulette—and so to this ultimate, ghastly blunder.

Up till this minute, I had not even been conscious of the little girl opposite me. I was not seeing her, or anybody else, during the time my bill slowly rose to the top of the croupier's stack. And as the bill neared the payoff position, I was all but holding my breath.

When I estimated my twenty to be about four or five from the top, I dared not wait any longer. As the croupier's drone called for bets, I laid out every bill I had, covering the table in all directions. I could not help but win a sizable number of the bets and with even a touch of luck, my all-important twenty would rain down on one of my wins. Damn it, it *had* to....

But it didn't.

The wheel spun merrily, came to rest. The sing-song of the croupier falsettoed off the winning combinations, His nimble thin fingers cascaded out bills, came to mine and— tossed it carelessly down on a bet just across from me.

Some of my now-growing nervousness must have been in my eyes as I watched a dainty little white hand come down on the bill and pull it in. I jerked up to her face to see what she looked like—and let go the breath I had been holding.

SHE WAS a dainty little girl, in a short black caracul coat and a pert little black pancake hat. Her face was like milk, with tiny, wistful features framed by dark auburn curls, her eyes granite-blue, long-lashed, starry. Her coat was thrown back to show a dress of dark blue silk that stretched across her tight, round breasts and neat little waist. She had the flawless, fresh skin that said she was young, but there was a relaxed charm about her that made me think of her as capable—I don't know why. There were little spots of excitement in her velvety cheeks.

I finally got my eyes down again to her money—she had quite a little stack of bills before her—and considered this new complication to my alarming problem. I had to wait now till she lost my bill, wait while it traveled again through the croupier's stack, pray once again for the twenty to come my way on a win.

It began to look damned serious.

And even while I watched her fingers—watched without realizing what her riffling the corners of her bills actually signified—it got more serious. The fingers suddenly gathered the bills together—and vanished.

I looked up, startled, just in time to see her slip back into the crowd, be instantly swallowed by people waiting to take her place. Then I realized she had been counting her money preparatory to leaving.

I grabbed up my funds and slid away from my side of the table. People were packed almost solid behind me and I had to squirm and wriggle to get through into the less crowded outer fringes.

I got through—and came face to face with the little headquarters conniver, Lieutenant Cullen. He showed up, directly in my path, and his mild blue eyes beamed as he planted himself to block me.

"Ah, Acme. Back in town, I see."

"Some other time, Lieutenant," I said. "I'm late for a date."

He turned and fell in beside me promptly. "Wasn't there some little discussion last time I saw you—about how it would be best if you had your company keep you operating out of New York?" he asked blandly.

I stopped and faced him. "I wouldn't remember," I told him. "Was there anything else you wanted?"

"No, no." Deep in each of his eyes there was a little pinpoint of red. "No—just that. We—ah—sometimes don't like the way you operate, you know."

"All right. I'll bear it in mind. Is that all?"

He said it was, and I broke away from him, cursing in ten languages. I fought my way to the exit, far down at the other end of the noisy roiling room, bought back my hat and coat and got to the door.

I asked the three-hundred-pound guardian of the ornate portal: "A little red-haired girl in a short black coat and pancake hat—blue dress—looked like you could eat her with a spoon. She didn't...."

"Just went out, pally—a minute ago."

I sweated as the elevator dropped me to ground level, hurried out onto the dark little side street and braced the lookout in the adjoining doorway. He pointed a skinny finger down the street.

"She flagged that hack—the one with the cockeyed tail-light—there—about half a block down. See it?"

I trotted the thirty yards to where my convertible was parked, kicked it into motion and got away, just before the star-shaped, cherry-colored tail-light of the cab vanished around the corner two blocks east.

IT WAS a short chase, but no merry one. I kept turning corners, just in time to see the hack ahead turn one, until we got over to Fifth. Then we made a long run south. I turned onto Fifth six blocks behind her, but by the time we got down around Fourteenth Street, I was ten behind. Her hacker was evidently under orders to hit it up and he seemed to be able to get through one traffic signal after another that snarled me up.

I was sweating in front of a red light when I saw them turn off on Eighth Street, and by the time I could slow my car down and turn in after them, the star-shaped tail-light had completely run away from me.

There was nothing to do but go shooting through the Village streets, crisscrossing and doubling around, in hopes of picking them up again. I did that for ten minutes without the slightest result, trying anxiously—and unsuccessfully—to convince myself that the girl was no crook, was not likely to know any crooks, and that my incriminating bill would probably pass into safe hands. At the end of ten minutes I gave up the chase and settled down to steady sweating. It was in my mind at least to warn the little Frenchman and give him a chance to duck out of town.

I swung around a final corner and almost ran into the rear of the cab with the star-shaped tail-light, parked in front of an all-night doughnut-and-coffee shop. The hacker was just pushing into the restaurant.

To my "Hey!" he strolled over, and for my five dollars told me: "I dunno exactly. First she says Sixty-A Jane Street, then when we get down here, she changes and jumps out at the corner of Jane and Eighth Avenue. I dropped her there."

I saw no moving thing on Jane Street as I drifted by the corner where it intersected Eighth. I parked my car just past the corner, hurried back and into Jane Street—a black little slot, lit by hissing blue street lamps. Tall, blank-faced, old-fashioned houses loomed on both sides as I walked along looking for Number 60-A.

It was four doors from the next corner on the other side—four stories of faded red brick. I could read the number from across the street. The corner arc lamp shone brilliantly on its high, parlor-floor-level stoop. I started across toward it—and stopped, with one foot in the gutter. The house had a vaguely dead look. Every shade in the place was drawn, dark. There was a sign on the door reading, For Sale, and giving the name of the broker handling it.

In consternation, I damned the cabby. He had undoubtedly given me the wrong number. I swung back the way I had come, with the desperate hope that I might catch him before he finished his coffee at the dirty-spoon and give his memory a jog, but the futility of that occurred to me before I had gone ten yards. I stopped, turned back—and there was a whine of metal from the areaway of the for-sale house. A door clanged shut faintly.

I stood staring, while a man emerged. He came up on the far side of the stoop from me—an old man, stooped, short, in black felt hat and long black topcoat. In the moment that he mounted to street level his face turned, first one way, then the other, as though surveying the street. The blue-white street lamp caught him full for an instant and I could see a mummy-like face with a long, tubular chin. He tucked the chin down, turned and stumped off silently around the corner.

I stood dopily, wondering if I ought to take after him and brace him about the girl—till it was too late. It didn't make sense anyway. Even through the fog of my own worry, it struck me that there was something funny about anyone coming from a house so obviously unoccupied. Then there was that click of metal again from the areaway and I realized that there was *still* someone inside—someone apparently watching the old man out of sight.

I STEPPED back into a doorway to consider and curse the luck that had suddenly made my twenty-dollar bill a really difficult problem. Maybe sleuthing for Acme for twelve years has colored my viewpoint a little, but—fantastic if you like—I suddenly smelled something off-color about the house opposite me. If the girl *had* gone in there—if she were doing business with hustlers, my bill might even now....

This was the first time I'd really considered the girl in a personal light. And I was prepared, the minute I did think of her dainty poise and her winsome, solemn face, to swear that she would not be doing business with crooks—at least, not willingly. I don't set myself up as any Galahad, but I suddenly had a growing curiosity in my mind about her—a wonder if anything sour was maybe happening to her. I found the possibility unpleasantly getting under my skin and had an abrupt, irrational urge to lend her a hand if she needed a hand. All this quite apart from the fact that her personal safety was vital to me, if I were to recover my twenty.

I considered walking boldly up and knocking on the front door—but not very seriously. For one thing, I was unarmed. My gun was in my car where I had left it before entering the gambling joint where a frisk always awaits the customers. For another, I couldn't figure anything to say to whomever might answer the door—if anyone did answer the door.

Intent on looking the house over from my little recess, I wasn't paying much attention to the street. I did not see where the girl came from—but she was suddenly there, almost at the foot of the steps of the gloomy-looking house across from me, running swiftly.

The rest of it happened so smoothly and with such speed that I could not have interfered then, even if I'd known how to begin.

In the moment that I saw her and came alert, she had reached the steps, was running up them. I opened my mouth, started out of my doorway, realizing that she, too, must have been concealed in just such a spot as mine until this very moment.

I stopped the "Miss!" I had ready to call, as the door at the top of the steps suddenly, silently opened to let a man slip out.

Spotlighted as he was by the blue-white glare of the street lamp, I recognized instantly his stock, gray-clad figure, his dark, shining, round-featured face, and little painted rosebud of a mouth. His name was Chain—known by his own choice as "Daisy"—a cold-blooded, ruthless, professional thief and killer, as deadly as a rattlesnake.

He was obviously taken aback at meeting the girl. He stopped stock-still as they came face to face on the stoop. So did the girl.

I was unconsciously moving toward them—then I wasn't. Daisy Chain's hand had suddenly dipped in and out of his pocket, and the street light caught a flash from metal. The little red-haired girl gasped, put the back of one hand to her mouth.

And in that instant the shots came—two of them—from the upper part of the house.

There was a man's thin scream—then a terrific crash, somewhere on the third or fourth story.

For an instant, both Chain and the girl were frozen, their heads snapped toward the still-open door at the top of the stoop. Then Chain suddenly whirled and started down the steps, pocketing his gun—while I stood like a gawk. But he didn't continue on down. As though something had suddenly occurred to him, he stopped halfway, swung back. The girl was stumbling backward down the steps, her hand still to her mouth.

In one quick motion, Chain again yanked the gun out of his pocket and jammed it into her back, sent her stumbling up the steps again.

She cried out, "Oh, don't…" and I was dopey enough— gun or no gun—to be hot-footing it across the street, by now.

Neither of them saw me. The girl, because she was being manhandled, and Chain because he was intent on hustling the girl back into the house as fast as he could. Then he had her in, was in himself, and the door closed softly, swiftly, long before I was even at the foot of the steps.

CHAPTER TWO
THE MAN WHO WANTED
TO BUM

I'**M DUMB,** but not dumb enough to go storming into locked houses where gunmen are shooting—unless I can do some shooting myself. I turned and ran down the street, back toward my car, keeping my neck cricked to hold the house in sight. No one had emerged by the time I reached the corner, and I was not out of sight around it more than a half-minute. Then I was hurrying back, a gun in one hand, a steel jimmy in the other.

I sprinted up the steps, yanked at the door. It did not budge and I could see it was not going to. I looked over the railing, slid a hip over the side and dropped to the areaway, landed ten feet down, on cement that did my heels and legs no good. One of my feet skidded and I saw that I had landed on a tiny black silk purse—the girl's, no doubt, lost in the scuffle. Even as I snatched it up to jam in my pocket I squeezed it hopefully, but it held no bulge such as the roll the girl had been carrying would have made.

I went to work on the iron-grille door of the areaway with the jimmy. The thing was a million years old, a simple mortise lock, but it had the strength of Gibraltar. It took me a good minute and a half before I wrenched the latch out of its moorings and ran into the basement hallway of the house.

At the foot of carpeted stairs, I stared up. There was not a whisper of sound above. I slid the safety off my gun as I ran up a flight. Musty smell rolled down in waves to meet me. I paused on the parlor floor. Nothing moved. Doors stood open along the hall and I got out my flash, threw a little light into each—a series of empty, dust-laden chambers. The same went for the second floor. Not till I reached the third did I catch the sharp stink of gunpowder.

I did not have to be psychic to suspect what had happened in this house, and so the dead man did not surprise me too much. He lay, a little man in black clothes, with white goatee and imperial, in the only furnished room in the place—an elaborate little office. He lay on maroon carpet, an overturned swivel chair beside him. He had been shot, high up in one cheek and the glaze in his eyes left no doubt that he was dead or dying—even if the two tiny blue-red holes in his antrum had not told the story. A cupboard and a wall safe in the room stood wide-open, both empty save for tracked-up dust. Of the girl or Daisy Chain, there was no sign. I ran downstairs to the rear of the cellar.

The back door stood open a crack. I ran out and into the back yard, found myself confronting a board fence. I went over it scrambling and was in the back yard of an apartment house. The dimly lit basement corridor of the apartment house stood open, three steps down, and I ran on along it.

When I came up, I was on another silent, blue-lit street. Not a thing stirred on this one either. Chain and the girl were gone—and my twenty-dollar bill.

Now I was in a mess. Although, queerly enough, the fact that Daisy Chain was who he was—a dangerous, big-money criminal—gave me respite, at least. The gunman was strictly a lone wolf—so strictly that even if he did read the damning message on my bill and understand it, he would not be bothered passing it on. In that respect, I had a little time in which to catch up to him. But somehow the bill didn't seem so important at this point. What did worry me was the dainty, frightened little red-head. What was she caught up in? What sort of a mess was this—and what part did Chain expect to make her play?

I had enough intuition, even then, to know that Daisy Chain would not be easy to get to. Not after this. If I were going to get a line on this thing, get some clue as to what he was planning to do with the girl, where he would be taking her, I'd have to try some other tack.

I WENT back to the house, the way I had come, with my ears open for the sound of a police siren. It was even money whether the two shots and the noise following were loud enough to cause a neighbor to send in an alarm. And, if an alarm had gone in, I had no wish to be caught up in the police investigation.

The police siren came all right—but before it came, I had covered the house. Not as leisurely as I would have liked, but adequately.

In the death room—the corner room on the third floor—black felt was tacked over the windows. A door in the rear wall was nailed shut. The one room constituted the whole apartment. There was nothing in closet, wall safe, or the drawers of the desk but dust. However, in the top drawer the dust showed where a very small pistol had lain for some time. I could not find the pistol.

The dead man wore white piping around his black vest, a bat-wing collar and a maroon tie. He looked a little pompous, rich, and frightened. There were bruises around his neck and two little veins of blood paralelled down his cheek from the two bullet holes. The holes were small enough to suggest that he had been shot with a small caliber pistol—possibly his own, the one that had lain in the drawer.

I had a feeling that his face was somehow familiar. That was no delusion.

Searching him, I found one paper in his pocket—a rent receipt, in advance, for the use of this room for six weeks. It had been made out—a month ago—to George Grantland Hessian.

He was, of course, the nationally famous swindler. At one time he had been known as the greatest stock promoter in the business, with a take of thousands a day. His specialty was the ferreting out of "literary" properties—that is, properties which, while utterly worthless, could, by clever phrasing, be made to sound on paper as though practically adjacent to rich and established oil fields. Having bought—or stolen—a long-term lease on the property, another glittering corporation would be formed with, if possible, some gullible citizen of outstanding integrity and reputation as a figurehead. From his Chicago, New York, and San Francisco offices, another gaudy prospectus would flood the sucker lists, via the mails. Success had made him incautious and he had plastered the mails with one too gaudy, giving the long-suffering postal inspectors their chance.

George Grantland Hessian became a federal number, with a long string of years in which to ponder. A hasty dig into my memory and a vague rule-of-thumb calculation made me conclude that he must just barely have gotten out—within a few weeks, at any rate. There was nothing to indicate who had shot him.

I had gone over the rest of the rooms in the house—all completely blank—and was in the basement, when the siren came. I had just recalled the black silk purse in my pocket and was in the act of opening it, when the shrill scream sent me scurrying out the areaway entrance, and back to my doorway across the street.

From there I watched the police circus descend.

I DID not care to make a light to see if I had anything in the purse—at least not till a crowd had formed to give me a little privacy. And the crowd simply did not form. I waited impatiently in my black doorway, while a few scattered curious drifted around, attracted by the car after car of police and officials, but at the end of fifteen minutes, there were actually as many newspaper reporters as idle spectators.

I was intently watching the obscure activity in the house opposite, hoping for some bit of information, some faint clue that would give me a bit of light on the whole business. Naturally, I kept my eyes on the door at the top of the stoop, but when it suddenly opened to let three men out abreast, I really thought I was having hallucinations.

The high stoop was a miniature stage, fully lighted by the corner street lamp. Of the three men, two were homicide detectives, of Lebaron's command. Light glinted on the handcuffs with which the two detectives held the third man between them. Photographers' light bulbs flared and cameras clicked, while I stared with my mouth open.

The third man was Daisy Chain, the red-lipped, dark-faced little gunman—the one man in the whole world whom I knew could not have fired the two shots that had killed George Grantland Hessian—could not, because he was squarely in my sight on the stoop opposite as the killing was done. Having stored the girl away somewhere, some vital business must have brought him back—brought him back only to be promptly collared by Lebaron and his men. It was fantastic.

But it was not one-tenth as fantastic as what occurred the next moment.

Lebaron—tall, green-eyed, bony-faced—suddenly appeared behind the three men, stepped around them and patted air for silence. When he got it, he said loudly: "Mr—uh—Chain wants to make a public statement—for the newspapers. He'll make it now and you boys can catch the early editions. You better get it down, because he *won't* see you once he gets downtown."

Daisy Chain's face was leaden, shining, his voice dull, flat, carefully enunciated as it came from his little painted-smile of a mouth.

He said: "I came here tonight because I had a tip that Hessian had big dough around. I got there at eleven o'clock exactly and hid in his closet. I had to wait for an hour and a half before he came in and opened the safe. I came out and held him up but the dough wasn't there. I tried to knock it out of him where it really was. He pulled a little gun on me and it went off and cooled him. Yeah, I know it's first degree—in commission of a felony. The cops caught me fair and square, coming back to look around when I thought nobody'd heard the shots. No, I got no lawyer. Let's go, Lieutenant."

I GOT to my car, sat there with my head buzzing. I had heard some wild monologues in my time, but never anything that ranked with this. There was no question of the cops having beaten it out of him. He was simply not the type. That statement had been a voluntary confession! I racked my brains to try and make sense of it. And it simply would not make sense.

I went over and over that scene in my mind's eye. The girl—barely at the top of the stoop. Daisy Chain facing her. The sharp, staccato sound of the shots. Chain starting to leave the scene—the natural urge for a crook with his record. His sudden decision to herd the girl hastily back inside and—it now became apparent—down and out the basement entrance to—where?

And now his voluntary return, his voluntarily confessing to murdering the recently released ex-convict oil-swindler. Why? What possible compulsion would make Chain literally put his head in the noose to shield the actual murderer? And why had he suddenly decided to abduct the girl? What had he done with her?

The impossible premise that he, Daisy Chain, was deliberately shouldering the crime to save someone else stuck in my mind. It seemed impossible—but what wasn't? And in that light, a possible reason suddenly popped up for his carrying the girl off. For she—as far as he knew—was the one person who could give him an alibi! She was the one person who could positively give the lie to his confession. She, alone, could smash his attempt to go to jail for a killing he hadn't done—and, for that matter, finally to the chair. This was getting beyond all reason. He had kidnaped the girl, put her out of the way, in order that she might not block his taking the rap for murder!

Who, then, was the actual killer? Was it someone with whom Daisy Chain was tied up? Was his gesture really one of self-sacrifice? Even as I formed the question, I knew it was not any such thing. Daisy Chain was a cold-blooded, heartless little crook, with ice in his veins. He was temperamentally incapable of doing an unselfish thing. Whatever wild reason was behind this move, it was sane, logical, and—profitable for Daisy Chain. That had to be so!

Then I remembered the old, stooped man with the tubular chin, who had stolen away from the house just prior to the shooting. Who was he? Where did he fit in this picture? Not the killer, certainly—any more than Chain—although, on second thought, he might conceivably have circled the block, come in the back way and....

Not any of this feverish speculation got me any nearer to the one question that really bothered me: Where was the girl?

Not till then did I open my hand and look down at the crumpled silk envelope. I threw a hasty look out the car window to make sure I was in no danger of being observed, quickly ripped open the purse.

There were two letters within.

One was yellowed with age, cracked here and there. I took it out of its envelope—addressed to a Mr. R. Robinson, Greensite, Texas—and had a communication in rusty ink, meticulous handwriting. It was on a letterhead reading: *O.E. Murray—Consulting Geologist.* The date line was Fanfield, Texas, thirteen years ago. The letter read—

Dear Mr. Robinson:

Your letter of inquiry regarding Tiger Flow Exploration Company received. I am able to state without reservation that I know every statement to be contained in the company's prospectus to be literally true. An investment in this company (which I myself, incidentally, am making, to the limit of my available funds) is as sound as government bonds. Their properties are definitely proved and await only the proper financing for drilling. I have myself examined their tracts and can positively state that there is oil-bearing mineral in every square yard of it. That the company makes much more modest claims in its literature, is due solely to the conservatism and modesty of its brilliant banker—and my esteemed friend—Mr. George Grant-land Hessian.

Yours very truly,

(signed) O.E. Murray, B.Sc.

The other letter, a freshly written, unstamped, unsealed one, was a note addressed to the Chalfonte Hospital, Houston, Texas, to the effect that the enclosed two hundred dollars were to apply against the bill of the Rev. Charles Hare, currently in their care, and was signed, *Respectfully, Dorinne Hare.*

There was no two hundred dollars in it, but it was enough to send me hot-footing it back to my hotel, where I got on the long-distance wire to Houston, where Acme Indemnity maintains an office of sizable proportions. I was lucky enough—after about an hour—to locate Jimmy Poore, an ace investigator out of that office, and get him to go to work.

CHAPTER THREE
MONEY MAN

THE REST of the night ran away from me—and a good deal of the morning—before I got everything that I could. In all, I got five calls from the West. Between times, I went to work on what stoolpigeons I could locate, dropping the word that I wanted any and all information regarding Daisy Chain. I did not get much encouragement.

By the time all the returns from Houston were in, it was noon—and I was deflated. I had information, yes, but not so much as one active lead in it.

The red-haired girl was the niece of one Charles Hare, I was informed, a retired clergyman of unknown denomination. Sixteen years ago he had become involved in an oil-stock swindle, engineered by George Grantland Hessian, had appeared as executive vice-president of the company. The whole thing had been exposed—in Fanfield, Texas—though no one had ever been brought to trial for it. There had been some mention of O.E. Murray in the complaints entered, as "a brilliant young geologist who had moved away from the state at about that time, following a scandal with a married woman!"

The Reverend Hare had been so stricken by the exposure that he had suffered a stroke. He was a bachelor, without close relatives, save a niece, Dorinne. Five years ago, this niece arrived in Houston from Chicago to take care of him. They lived in an obscure boarding-house where little was known of them. Recently, the old man had suffered a relapse and had had to be moved back to the hospital. Their former landlady was of the opinion that a telegram the old man received from New York had caused this relapse. The same landlady volunteered the information that, subsequent to the old man's removal to the hospital, Dorinne Hare had done a great deal of searching through old boxes of papers stored in the cellar, and had subsequently left for New York, though reserving quarters against her return.

It gave light, all right—of a sort. It cleared up the girl's motives. Her uncle, involved with Hessian sixteen years ago, had evidently retained certain papers. Hessian, coming out of prison, had needed one of them—probably the O.E. Murray letter—and had wired, demanding them, probably on threat of raking up the old disgrace. The girl had come to New York with the letter, had found herself short of funds for paying the old man's hospital bill, and had desperately tried to acquire some gambling. She had won—including my twenty-dollar bill—and in making delivery of the letter—or attempting to—had stumbled into the vicious little drama with Daisy Chain.

All of which left me knowing no more of them than I did before about where or what or how to do for the girl.

My stoolpigeons could only report that nobody seemed to have been aware that Daisy Chain was even in town.

The morning newspapers carried nothing that helped. Every sheet gave front-page prominence to Daisy Chain's amazing public confession from the stoop of the murder house. He was in the Tombs, charged with murder in the first, awaiting arraignment.

Futilely cursing the fact that the little gunman was out of my reach, was in the one place where I could not reach him for the purpose of squeezing answers out of him, I suddenly saw the really amazing thing that I had.

Daisy Chain had gone to unbelievable lengths—had connived, schemed, perjured, and even kidnaped, evidently—to get himself into the Tombs. It was apparently important to him that he be behind bars. Whatever the obscure reason, he wanted to be there—desperately.

And I could turn him out! I could come forward, establish his alibi, tell the D.A. exactly what I had seen, omitting, for this purpose, all mention of the girl—and Daisy Chain would be on the street in no time. That is, I could—if he refused to answer my questions!

I JUMPED for the telephone. If I had it right, this was probably a new high in fantastic situations. Daisy Chain had gone all the way—to get himself started for the chair. I stood in position to blackmail him with threats of proving him innocent. It was beyond all belief—and yet it was so.

I got Preeker, the long-nosed, unbelievably shrewd little head of Acme's investigation department—my boss—and gave him a long story, none of it true, ending up in a plea for him to get me permission from the D.A.'s office to visit Daisy Chain in the Tombs. He didn't believe a word of it, but after twelve years he is prone to indulge me now and then, and he grudgingly consented to try.

At that, it was four o'clock before the messenger came up with the pass from the D.A.'s office. I grabbed up my hat and my green morocco box—it contained my spare gun and, for the moment, the two letters and the girl's silk purse—and took it down and deposited it in the hotel safe. I wasn't taking any chances on the cops finding these just at the moment.

I went downtown in the subway, taxied to the Tombs, and took an elevator to the waiting-room.

The red-faced, blue-eyed Scotchman behind the desk shoved back his uniform cap and told me cheerfully: "I can't make him see you. He's refused everybody but his tongue."

"He'll see me," I comforted him. "Give him this."

I had the note already written out—*Talk to me or I'll blow the whole racket sky-high. I can do everything the girl could.*

The turnkey shaped his lips to a worried whistle. "Hey—I don't know—"

"It's all right. It's just a bluff to maybe scare a little information out of him."

"Well—" He shook his head, but waved one of the uniformed attendants over. "Take this in to Daisy Chain," he told him. "Gentleman waiting."

The attendant said: "His lawyer's in with him now. He ought to be through any minute." He turned and looked at the door at the other end of the musty room. It opened as he looked.

A tall, spare, distinguished-looking man of forty-odd strode out. He had shortcurling brown hair, a clipped brown mustache and straight eyebrows over cold blue eyes.

"There he is now," the attendant said.

"Chain's lawyer?" I asked the turnkey.

"Uh-huh. *Some* lawyer, too. Osborne, of Fairfield and Ritchie."

"*Wha-at?*" I gulped.

"Yep."

"The Wall Street…?"

"Yeah. Funny they'd take a criminal case, ain't it? Especially a hood like Daisy."

"Yeah. Listen—I just thought of something I'd forgotten. I'll have to come back later."

I skipped out while he was complaining.

I was struck dumb. The firm of Fairfield and Ritchie were Wall Street's oldest, most supremely exclusive. Their clients were all multi-millionaires. Here was money and no mistake. Fairfield and Ritchie did not represent Daisy Chain. As well expect the angel Gabriel to plead that thug's case. Who did they represent?

I missed Osborne at the elevator landing, rode down in a sort of daze. If I said I wasn't a little shaky in my knees at this unexpected turn, I'd be a liar. There are three things in New York that scare hell out of me. The first is money. The second is money—and so is the third. The cop—private or otherwise—who tries to buck heavy dough in this town might just as well go out and hit himself over the head with an axe. And if ever it looked like a person was bucking money, I was, here and now.

I looked round the lobby of the Criminal Courts building a little wildly, trying to catch sight of the tall, English-looking lawyer. I had evidently missed him but that was no great blow. I knew where Fairfield and Ritchie had their offices. I started out.

Osborne turned away from a cigar stand, lighting a cigar, and fell in directly in front of me.

I followed him, of course, while I tried to get rid of the daze in my think-machine. What client of this ultra-snobbish firm could be mixed up in all this? How could one of the tycoons whom Fairfield and Ritchie represented possibly be involved with Daisy Chain—with George Grantland Hessian? It didn't make sense.

I STUCK with Osborne down to the A Broad Street skyscraper. The bulletin board gave Fairchild and Ritchie's suite as the twenty-first floor. Naturally, I expected the lawyer to disembark at that level.

He didn't. Instead, as we were passing eighteen, he said crisply, "Nine," and got off at the nineteenth. Hastily I had to call for twenty, get off and hurry back down to the marble stairs at the end of the hall.

I ran down the flight, bent down from the last shadowed step. I was just in time to see the lawyer stop before a ground-glass-paneled door reading: *Private. Entrance 1904.*

A girl opened the door to his knock. His crisp, English voice inquired for, "Colonel Lamson."

A small, twinkling pair of men's feet, crossing the office just above my line of sight stopped, and came back and the owner appeared, urged the lawyer inside. The door closed.

I stared. The owner of the small feet was, I would swear, the stooped, elderly man with the long tubular chin whom I had seen doing a sneak from Hessian's house the night before—minutes ahead of the killing.

In business clothes, with his strange, yellow eyes visible, he did not look nearly so feeble as he had last night. Multi-millionaire or not, he was one tough little party, if my judgment was worth anything.

Ten long strides took me to the door numbered *1904*— the entrance to the suite that comprised the whole floor. Then I knew the worst. The legend on this door was: *C.J. Hollingsworth and Co., Private Bankers.* Down in one corner was, simply: *London, Liverpool, Paris, Berlin, Buenos Aires.*

I placed the "Colonel Damson" then. Thirty years ago, he had headed his own firm. Damson & Co. were—like most of our Wall Street demi-gods—at that time plain pirates, freebooters, highbinders. They were behind half the really big, ugly operations in railroads, mining, oil—anything you want to name. A Congressional investigation, a newspaper crusade, had finally put so much of an odor to the name Damson that he had thought it best to blend with the deaconish, butter-wouldn't-melt-in-their-mouth firm of Hollingsworh & Co. Their saintly reputation, legitimate enough, had been sufficient to smother Damson's questionable past. No doubt he had promised to reform—why shouldn't he, with all the money he or a dozen like him could ever need?—and the firm had wound up as one of the six largest, most conservative, private bankers on the Street. No breath of scandal had touched them in fifteen years.

I was up against money all right. But how? It was pure madness. How could a firm like Hollingsworth—even if one of the partners had a heart full of larceny—be tied in with plain crooks like Hessian and Daisy Chain? Whatever Damson's past, his present was as spotless as white linen. It had to be, for his firm to stand out as it did. One intimation in the Street that he was—in any way—doing business with such as Chain and Hessian, and Hollingsworth's prestige would melt like lard on a hot brick.

I even tried to think up some way I could hold that as a threat over Damson—that I would reveal how I had seen him stealing from the house on Jane Street, unless he did so and so—but I knew I would never have the brass to try it. He would squash me like a fly under his thumb if I got in his hair—at least, if I showed up without a lot more than I had now.

I BLESSED the chance that had let me run into Osborne, the lawyer, at the Tombs, before I had seen Chain. My little hold on Chain was the one shot in my locker that

looked valid. To have fired it blindly, in my present mysti-
fied state, would be madness. Once I could grasp—even
in a general way—what was going on, I might be able to
use it with ten times the effect.

The torment of that was that every passing minute
increased my worry about the little red-haired girl, and
the fate of my twenty-dollar bill—though the truth is
I was more interested in the girl now than in the little
Frenchman. Not that I had forgotten him, but my urge
was primarily to get her out of danger.

Once again I sorted over the items in my head that
might hold—must hold—the answer to what lay behind
this crazy merry-go-round. And once again I found myself
just where I'd started, my questions still unanswered.

What murderous equation was there between Hessian,
Chain, and Damson? Why had Daisy Chain voluntarily
jailed himself? Above all, what had he done with the girl
before he surrendered to the cops?

I could get an answer to none of these questions from
my buzzing brain and so I finally got back to brass tacks.

Trying to do anything with Lamson was simply beyond
my depth. I might scheme a dozen schemes, work out a
dozen gambits on the banker—and the closer I got to the
truth, the closer I'd be to a few ounces of lead in my fat
head. No, I'd have to work from the other end—on Daisy
Chain's trail. I understood thugs like Chain—or even swin-
dlers like Hessian—could cope with them where a Lamson
and his money would make me a babe in the wood.

It suddenly occurred to me how odd it was that none of
the wires I had out had brought in anything about Chain.
I'd gleaned absolutely nothing. I wondered where the little
gunman could have been lately that he was a total stranger
in his customary haunts in and around New York.

One disadvantage in being moved about the country constantly as Acme moves me, is that you lose intimate touch with the crooks in any one city. I had very little knowledge of Daisy Chain's recent activities, but I did the first thing that anyone would do in trying to dig back. I went down to a pay phone in the lobby and called the Parole Board office. More deadly little killers than you would think possible, somehow seem to manage somehow to be on parole.

I had a good friend—Taylor Hicks—in the parole office, but the best he could do for me was: "No, he's not on parole. I think he's been out of the state for a couple of years. Wait a minute."

I waited and after a bit learned: "Charley says Daisy came to town about six weeks ago with that skinny blond wife of his. I don't know where from. I'll ask around for you, though, and phone you anything I can get."

I hung up, looked at the clock. It was getting on toward five. Workers in this section quit early and the building was draining.

I GOT an inspiration and walked over to the newsstand, bought a city map. I made a quick estimate and circled a part of Greenwich Village lying within a certain radius of the house on Jane Street. I made the circle large enough to include every possible point to which Daisy Chain might have taken the girl last night in the few brief minutes he'd been gone from the murder scene.

Studying the circle got me nowhere. I folded the map, put it in my pocket—and the break came.

As I turned away from the counter, I saw Lamson's lawyer—the crisp-looking Osborne—come out of an elevator, walk briskly across the lobby. The lines on his intelligent face were drawn and unhappy. I had a hunch that he liked no part of having to assist Lamson in this business.

I was watching him so closely that when his expression changed, I caught it before I saw what had caused it. His face suddenly had an even more worried look and he hastily shook his head, ever so slightly.

My eyes jumped to where he was looking and I said *"Unh!"* under my breath. A stocky, powerful little Latin, with a genial, glowing face and warm, liquid brown eyes, had come into the lobby. He had stopped, momentarily, but at the hasty negative of Osborne's nod, he strolled leisurely on. Osborne sailed right on past him and out the door. The Latin continued on, boarded an elevator, while I let this final addition to the cast of characters of this little drama sink in.

He was Jack Enz, a private detective. That was not the half of it. He was shrewd, ruthless, completely unscrupulous. His agency was not even listed in the telephone book. His clientele were ultraselect—as select as were the lawyers, Fairfield and Ritchie, but in a more sinister way. The service his organization rendered—no one but his clients knew just what services he did render. There had been a time when he was a labor-specialist, but he'd had sense enough to give that up before it got too hot. I wouldn't have bet a dime, however, that in Colonel Lamson's pirate days, this same little schemer might not have worked for him.

Osborne's apparent ignoring of Enz told more of the story than if he had stopped to chat. Plainly, the stiff-necked lawyer would not go so far as to be publicly seen speaking to the private detective. Just as plainly, that seemed to indicate that Enz was immediately connected here.

I tried to keep the touch of desperation out of my mind as I recalculated the folks lined up against me. Lamson—Daisy Chain—now Jack Enz—not to mention the lawyer Osborne and probably the police, sooner or later, if they stumbled on my trail. I was in a tough spot and no mistake, but that poor little red-head was in an even tougher one—as was my Frenchman—and I had to stick with it.

I was too late to board the elevator with Jack Enz—which I would not have done anyway as I had no wish to have him see me. But I tried to spot where he got off by watching the elevator indicator. I learned nothing. The car did not stop at nineteen—Lamson's floor—nor at twenty-one where Fairfield and Ritchie were. It did stop at twenty and I assumed the glowing-eyed Enz was merely being cagy. However, that made it useless for me to go up after him.

And as I stood, hastily trying to cook up a move for myself, Osborne came back, walking as stiffly as before, distaste writ large on his face. For a moment I had a foolish urge to brace him.

He barely missed seeing me—I didn't know but that he might recognize me from the visitors' room at the Tombs—and I quickly turned my back, lit a cigarette. Watching the elevator indicator again still left me without knowing where to go, even if I did decide to try the upstairs. The car happened to be packed full and it stopped at every single floor on the way up.

THERE WAS nothing for me to do but wait in the lobby till Enz came down—about twenty minutes. I almost got in his way. I was waiting in the niche by the telephone booths, not thinking of the possibility that he might want to use one of them, and when he turned and walked straight from the elevator toward me I had to retreat into one of the two vacant booths, hunch over to disguise my face and begin an imaginary conversation in a mumble.

Jack Enz took the next booth. After dialing a number his lazy voice said quietly: "Check that address. Wait a minute." I heard him tear paper, then, "Go ahead." After a minute he said, "Right," and hung up.

I felt excitement begin to churn inside me. In my bones, I knew that I had finally caught up to something—that the address he was discussing was something I wanted. I eased my door open a crack so that the light would go out.

Enz didn't emerge at once. Instead, he dialed another number, while I held my breath to listen for the second time. This time he said: "Corky?... Check back with that address." There was a long period of silence, then, "Right. All right—go ahead the way I told you, and don't miss... Yeah."

He strolled leisurely out, twisting a scrap of paper idly between his fingers. I held my breath, waiting for him to throw it away—but he didn't. He strolled to the door, aimlessly, as though he hadn't any place to go—and casually slid the scrap of paper in his vest pocket.

I groaned, stood first on one foot, then the other. I wanted that slip as badly as I ever wanted anything in my life. Obviously, some important further move was, this minute, taking place. I had no idea what it was. I had no idea where it was—but I knew that the where was on that carelessly crumpled bit of paper. I had to get it, somehow, and quickly. The whole wild business was suddenly focused, for me, on that slip.

Enz stood there, idly, lit a little cigar and puffed it absently, while I felt sweat on the back of my neck. Minutes were slipping away.

Finally, he strolled out onto Broad Street. It was almost dark now. The sky was heavily overcast. The district—it was way after five o'clock now—was practically deserted. Only a thin sprinkling of pedestrians drifted past us as we walked up to Wall, and then up Wall to Broadway. I was going nutty, trying to figure a play—when he turned absently into a building.

It was a bank, and it was closed. The recess of its front facade was not more than ten feet deep. But I didn't realize it was a bank, or what it was, till I hurried around the corner of it after him—and found him coming back out, straight at me.

There were people fifty yards away, in both directions, but I didn't think there were any close enough to see me. I had had my fingers wrapped around my blackjack from the moment we left the Broad Street building, and now I whipped it out and up under his chin with a whack you could hear. He just folded up and fell forward against me. I jammed the blackjack back in my pocket, eased him into the dark entrance niche, my fingers digging for his vest.

Then I had the slip, and was making tracks away from there fast. I was around the corner of Wall again by the time I heard somebody shout for the police. I swung into a tobacco shop, casually ordered cigarettes and unfolded the paper. It was no false alarm. The address was plainly jotted down. I got my butts, ran out and to the subway.

I had an anxious moment while I considered the possibility that Jack Enz had recognized me as I hit him. I make no bones about the fact that I was scared of him—plenty. However, it seemed almost certain that the darkness had been too deep for him to get a square look at me and I dismissed the worry. I was too intent on getting where I was going, anyway.

CHAPTER FOUR
THE BLUE FOLDER

IT WAS on Fourth Street, not far from A Sheridan Square—an artistic-looking, small stone house—and my old pump was speeding up as I realized it was well within the circle I had drawn on my city map. I forced myself to spend minutes in a doorway opposite.

There was no light in the house but, somehow, it did not seem deserted. There were iron bars across the ground-floor windows—ornamental, but still iron bars. There was a scrolled-iron gate at the side of the house, screening a little service alley leading around to the back. There were curtains inside the windows and the shades were not quite drawn.

In three minutes, I could not detect a single sign of activity. I walked up the street a few rods, crossed over and hugged building fronts coming back. If there were spying eyes in one of the darkened windows, they couldn't have seen me.

Then I got my hand on the little servicegate—and lost some of my starch. The lock on the gate was broken. It swung loosely under my touch. I turned in and ran as quietly as I could, through a cement-floored slot, into a tiny back yard.

A flash from my torch showed a back door—and I groaned. A square piece had been cut from the glass panel in the door. It, too, opened under my touch and I was in a kitchen.

There is a strange feeling about a house that has recently been emptied, and I knew this one had been. I knew it in my boots—that's where my heart was—even as I ran through into the front part of the house—knew that I had missed the boat. Hurriedly I covered the house—upstairs and downstairs—and finally got the whole heart-breaking picture.

In the living room, on the ground floor, there was a faded blue kimono and a pair of blue silk mules, scuffed and old. There was a box of blond hairpins, a scanty wardrobe for a slender, tall girl, mixed with clothes that were obviously Daisy Chain's. Taylor Hicks' words jumped into my mind: "... hit town with that skinny blond wife of his...."

Every piece of furniture in the house had been upended, searched mercilessly and destructively, as though for some small object.

The basement was the payoff. I wound up there, staring into a solid box of cement with a steel door—a wine-cellar, by design. The door was open and there was a single bulb burning on a ceiling cord. There was a cot under the light and a table by the cot. The table held a pitcher of water, a tumbler, and a cardboard box of morphine tablets, half spilled on the floor. A tiny, balled handkerchief was on the cot, in the depression where some small person had lain. The handkerchief was daintily scented.

The picture was inescapable. This was where Chain had hidden away Dorinne Hare. This was where she had lain, doped—and re-doped, I didn't doubt—under the care of Daisy's skinny blond wife, until—until what?

Until Jack Ena's men had discovered the hide-away—discovered it and swooped down, cleaning it out, making off with both girls and, apparently, whatever object it was for which they had been searching.

Suddenly, as I stood there with my forehead burning, a little chain of reasoning linked itself into place in my mind.

Daisy Chain—I was almost positive of it now, though the reason was still an utter mystery—*had* snaked the red-head away last night because she was his alibi. Snaked her away and put her on ice. Some scheme had occurred to him in the moment he stood on the stoop with her— some scheme that necessitated his being taken up for the killing. But—now I got it—the scheme also involved his having the girl ready at hand, to produce when needed, so he'd have his alibi only when he wanted out and no sooner. Though I was damned if I could see what he wanted to be in the Tombs for in the first place.

IT DIDN'T take much reasoning to see what had happened now. Someone had stolen his alibi—had coolly taken away his ace in the hole! Someone—Lamson, via Jack Enz—had suddenly pulled away the vital prop that supported whatever scheme the gunman had been attempting! Someone had determined that Daisy Chain should stay in jail—and, with his record, it was more than an even chance that the vicious little killer would face a murder trial! With his alibi destroyed, he was suddenly in a very hot spot.

The ominousness of that word—destroyed—congealed my thinking apparatus for a minute. I could not blind myself to it. If those who sought Daisy Chain's down- fall really wanted to ruin him, they could do so only by complete elimination of the lovely little red-haired Dorinne Hare!

The thought gave me a cold wallop. Then I saw a possible out.

Now Daisy Chain would *have* to talk to me—would *have* to throw himself on my mercy! I was now his only chance of avoiding a murder trial. I could give him the alibi he had thought only the girl could furnish. I could get him out of the Tombs. And without me, facing the behind-the-scenes pressure that the powerful Lamson could exert in the D.A.'s office—well, Daisy Chain would be just as hep as I to what he was up against. Now—and I prayed it wasn't too late—I had the red-lipped little rat in the hollow of my hand!

I ran upstairs, praying that that the turnkey at the Tombs would not get stuffy about my visiting Daisy at this hour, running over schemes to get around him if he did.

I remembered to switch off the lights I had turned on, ran out the back door, closed it quickly—and three electric torches blazed in my face.

Unconsciously my hand went to my hip as I stumbled, trying to stop. I nearly lost my head and grabbed my gun out, I was so demoralized.

A voice behind the middle flashlight drawled, "I wouldn't do that, my friend," and I recognized the soft tones of Jack Enz.

"Move wide, boys, and keep him covered," Enz continued and stepped into the beam of light himself. I could see the welt under his jaw and wished it had been an axe instead of a blackjack I'd hit him with down in Broadway. He dropped his flashlight into a pocket of his belted camel-hair coat and juggled his gun with the other hand.

"Hadn't you better turn around and get your hands out of my way?" Enz inquired.

I turned and put my hands up, while he took my gun and ran a hand over me. Then he said: "All right. You can put them down. You'll have to wait a few minutes, my friend, till I do some phoning. But the boys will keep you company till I get back."

A voice behind one of the flashlights said: "The phone in the house is working, chief."

"I thought it was unoccupied—except for Daisy and his harem."

"Yeah, but it belongs to a crazy woman. She's in a loony bin and the house is all tied up in the courts. Nobody can sell it or rent it. When Daisy decided to squat here, he had the nerve to have the phone hooked up so he wouldn't have to go out much."

"*Tsk! Tsk!*" Enz said, and walked into the house.

When he came out again, five minutes later, he was still playing with his gun. I couldn't tell from his manner whether he knew I was the person who had socked him downtown. He said to me, "Well, it seems that certain people would like to see you," and then, to the two behind the still-steady flashlights, "You two take that house apart. The blue folder is positively there."

I jumped on that. A blue folder. It could be anything, and—

"You won't mind a little band of felt around the eyes? I promise you I'll drive carefully," Enz was saying as though he really didn't want to offend me.

I gave him a dead-pan and said nothing.

I DON'T know where we drove in the limousine. I was fighting to get up from the depths of hopelessness and not making such a good job of it. I didn't even try to guess where we were going, nor, when we finally tracked on gritty cement in a place that reeked of garbage smells, then rode in a wooden-floored elevator, did I worry about where we were.

Not until we walked down a lush-carpeted corridor from the elevator did it dawn on me that we had come in through the service entrance of a hotel.

"Stop here," Enz said, and his knuckles beat a cadenced tattoo.

A door opened and I was pushed in.

A dry, cackling voice said, "I will let you know when there is anything further, Mr. Enz," and the door closed. The voice men told me: "You may remove the bandage."

The aged, mummy-faced, tubular-chinned little Lamson looked at me with yellow eyes that were like ice, yet somehow seemed glad to see me in a sardonic way. The cold blue eyes of his lawyer—Osborne stood uncomfortably by a refectory table, with hat and black chesterfield still on—were not glad to see me in any way whatsoever. His English face was still unhappy and bleak and he held a pistol as though it had been stuck into his gloved hand.

I tried to look nonchalant. "A surprise to meet you here, Colonel," I told the yellow-eyed little gnome.

The yellow eyes got a little smaller. "So," he said, without too much surprise. He thought it over and then, "I think it best that we hear exactly what your interest is in this little affair, so that we understand each other perfectly."

"A girl," I told him.

The yellow eyes regarded me expectantly, so I went on: "The little auburn-haired girl whom you had removed from that house a couple of hours ago."

There was a little puzzlement in his eyes momentarily but he blinked back. "Ah, the girl. Yes. Who is that girl, by the way?"

Truth couldn't hurt here. "The niece of a retired clergy-man out west. Her uncle is bedridden. He was tied up with George Hessian in some swindle, years ago, and apparently had some papers left over. Hessian sent for them and the girl came to deliver them. She knows nothing about all this business. She just happened to arrive at Hessian's place on Jane Street last night, within minutes of the time you left."

I didn't know if that were the worst possible thing I could say—or the best. I had no guides of any kind, had to play it as it occurred to me. I was down to rock bottom, the way I figured, and I could hardly make things worse no matter what I said.

I went on, casually, as though it were not a very important item: "She was trapped, at the moment of the shooting, on the steps of the house, just as Daisy Chain came out. He grabbed her, rushed her away. He had his wife keep her doped, a prisoner in the house on Fourth Street, till your henchman got hold of her."

The yellow eyes were boring into my face. There was not the slightest flicker of expression in them. "Scarcely possible," the little tycoon decided after a moment. "Daisy Chain, by his own confession, was not on the steps at the moment of the shooting."

I let that go with a tired sneer—and instantly cursed myself.

"Ah. So you know that he was?"

HAVING FALLEN into the trap, there was no point in not making the best of it. "Certainly," I said. "If you'll give me a chance to talk without interrupting, I'll tell you. I was across the street in a doorway during the whole proceeding."

"Doing what—if I may interrupt?"

"Trying to keep the girl out of trouble."

About the only hope I had was to get him puzzled about me, unsure of me. And the only way I could see to do that was to try to say exactly the things he wouldn't expect. From his long, careful stare I began to have hopes that I was succeeding.

"Let me see," he said thoughtfully. "You—a sort of detective…"

"A damned good detective," I said heatedly.

"Yes, of course, but—not a police detective. In fact you—to my eye—a rather, shall we say, sophisticated individual—know this little lady. You've known her some time, I take it?"

"I never saw her in my life till last night."

"*Ummm*. Yet you suddenly play Galahad to beauty in distress. You involve yourself. You follow her into a murder. You risk trouble with the police—take various serious risks—threaten Mr. Chain in the Tombs—interfere with business of which you have no knowledge. You have no motive from first to last, save to shield this young lady. A little odd, don't you think?"

"Why? I'm not forty yet—and she just happens to hit me. Anyway, that's how it is. Take it or leave it."

He nodded as though confirming my words. "Yes. Well, I'm afraid I shall have to leave it. It just won't wash—won't wash at all. Let me suggest an alternative theory."

He took a careful breath, and suddenly there was crackling electricity in his voice. He leaned forward to drive at me: "You learned—through an underworld tip, let us say—of a bit of blue paper. You learned its value—probably through some unwise or drunken talk of Hessian's—and you learned, apparently, of my interest. You went to the Jane Street house last night to steal it. In doing so, you murdered Hessian. The girl knows your guilt. Hence you seek the girl. Meanwhile, you hold the blue folder. No?"

"No."

"You know nothing of a blue folder, I suppose?"

"Who said I didn't? Certainly I know about it."

For the first time I saw a flicker of real uncertainty in the yellow eyes. I jumped on it. "To get down to brass tacks," I said, "how much is it worth to you—exactly?"

"I offered three hundred thousand dollars."

"How much did Chain want?"

"Three times tha…" The old man cut himself off, as he saw that *he* had taken a tumble.

I pretended not to notice it, said carelessly: "Well, we can make a deal, Colonel Lamson. You know, it might just possibly be that that was why I came here."

He did his best to read my eyes, but I made them bland. He snapped: "That's my price."

"It's not exactly mine," I said. "First and foremost, I want the girl free and unhurt."

The yellow eyes darkened. "We haven't any girl."

"And I haven't any blue folder."

The little gnome jumped up. "Then what in God's name—"

"But I can get it," I assured him.

The yellow eyes suddenly blazed. "Listen, my friend. Lying to me is unhealthy. I have had enough of it."

"Suit yourself," I shrugged. "I can get the folder for you. I'm the only one who can. You can have it—for the girl. All right, we'll say that you haven't got any girl, but put it this way, if it makes you happier. You *get* the girl. Meet me at the bus terminal in Washington Square in a couple of hours and the bargain's made. Otherwise—kiss the folder goodbye. What is the folder?" I asked as though the sudden inspiration had not just that moment hit me. "One of Hessian's old phoney properties that did a miracle and turned out to have oil on it?"

I GOT no answer to that. I didn't really need one. I knew I had hit it. And even the infinitely long minute that he took to look me over carefully did not disturb me. I knew I had got over this hurdle—that I was back in the game again—and more. The mists were suddenly rolling away, one by one. I rattled pictures through my brain—

George Grantland Hessian, suddenly finding himself owner of the one thing his wildest dreams had never embraced—a real oil well, a fabulously rich one, from the price Lamson had quoted. Hessian interesting Lamson in the deal, dickering to sell him the lease on the property. Daisy Chain, getting wind of it, snooping around, hiding— and as I suddenly remembered the front-page stories in the morning papers I knew there could be no doubt about it—hiding in some spot in that house so that he overheard Hessian's last night's talk with Lamson. Then—knowing for the first time what the blue folder actually was— snatching it and ducking out while Hessian was down letting Lamson out through the areaway door.

Then Daisy Chain, with a fortune in his pocket—a fortune, that is, if he could make a deal with Lamson. His own shrewd knowledge of the dynamite with which he was playing even in trying to dicker with the dangerous old man—and his equally shrewd knowledge of the power of blackmail he held over Lamson. Above all things, Lamson could not afford to have it known that he would deal in any way with a swindler like Hessian. That would be a jolt to the prestige of his banking firm and would probably infuriate his partners.

The pictures were dropping into place like the symbols on a slot-machine, building up in my brain with incredible speed, once the first barrier was down. Daisy Chain's weird actions were suddenly all clear and sane—brilliantly sane. He wanted to dicker with Lamson. He knew as well as I did that he was flirting with disaster the minute he tried to blackmail the old pirate. So he had concocted, on the spur of the instant, the supremely smart move of getting himself into the Tombs, where even Lamson's influence could not reach him and where nothing on earth could get him out—till he was ready to produce the girl and get himself out.

And even as I cursed him, I had to acknowledge the braininess of his split-second thinking in those few minutes last night. He not only got himself into jail, but he managed to use the newspapers—every paper in town— to carry his message to Lamson as to just what was what. It came back to me—the rather meaningless insert in that little front-stoop speech—*"I was in the house from eleven o'clock on—in the closet,"* or words to that effect. And, *"I have no lawyer."* If he had written a note to the yellow-eyed little banker saying, "I was in the closet and overheard your entire interview with Hessian. I have the blue folder. You had better send a lawyer to see me and talk it over," it could not have read more plainly to Lamson's eyes.

THIS WENT through my head like a flash, in all its painful clarity, while I waited for the old man to decide what he was going to say.

He said: "Think very carefully, my friend. You have said enough to make me very deeply interested in you. I do not like people to try to outwit me. It annoys me. For instance, it is in my mind to let Daisy Chain rot in jail for his efforts along that line. And, if I do decide so, I realize fully that

I shall have to do something about both you and the girl, who could provide him with an alibi."

He hesitated, and I came back to earth fast under the threat.

"You may imagine that you, too, are playing a crafty game against me," he went on. "Very well. I am going to give you a little rope. As long as I secure the blue folder in the end, I shall be quite satisfied to hold no animosity. But if I do not get it—and get it by midnight tonight—I am going to be damned good and fed up with the lot of you. Is that clear?"

"Oh, sure."

"Need I remind you that there is nowhere in the world you can run to from where I cannot drag you back?"

"Who's running?" I said. "You see that the girl is unharmed and on hand—that's all you have to worry about."

The little czar snapped from the side of his mouth at the lawyer, "Mr. Osborne—kindly get in touch with our friends regarding that," and the lawyer gave a start, ran a finger inside his collar and nodded.

The old man fixed his eyes on me and said softly: "You are free to go. Maybe this seems like an old man's folly to you—but I have set my heart on having that property. I want that blue folder."

"I believe you," I assured him. I did, too. After all his years of toeing the straight and narrow line, he did not have to tell me he was itching to get at it.

Now, somehow, I didn't care about George Grantland Hessian being killed. I saw my way clear at last—my way out of this mess, and the girl's way out. Ten minutes with Daisy Chain and I would know where to find the blue folder. Ten minutes with the blue folder and this old pirate, and I would have the girl free and clear—and my twenty-dollar bill. Beyond that, I had no interest.

I picked up my hat and stuck it on, turned at the door to say, "I'll see you in a couple of hours."

When I stepped out and closed the door behind me—and ran—I thought I had the thing licked. I suppose that's funny—if you like your humor macabre.

CHAPTER FIVE
DAISY CHAIN

I RAN off the elevator into the visitor's room at the Tombs with my pass out, waving it in the Scotchman's face, bringing him out of his nap over a newspaper. I was relieved even to find the room open. It was empty, too, except for its custodian, and that was an added break.

"You again? You can't do no business now. Too late," he said.

"It's life and death," I told him. "I've got to see Daisy. I promise you—tomorrow the commissioner himself will thank you for it. And every second counts. Besides that, there'll be a hundred in it for you. You'll be breaking a murder case and maybe saving two more lives. No—don't phone anyone—you might as well say no. If I have to wait as much as a few minutes, I'm licked." I would have told him anything.

His eyes were ludicrous. He had been shaping words with my last four sentences. "But—but—hey! It could mean my job—"

"Not with Acme backing you—come on, hurry up, there's a good guy."

And then, somehow, I was outside Daisy Chain's cell and the red-lipped little thug was staring at me with shiny, contemptuous eyes. "How did you get in here? Listen, scram—"

"Save your breath—and your life," I told him through the mesh. "Get this—and get it the first time. The whole works are blown. Your life and mine on the counter. The deal—the oil business is done—gone, napoo. The old boy has decided to pass it up, and to send you to trial. Play with me and I'll get you out of here—"

"Save it, pal. I can get out anytime I feel like it."

"Not now, you can't. Let this leak into that numb head of yours. Lamson's got the red-head. Your alibi's gone! You're in—and you'll stay in—unless I get you out. They found your place on Fourth Street. You're sunk without a trace, except for me. I can give you an alibi. I was in a doorway across from the house on Jane Street when Hessian was killed. I can clear you."

His face had paled a little, but the ugly sneer was still on his face. "What am I? A sucker? Go peddle your papers!"

"Wake up! You asked Lamson too high a price. He got mad and put Jack Enz to work. Enz found one of your hiding places in jig time. Lamson figures he can find the other presently. So he's giving you the miss. He's going to see you railroaded to the chair. Nobody'll listen to your story about his dealing with Hessian, while you're in here charged with the killing.

"For the last time—I'm the only one that can save you. The money's gone—forget it! But let me try to save your skin—all of our skins. If Lamson is going to send you over, he'll have to put me out of the way—and the red-haired girl. I can buy us all out of the hole with that blue folder, if I can get it quick. Clam up on me, and we're all done for. And your wife, too. They've got her."

The last of the color drained from his face. "Carol? They've—" he gulped. "You—you're lying, damn you!"

I pounded at him: "Waste about five more seconds and you'll find out if I am. Why? Does your wife know the hiding-place of the folder? If she does, they'll be working on her now. They'll get it out of her—and then I won't have anything to trade with. You fool—open up! Does she know it?"

"Yes! Yes!" he croaked. "She—but she'll never tell—"

"Do you think—with one murder already on the cards— they're going to be nice about working on her? If you're damn fool enough to want to burn yourself, for God's sake, crack to save her. She'll be getting it—plenty—until I can get to them with the folder."

He blurted out: "It's in the Fourth Street house. Look, copper—you'll play square with me? You swear it? You'll get me out of here?"

"Absolutely. Go on—hurry up!"

"It's in the living room. There's a tablelamp with three big bulbs—one bulb is phoney—unscrew it. The folder's wadded up inside. For the love of God—"

I wasted no time getting back down the corridor. Flinging a hurried, "Thanks. You did something," to the red-faced Scotchman, I dropped to the street. I made time heading for the subway, too.

Dummy that I was, I thought I had scored the whole way. I was so preoccupied with getting the girl safe and myself safe that the grim specter of murder in the background simply didn't get home to me.

And then it did.

I ran in to a drugstore to phone the bell captain at my hotel. Jack Enz still had my gun and I didn't think this was any time to be without one.

The minute I got Jerry on the wire I knew from his tone that something was wrong. His voice was too careless as he said: "Oh, hello, Mr. Green."

I got it. I said, "Visitors? Cops?" wondering why it hadn't occurred to me that my visit to the Tombs earlier would have been reported long since.

"Yeah, Mr. Green."

"Can you bring my spare gun down for me? It's a matter of life and death—that green morocco box in the safe. Get it to me somehow, on the corner of Fifth and Waverly before eleven thirty and there'll be dough."

"Sure, Mr. Green. Glad to see you."

Even that didn't worry me now—that the cops were closing in on me. I figured I could run ahead of them, be clear by the time they caught up to me.

I hurried out of the drugstore onto the dark street—and was blackjacked instantly into unconsciousness. I didn't even feel myself fall.

I WOKE up to find my fingers dug into a woman's cold flesh, my frame half sprawled across her nearly naked blond body.

I was back in the living room of Daisy Chain's Fourth Street hideout and somewhere a clock was chiming midnight—the hour of my appointment with Lamson.

My stomach almost came up in my throat as I scrambled hastily off the woman. She was quite dead. Livid bruises on her throat, her brassy blond hair in disarray, angry red-and-black burns on her naked belly, a small hole over the bridge of her nose and exquisite agony in her thin tortured face, told me the whole ugly story. The bullet hole had leaked surprisingly little blood.

My head was dizzy, pounding, and it was a minute before the whole impact of the situation got to me. I stared giddily at the girl. She had on the kimono and mules I had seen here earlier—nothing else.

Unconsciously my hand went up to my cheek and I realized it was smarting.

That brought me to. I jumped for the mantelpiece, ducked to look in the mirror—and saw the three parallel scratches down my cheek. I swung back, dropped down and snatched up the girl's skinny hand.

Under her red-tinted fingernails were black red adhesions—and I knew it was my own flesh. Something new in frames.

Not till then did I really see the tiny bullet-hole over her nose. It dawned on me that it *was* tiny—that it was undoubtedly from a small-caliber gun. It looked—and then I got the picture—it looked exactly like one of the holes that had put a period to the life of George Grantland Hessian.

My scalp crawled. Too late, I realized my criminal folly in not nailing down someone for the murder of Hessian. Now the killer had become a double killer—and I was stuck with both feet in the mess. In a rush of frightened fury I cursed Lamson wildly. I had thought I was outsmarting him and all the while he had been making this kind of sucker of me. Probably he had the blue folder all the time....

I swung round dizzily, saw the three-bulbed lamp on the refectory table and jumped for it.

To identify the phony bulb, I jerked the chain.

That about finished me. All three bulbs lighted! There was no false bulb! I yanked all three out and pounded them to pieces. All were regular, large-size bulbs. There was no sign of any blue paper.

I started to curse Daisy Chain—and then I swung back again, stared down at the brassy, tubercular looking dead girl on the floor, and I understood. She—Daisy Chain's wife—had told the hiding place. Told it—and then died—probably thankfully.

Women-torturers always drive me insane. I was half off my nut now anyway and I got a red fog in my brain. Now, too late, I realized that I wanted to get my hands on the killer of this girl—and the killer, incidentally, of Hessian—more than anything in the whole picture. If I had him—and had enough evidence to ram down his throat—then, I could choke safety for both myself and the red-haired girl from him—or kill him in the attempt.

Not till then did the striking of the hour work through to my intelligence. I swung round, saw the hands of the mantelpiece clock at two minutes after twelve—and at that exact moment, the distant, far-off wail of a police siren filtered in.

It was blocks away—but it sent sweat out all over me. Maybe it wasn't coming here—but even as I tried to think that, I knew it was. The miracle was that it hadn't come sooner—that someone had underestimated the thickness of my skull. Nevertheless, I had to get out and get out fast. There was simply no choice. No disaster could be worse than my being caught here now would be. I had to leave the frame—leave it and run, not even knowing what else had been planted here to incriminate me.

I DUCKED out the back door, into the board-fenced back yard, got across that and moved a few houses sideways, going over one fence after another, till I found one

with an alley that would put me out on the street above—
Waverly Place.

The minute I slipped out onto the street, I realized that
the original siren had been joined by others—two, three,
four—I couldn't tell how many. And they weren't all heading for Fourth Street, as far as I could distinguish. They
were coasting back and forth, through the vicinity. I got
it, then—or thought I did. The alarm was out for me. The
bright little mind behind my frame had taken no chances,
had dropped a hint somehow to the cops to sew up the
district.

I hugged doorways, sweating. Gradually, I slipped across
Waverly, reached Fifth after an eternity, not daring to hope
that Jerry would be there with my gun box. But he was.

I blessed him, snatched the familiar police positive out
and pocketed the papers that were also in the box. Then I
told him: "Beat it. Forget you ever knew me!"

I cut off his aghast whisper, "Gosh-hell, are they after
you…?" with a push that sent him out onto the sidewalk.

I sent one grim glance down toward the south end
of Washington Square—the spot where the little master-
schemer had blandly agreed to meet me. I knew, of course,
that he would not he there, but how I wished that he were.
As things stood now, my goose was cooked—mine and the
lovely little red-haired girl's—and Daisy Chain's as well,
for that matter. But I could take it without batting an eye
if I could have five minutes alone with the cold-blooded
little monster back of all this.

Why hadn't I had the brains to get something on him,
get some evidence lined up that would tie him to his two
rotten killings?

And then, suddenly, I realized why I hadn't.

My brain shot off like a pinwheel and I caught my breath. The whole panorama suddenly spread out before me as I saw the black bulk standing motionless down by the bus terminal at the bottom of the park.

Could it be—and I realised that it had to be—that this game was not yet played out? There was still one last chance left.

Sirens were shrieking in the blocks all around us, but there were no police cars around the park itself. I doubled over, shot across the street and into the shrubbery. In little sprints I worked my way across, till I was in the bushes ten yards from the black bulk. I could scarcely dare to believe my eyes—to believe that Lamson had actually shown up. But he had. He was standing beside his car, smoking, exactly where he had arranged to be.

Just as I got ready to call him, two green-lighted police cars shot into the square—one at the top, one at the bottom. I had to swallow my tongue. I took a good grip on the gun for I thought I had been spotted, but it wasn't quite that bad.

THEY WENT away and I got my throat to work. I called out to Lamson: "Stand perfectly still and get your hands away from you."

Even then, I think I would have given it to him if he had made one false move, but he didn't. He obeyed, without showing the slightest expression.

I said, "Turn around and back over here," and he did that too.

I frisked him. He had no gun. He asked innocently: "They looking for you?"

"Go back to your car—slowly—so that I can see every move," I growled at him. "Open the door and turn on the dome light. Then stand clear."

When I was certain there was no one else in the car I told him to turn the light off and stand away. I went across the sidewalk in one smooth motion and into the tonneau of the sport sedan.

"Get in," I told him.

If he was the slightest bit scared he didn't show sign of it. He got in calmly and asked me again: "Are they looking for you?"

"Yeah," I said. "And if they get me, you get a bullet in the back of your neck. I promise you that."

He was silent a minute. Then he asked: "Have you got the folder?"

"Produce the girl, and it's yours," I said. "But get me through this dragnet first. I want to talk to you a little."

After a second he said coolly: "All right. I have a little private office not far from here. I keep it for confidential meetings. I was going to suggest it anyway. I can get you there, if you'll lie down in the rear there and put the blanket over you."

The sirens seemed to be deliberately congregating around the square. I set my teeth and said: "All right—but don't forget what I said."

I don't know whether I was surprised or not when he made good.

To the copper who yelled us over to the curb, five blocks above the square, the old man said irritably: "What's the meaning of this? My card, officer." The uniformed man stammered: "Oh—uh—excuse it, please, Colonel Lamson. Looking for a killer—somewhere in the neighborhood."

Then we were away, through the Twenties, into the Thirties. We turned east a block and the car came to a stop.

I was up in the seat with the gun in my hand as he climbed out and waved at a modest apartment house of yellow brick. There was a small, obscure door sunk in the gray stone, its panel clouded-glass-and-wire. "This is my private entrance."

I got behind him without saying anything and he produced a key and opened the door. We stepped into a tiny elevator, direct from the street, and he switched on the light.

"I hope there's no monkey business," I told him as we sailed up. "I'm in about as bad a state of nerves as I can remember ever being."

"Why should there be monkey business?" he asked.

Nevertheless, I kept the gun six inches from his back as we stepped out onto a turf-garden-and-shrub-covered roof and faced a darkened Spanish-looking bungalaw. Lamson touched a switch in the structure of the elevator shaft and light went on in a living room at the front of the bungalow. The dew-drenched greenery sparkled.

"All right," I said and we walked across. The door was unlocked and he strolled in, threw his black hat on the table, walked over and touched buttons by the fireplace. Somehow, that lighted an already-laid fire of apple-boughs. Flames crackled upwards. He turned his little mummy face toward me, his yellow eyes thin.

"Now, my friend."

I said grimly: "The price has gone up since I talked to you last."

CHAPTER SIX
THE MAN WITH
THREE LIVES

FOR JUST a second wild consternation flared behind his yellow eyes. He bit shrilly, "What?" and his forehead flushed. His eyes became hot, driving. "My God, have I put my faith in a fool?"

"No. But I've got to have the killer of George Grantland Hessian as part of the deal."

"Killer? I know nothing about any killer. I'll get—I've got—the girl—" My heart dropped as I saw the slip of his tongue. He hadn't the girl yet. "—and I want the blue folder."

"To get the girl, you'll have to take her from the killer. I've just wakened to the fact that you aren't the killer yourself."

"What?" he shrilled. "My God, what drivel are you—"

"I'm no brain trust," I admitted, "but that threatening act you put on downtown, plus what I'd heard about you, would have fooled anybody. Now shut up and listen. You've got to get that killer to get your blue folder. Getting him, you'll get the girl."

"What? You mean—this thug, Daisy Chain—"

"Daisy Chain hasn't either the folder or the girl. The murderer has them both. He hi-jacked them from Chain. And for God's sake, wake up to this. This killer is desperate!

He's tortured and killed one girl tonight. He may be doing the same to Miss Hare this minute. If anything happens to her, I swear you'll get no blue folder—and you'll get everything else you don't want."

"Wait a minute! What's he want to torture her for, if he's got the blue folder?"

"Because he doesn't want it," I stormed. "You fool—he got that by accident—*while he was looking for something else!*"

His eyes were electric, driving. "Who is this killer?"

"A man named O.E. Murray."

"What!"

"If you keep on interrupting," I swore through tight teeth, "you'll ruin us all. I'll give it to you in words of one syllable—and for God's sake get it the first time."

"Yes, but who is this O.E. Murr—"

"He *was* a brilliant geologist, while he was still practically a kid—out in Texas. He got in some jam with a married woman, had to blow town, and, apparently, to raise a stake, he sold out to George Hessian, thirteen years ago, and wrote a letter—nothing to do with this deal you're interested in—which was absolutely criminal and which could still put him in jail.

"When the swindle eventually blew up, this letter did not come to light. It was with other papers that got into the hands of one of Hessian's stooges—Miss Hare's father. But Hessian knew where it was.

"When he got out of jail recently and found he had this valuable oil well on his hands—or this blue folder—this lease that had been part of his collection of sucker-bait and had suddenly bloomed—he knew he had a potential fortune. But being who he was, he couldn't have raised a dime to drill and finance it. He had to sell. There aren't many people with the money to buy that sort of thing these days. He thought of you.

"He got in touch with you. In your position, everything had to be secret. The slightest hint in Wall Street that you were dealing with a swindler like Hessian and your own partners would probably throw you out. Hessian took that secret apartment on Jane Street so you could negotiate privately.

"Unfortunately, Daisy Chain was nosing into Hessian's affairs—keeping very close to him. Close enough so that he, apparently, knew the location of the blue folder long before last night, but didn't know its value.

"Last night, he found out. He was hidden within earshot while you had your final talk with Hessian. While Hessian was downstairs letting you out the areaway, Chain snatched the folder and ducked.

"And the killer came into that house—through the rear, probably—about that time. At any rate, he was upstairs in Hessian's office, by the time Daisy Chain let himself out the front door."

THE YELLOW eyes bored into mine. "I know all that—but go on. You said this O.E. Murray got the blue folder while looking for something else. For what?"

I swore at him. "I'm giving you the whole picture, so there'll be no questions. Shut up till I finish. I'll clear up Daisy Chain first.

"He is no fool—he's sharp and cunning. He knew exactly to a hair how much of a hold he had on you—not only the folder, but the damaging knowledge of your deal with an ex-convict. He also knew exactly his own danger, if he should try to shake you down. But he got a break—and thought fast enough to take advantage of it.

"He ran into the girl on the front stoop, just as the shots that killed Hessian were fired upstairs. He saw what he had—a perfect alibi for the killing. So he grabbed it—grabbed the girl, that is—spirited her and the blue folder over to his house on Fourth Street and hid them away in the care of his wife.

"Then he came back and coolly put himself in jail. Because in jail, with an unbailable first-degree murder rap hanging over him, not even all your influence and money could get at him. He could sit coolly in his cell and dictate terms to you. Then, when he had closed with you and felt it safe, he could produce the girl and walk out. He was even smart enough to stage that little speech on the death-house steps, knowing it would make front-page prominence and get his little message to you.

"It worked. You sent your lawyer to dicker with him. But apparently he asked too much and you—or Osborne—turned Jack Enz loose to try and find the little thug's hiding place. Enz found it, but got there too late. All he caught was me.

"And that is positively the end of Daisy Chain's connection with this mess. He didn't kill Hessian. He was in jail when his wife was killed. This O.E. Murray killed both of them—and wound up, accidentally, with the blue folder... Don't interrupt, damn you!"

I gulped air, went on: "This killer, blackmailed by Hessian, evidently was on hand the moment you left that Jane Street house. He had been promised his incriminating letter back at that time. Hessian couldn't produce it—couldn't, because it was in the possession of the girl on the front stoop at that moment. O.E. Murray thought he was being given a stall, and tried to choke it out of Hessian.

In the struggle, Hessian drew a gun and got killed with it. The killer fled.

"Next morning, when he saw what Chain had done, he at once concluded that Chain had gotten the thirteen-year-old letter among his loot. He—O.E. Murray—also set out to find Chain's hiding place. And did.

"But, after torturing Chain's wife to death, all he could get out of her was the blue folder. He got that—but he is still looking for his letter. He thought I might have it—and waylaid me. Having me, he decided to pin the two killings on me. Now, he must be desperate enough so that he won't be rational. He hasn't anybody he can look to, to tell him where his precious letter is, except Miss Hare. If he has discovered her identity, the chances are that he won't be reasonable—that he'll ignore all the reasons she gives and will simply bear down on her till she dies. Because—make no mistake—this O.E. Murray is an important man.

"He faces ruin, the collapse of a brilliantly successful career. With one career ruined under him—his geology in Texas—he came to another city, learned another business and was good enough to make his way high up the ladder in these fifteen years. Maybe he wouldn't have gone this far in the first place, but he's in blood up to his boot-tops now and he won't stop. He's going to save his career at any cost, now that he's gone so far.

"I've got to get to him—to keep him from killing the girl. You've got to get to him—to get your blue folder. Everything comes down to that. Now—for Heaven's sake—get him and get him fast!"

"But—but I don't know anybody named O.E. Murray. How—who—I—"

I FLUNG at him: "You're not that dumb! It's all obvious enough. How did you get to know George Grantland Hessian in the first place? How in the world could a known ex-convict, a swindler, even get into your presence, let alone interest you in a deal?"

"I—why I was introduced to him—"

"Exactly. And look at the limb the party who introduced you was going out on! Suppose you hadn't been a damned highbinder with a heart full of larceny? You would have tossed this 'introducer' out on his ear! He knew that—but he had to risk it! Had to, because that was what Hessian demanded! Because that was the price of the O.E. Murray letter—that Murray should introduce Hessian to you and should father the deal. When the deal was settled, he was to get back the letter—the letter that would have stripped away his new identity, torn down the fifteen years of brilliant work that he'd put in getting himself somewhere—would have exposed him as the conniving, criminal geologist who had written that letter! His being overanxious about it—not giving Hessian time to get the letter—is what caused this whole fantastic business. Good Lord, it's clear enough!"

"Yes, but—wait! How do you know he *hasn't* got—where *is* this O.E. Murray letter?"

"Here!" I took it from my breast pocket. "He searched me for it a while ago, but it happened to be at my hotel at the time! Now—get him! We've wasted enough precious minutes. Hell and damnation—for a mastermind, you're certainly dumb enough not to have realized most of this before."

His yellow eyes were suddenly crinkled at the corners. He held out a skinny, gloved hand. "What makes you think I didn't?" he asked queerly. "Let me see that!"

A voice said crisply from the dark doorway at the rear of the room: "No. Let me see it!"

The English-looking, crisp, blue-eyed lawyer, Osborne, stepped into the light, a blued-steel gun in his hand. His eyes were bloodshot, hollow, but there was a wild gleam in them that told me not to try and raise my gun.

I CONFESS I was a fool—I thought we were done for. In tormenting succession, the thoughts went through my mind that this, Colonel Lamson's private little retreat, would, naturally be known to his lawyer, and that the old banker was a damn fool not to have considered it as a possible operating spot for the lawyer-murderer-geologist. Unfortunately, the hollow, unpleasant truth insisted on presenting itself—that it was I who had known the identity of the murderer, not Lamson, and that I should have thought to look through the other rooms of the bungalow.

Even at that, I think I would have taken a chance and let him have a shot at me. I couldn't prevent his getting in the first one while I was drawing a bead on him. I would have taken a chance that in his wild state his aim would not have been fatal—except that I suddenly realized that I could not kill him! *He was the only one who knew where Dorinne Hare was!*

Sweat came out on my neck. If I killed this maniac, she might die before we could find her, drugged with morphine. If I shot him down and didn't kill him, he could pump half a dozen shots into my carcass without my being able to do anything about it. I was stalemated.

He said, "Drop that gun!" and I let it slip from my fingers.

He said, "Toss that letter over here," and I was about to do that, but changed my mind.

"I'm damned if I will," I said. "Maybe you could shoot me and get away without the cops coming down on you. Listen—" the wailing of sirens were plainly audible. It seemed that the dragnet searching for me had expanded a little, was coming near us. "I'll give it to you, if you can show me that the girl won't be harmed."

"The girl is unharmed," he said through set teeth. "I have been unable to rouse her. She—they evidently kept her heavily drugged. You need have no fear—"

"I'll need more than your word."

Colonel Lamson broke in: "And, of course, the blue folder."

The lawyer's cold blue eyes and stony face did not change. "I am appropriating the folder," he told Lamson. "I do not plan to start my third life as I have the other two—penniless."

LAMSON'S VOICE was drawling, curious. "What! You're not planning to run away! You're crazy, Osborne—or Murray, or whatever the name really is. I can use you. You don't think I'm a man to let a little mistake made years ago stand between me and a man who—"

The other's British voice was clipped, a little weary. "You can save it, Colonel Lamson. I have been, you forget, in position to observe your cunning from the other side."

Lamson's voice grew ominous. "You think you can antagonize me and run far enough to get out of my reach?"

"No," the other said impatiently. "No. Since you and this gentleman came in, I have known that I could not go through with this—as long as you were alive."

"Oh." Lamson seemed mildly amazed. "You are going to kill me—us?" Then, seemingly irrationally, he said: "Bah!

I don't believe you have the real blue folder at that. There were two of them, you know."

The other's lips twitched tiredly under his crisp mustache. With one gloved hand he drew a folded blue paper from his inner pocket. "I'll take a chance on that, Colonel."

The yellow eyes seemed to shine like a tiger's. "Then there is nothing we can do to stop you shooting us?"

"Nothing," the lawyer said. "Damn it—it's no wish of mine, but I've no other course—none whatever—" His calm was breaking. Suddenly, he said in a tired, quick, voice of finality, "I don't know why I'm waiting," and swung the gun muzzle toward Lamson.

Well, what could I lose? He had declared his weight. I was going to get a blast from that gun anyway. I figured it better to hope for a million-to-one break and make a scrap of it at any rate. I dived for my own fallen gun, tried to whirl myself around an overstuffed chair.

Flame and roar jumped in his hand and a shower of floor-splinters leaped up in front of me, ripped my forehead open. Blood—my blood—spattered into my eyes and my heart was stone cold. Automatically, I jerked at the trigger of my gun. I could not see—I could only hear—and I was braced for the shock of his concluding bullet.

It did not come. I heard distinctly three thunderous reports while I tried to dig my eyes clear.

A voice said, "Cease firing, pally," just as I got my sleeve across my forehead and could see hazily for the first time. "You got him." I jumped up.

The lawyer was lying on his side. Half his face was blown away, but he was wriggling, squirming in wild agony, both gloved hands clawing at what had been his features. My forty-five at close range had done bad things. A whimpering mewing came from his lips. The blue folder lay a foot away, just out of reach of the spreading blood. I saw Lamson make a catlike dive—and the blue folder disappeared. I was focusing on the man who leaned in the doorway—the stocky, liquid-eyed little Italian private detective, Jack Enz. He was blowing smoke from the muzzle of his pistol, and even as I could see clearly again, he stepped over to the writhing man, aimed down.

I jerked my gun up and cried hastily: "No! No! Don't kill him! He's the only one who knows where the girl is!"

"Oh, no, he isn't, chum. You don't really mean that you thought Colonel Lamson was way behind all this play—"

"Where is she, then? How do you mean—" Below, I could hear the wild congregation of sirens, seemingly just outside the bungalow windows.

"Why, he got most of the picture, just after I brought you down to the hotel to see him. Evidently he guessed, from what you said, that he'd better contact me direct, instead of working through the mouthpiece here. Then we find that I been pulling this rat's chestnut's out of the fire for him, while I was supposed to be working for the Colonel. I trace him here and let the Colonel know so he brings you here to have it all out. Right, Colonel?"

I could hear the humming of the elevator on the roof outside. "But the girl—"

"Try the second bedroom down the hall," he said. Then to the Colonel: "Here come the cops. What's the story?"

"You two are working for me, investigating a swindle perpetrated on one of the bank's clients. You may be assured it will never reach the newspapers so as to involve any of us."

"That all right with you?" Enz asked.

"Positively," I said, and jumped as he coolly fired the final shot into the twitching lawyer.

SHE WAS lying on the bed, spread-eagled, her mouth taped. Her face was white, her eyes closed. There was a sponge and ammonia beside her on a table. She looked very still. Her clothes were pulled back, but evidently the lawyer-murderer had not touched her yet.

I grabbed for her pulse and for a moment I failed to find it. I rolled back her eyelid. Her pupils were dilated terribly, but there was plenty of warmth to her soft, satinlike white skin, so I breathed again. A bulge in the breast pocket of her tailored suit caught my eye. Hastily I dug it out. It didn't make me mad at all when I found my all-important twenty on the outside of the roll. I exchanged it quickly, touched a match to the greenback, stamped on the ashes.

I went back to the door, opened it. Feet were slogging around in the front of the house. I suddenly heard my name spoken—in the purring, gloating tones of Lieutenant Cullen.

Then the little banker's chuckle. "Nonsense, Lieutenant. He's been working with me. You'd embarrass me very much if you made trouble for him. Here—on the floor—is the murderer you want."

I closed the door, grinning, as I pictured Cullen's humble little Foxy Grandpa face. I found some witch hazel in the bathroom to stop my scratches bleeding, went back to the bed, and drew up a chair.

The girl was deep under the morphine, but I could almost feel her pulse strengthening. She would be out for at least an hour more, but that was all right with me.

I could wait.

THE SECOND LOOP

IT LOOKED LIKE A ROUTINE ASSIGNMENT WHEN I HIT THAT TANK TOWN IN THE STICKS. BUT ALMOST BEFORE I'D SET MY BAG DOWN ON THE DEPOT PLATFORM A KILLER WAS TAKING POT SHOTS AT ME FROM AMBUSH, AND I FOUND I'D WALKED INTO THREE MURDERS INSTEAD OF JUST ONE JEWEL HEIST WITH THE THIEF ALREADY IN THE CAN.

I **T WAS** the most desolate railroad station I have ever seen—a square little shack by a T-shaped platform, the paint peeled from it, its swinging sign almost bleached clean of its *Carmay*. Afternoon sun blazed down, reflected from the rotting boards like a furnace. The sky was pure, hot blue. There was not a living thing in sight.

Across the tracks rank swamp grass was hemmed in by a wire fence. The grass, high as a man's head, a huge tract of it, swept away and up to the woods that seemed to surround the swamp eight hundred or a thousand yards away. Behind the station a scrub clearing of what had once been gravel met the tangled, thick woods all around on that side. I could not discern the road that must lead out of it. I was alone in a silent, empty world.

I sat down on my bag, mopped the sweat from my face and cursed with a fervor I had forgotten I possessed.

I got out the wire from my boss, Preeker, that had caught me in Baltimore the previous day.

Go at once to Carmay. Have ticket agent work you out a connection that will get you there no later than tomorrow afternoon. Authorize you pay usual ten percent reward return Judge Hawkins jewelry on which we've already paid theft claim. Airmailing you care of Holland House, Carmay, previous oper-

ative's report and telegram from Carol Trent. Advise Trent by
wire, Carmay Daily Courier, time and place your arrival and she
will meet. Urgent.

Preeker.

I looked at my copy of the wire I had sent this Carol
Trent. I had made no mistake. The railroad agent in Baltimore had arranged the only possible route for me that
would land me here in time. I had sat up all night, switching
trains till I was dizzy, to arrive at this, the disused station of
Carmay. The town itself was now served by another line.
Making connections with that line had been impossible.
I had had to unravel yards of red tape to have the train on
this branch even stop to let me off here and, after all the
feverish rush, I was now left holding my hand on my neck.

I COULD have cheerfully murdered Preeker. It had
not occurred to me to question his instructions. After
nine years sleuthing under him, you lose the habit. But
the hotter I got, the madder I got, once I started to think
it over.

Carmay was a town of nine thousand people, I'd learned.
Somebody named Hawkins had had some jewels stolen.
Acme Indemnity had paid out on the theft. This Carol
Trent evidently had got wind of them and I was to go and
dicker for their return. A routine job. What the hell was
so urgent about that?

Only one blessed thing was urgent—and that was to get
myself out of the torturing heat before I melted. I looked
around the clearing again for the road, but it was only a
gesture. I knew damn well I was going to park right here
and store up wrath to blister this Carol Trent when she
finally did come.

The flashlight arced through the air and lit, its beam pointing straight at the killer.

I looked at the station shack. The windows were all boarded up and the whole place was in a state of decay. There was a padlock on the door, but, regardless, I determined to break in. It might not be cool inside but I'd be out of the sun at least.

I stepped over to the door—and a bullet *whacked* into the wood a foot from my face.

I nearly broke my neck jumping away from the door. A rifle cracked out in the lush grass across the road—once, twice, three times. The bullets smacked into the wood as I dived dizzily across the platform and plunged over the edge.

I was more flabbergasted than frightened. From the report, the rifle was of modest caliber, but even the smallest can do damage to the back of your head at a hundred yards or less. From a crouch behind my platform shelter, I sweated and cursed. I had no gun on me, naturally—I don't wear one on train rides with nothing more than routine in sight—and my bag, containing two, was well out of reach from where I squatted.

What made it all the more maddening was that I could have picked this Daniel Boone off with ease if I were heeled. I could follow his progress through the long swamp grass as easily as though he had been holding a flag over him. Having apparently finished his murderous little chore, he was now hotfooting it quickly toward the thick woods. I couldn't figure whether he thought he had potted me or what, but I took a chance presently on his not planning any more shots and wriggled up, went for my bag as fast as I could. Unfortunately buckles and straps defeated me, and by the time I had a gun out, the waving grass indicated that he had reached the woods. Hot silence settled down again.

I knelt there, wondering dizzily what anyone would want to knock me over for on a job like this. It didn't make sense.

It didn't make for comfort either. Whatever the hell was causing all this, it dawned on me that I had better get to the airmail reports that were, presumably, waiting for me at the local hotel, and without delay. Not unnaturally, I began to fry Preeker in my mind for sending me on a dangerous job without warning. I had told him a dozen times I'd skin him alive if he ever did that to me.

Then a welcome sound fell on my ears—the approaching hum of a motor. I slid my gun onto my hip and stood up.

A not very new Chevvie poked through an invisible road and came swerving around to shower gravel against the platform. A boy of fifteen with large brown eyes stuck an envelope at me. "Your train was a hour late. She couldn't wait," he informed me truculently.

I ripped it open and read: *Terribly sorry but cannot wait any longer, as I have a most important appointment out at the prison. Will you please let Jerry drive you out and meet me there?* It was signed: *Carol Trent.*

I asked the boy: "What prison?"

"Walkeela."

"Can we pass the Holland House on the way?"

"I guess."

TEN MINUTES later, as we hummed out the other end of town, I had a fat brown envelope on my lap, was digesting Moffet's report hastily. There wasn't much of it—

This Hawkins is all right and the robbery is legit. The big lug who stuck them up isn't human. They gave him everything they had at the station house but he won't give up the ice. They might as well have been working on somebody else. I swear he doesn't feel. I am writing this just after he has been plastered with a ten-year sentence, so I'd say we can kiss the ice good-bye. The enclosed news story covers everything.

It did. It presented the strange, sultry little situation in trim, orderly detail.

It was a six-weeks-old copy of the Carmay *Guide-Advocate*. The banner head was about the murder of a local newspaperman, evidently the editor of a rival sheet. I skipped that, at first. Our robbery got a fair play on the left-hand side.

JUDGE HAWKINS, REV. ALBEMARLE, SENATOR NUYS BURGLARY VICTIMS
Members of Citizens' Committee Robbed
While Awaiting Report of Editor Hess.
Thief Caught Within Few Minutes of Crime.

Tonight, at exactly midnight, at the residence of Judge Hawkins, the judge, the Rev. Mr. Albemarle, and Senator Nuys were held up at the point of a gun by one Finch, a gardener employed on the local estate of Senator Nuys. The victims were gathered at the judge's home on request of Editor Hess of the *Courier,* and his promise that he would phone them tonight sensational disclosures regarding his investigation of the ring which has allegedly been smuggling contraband into Walkeela Prison.

The tragic irony—tragic in view of Editor Hess's death—was that the editor did phone, at exactly midnight as promised, but was unable to communicate anything whatever. Senator Nuys' secretary, who answered the call, was in the very act of passing the instrument to the senator, when Finch appeared and forced him to hang up the phone at once.

The gardener, brandishing a gun, then proceeded to relieve all present of their valuables, including jewelry from the judge's open wall safe and a sum of money which comprised the treasury of the Citizens' Committee.

Instantly the robber had departed, the senator phoned in the alarm and Finch was captured as he was attempting to steal a car parked on Main Street. Unfortunately, none of the loot was found upon him and, to date, he has refused to reveal its hiding-place.

Finch had been employed on the senator's estate for some three years and, although dull-witted and of a morose disposition, had, as far as is known, a clean record.

Etc.

If I had not been going to jump across the page to the story of the murder of Editor Hess by then anyway, sight of the byline would have made me. The story was written by Carol Trent, the girl who had wired Preeker about our jewelry.

Under the banner, the sub-head read—

Courageous Editor Strangled in *Courier* Offices. Desk Looted. Evidence Against Crooked Prison Ring Vanishes. Clyde Daniels, Ex-Druggist, Sought in Killing.

Tonight, at ten minutes past midnight, the body of Editor Hess was found in his office-living-quarters, strangled by means of a hangman's noose formed in a short length of hempen rope. Bruises on his face indicated that the newspaperman had put up a struggle before succumbing to his assailant.

The body was discovered by Police Chief Maybee. Chief Maybee was informed by the local telephone operator, at fifteen minutes past midnight, that the receiver in the apartment above the *Courier* offices had fallen off the hook and that she had heard crashing sounds. Unable to get an answer, she called police headquarters, knowing that the *Courier* offices were only a short block up the street and visible from the station house. Chief Maybee, acting on the suggestion, looked out, saw lights burning in the upper part of the little building and hurried to the scene, where he found the dead man.

The office-living-room of the little two-room suite was in chaos, drawers upended, their contents dumped out. Editor Hess lay in a sea of papers, his face blackened, his fingernails broken in vain efforts to loosen the rope, which had bitten into his flesh. An extra hangman's noose lay beside him.

The time of the murder was accurately established. At exactly twelve o'clock, it is known that Editor Hess talked on the phone to another, distant section of town (see story opposite). At ten minutes after twelve, the telephone operator received the flash on her board which resulted in the alarm to the police.

Police are seeking Clyde Daniels who was seen by citizens running down Hester Avenue within a few minutes of the murder. So far, the ex-druggist has completely eluded pursuit.

Readers will recall that Editor Hess's investigation was instigated following the publication in a northern magazine of the memoirs of a Walkeela ex-convict, in which it was stated that narcotics, spirits, and various contrabands were readily obtainable inside the prison. Directly following this, it will also be recalled, Clyde Daniels abruptly left Carmay and his position with the Regal Drug Store here. He became the special target of Editor Hess's broadsides, the militant editor all but accusing the ex-pharmacist of being the brains of the ring. Editor Hess had also declared his intention, should he receive certain evidence for which he was angling, of turning the matter over to the Federal Narcotic Bureau. Police believe that this did eventuate and that Daniels, learning of it, returned to silence his accuser.

All highways and railways etc....

THE LITTLE Chevvie bounced on sanded tarvia, through burnt-over scrub woods. Even the breeze was hot. I stared down at the two neat oblongs of print.

One story or two?

It fairly cried, at first glance, to be all tied together, but the more I groped, the more ticklish the tieing-together process seemed to become. I didn't doubt it was Hess's investigation which had finally brought about his death. It seemed reasonable that this fugitive Clyde Daniels had done it with his little rope, and just in time, at that. For it certainly appeared that the newspaperman had—in view of his assembling the Citizens' Committee—come into evidence that would justify contacting the federals.

But why the holdup by the gardener at the other end of town? What bearing could that have had on the staging of the killing?

I didn't want to, but I had to recognize that the holdup episode was complete in itself. A disgruntled farmhand, tired of grubbing for a living, with the sight of a wad of money turning a none-too-bright brain—the holdup—the hiding of the loot—the dopey attempt at a getaway. I had run into a thousand jobs just like it. It didn't need explanation. Apart from the loose end of the loot's being undiscovered, it was all cleaned up.

Nor did the murder need further explanation. Apart from the rounding up of the fugitive Clyde Daniels, that too seemed complete in all angles. Whatever fuss might grow out of it regarding conditions at the prison would be another matter to take up later.

So that settled it. Apart from the coincidence of the phone call, the murder had nothing to do with our little jewel robbery. I could forget the killing and concentrate on my own business.

Yes I could!

Just to make it tougher, I suddenly noticed the yellow form I had overlooked in the fat envelope—the telegram

Carol Trent had sent to Preeker in New York and which had caused him to send me here. It read: *If you want to recover stolen jewels taken from Judge Hawkins last month, send experienced man capable handling a murderer here at once. Must arrive before tomorrow night or will be too late. Wire me and I will meet train.*

I gave up the mental merry-go-rounding. The girl evidently had the key that would set the two puzzles together. Yet—professional pride maybe—I would have liked to figure it myself, especially in view of the unknown gent who had tried to murder me. He was going to be plenty sorry when I got my hands on him.

I wished that I could see the robbery victims—this Judge Hawkins, the dominie, and the senator—and, promptly, I got my wish.

We were on this narrow tarvia road, winding through the scrub woods. Suddenly the prison appeared against the skyline three or four miles ahead of us. I knew of this Walkeela Prison. It had been a woman's jug—a very small one—until abandoned a few years before. Unfortunately, the men's prisons in the state started to fill up almost directly after that and they had to brush the cobwebs off Walkeela and use it for an overflow, a holdover. It was known as a soft stir where bad-behaved convicts did not go.

As we broke, momentarily, out of the woods, I saw that it sat high on a spur of hill. The road ahead of us led down, wandered through woods, then finally swerved sharply up in a long, banked climb on a sort of curved rib, leading up to the little eyrie on which the old pen perched grayly on the edge of nothing.

I WAS so intent on examining the prison, and I guess the boy beside me was too, that we almost climbed the rear

end of the big, five-year-old limousine we suddenly over-
took on a curve. It was just chugging along but we were
going fast and the boy had to turn aside for a moment
while we ran up beside it.

A bespectacled youth was driving. In the rear seat three
men rode. One was a dark-eyed tall man with a long, horse
face and iron-gray sideburns. He wore full clericals—even
to gaiters and a flat-crowned black felt hat. The middle one
was a short, dumpy man with straggling gray wisps of hair
sticking from under his broad-brimmed black hat and an
anxious, bewildered look. The third was a bony, hard-faced
individual with a perfectly square bald head and cold gray
eyes. They all gave us a glance as we pulled up beside them
for an instant. The boy instantly braked the car and we
dropped back.

By then, we could see all the road between us and the
rib leading up and around to the prison. "Go on," I urged
him. "Pass them and get up there."

He shook his head. "You ain't supposed to pass on this
road. That's Judge Hawkins in the car there. He'd see I got
a ticket."

"That's nice. Which is Hawkins? The little gray-haired
actor in the middle.

"Naw. That's Senator Nuys."

After a minute I said: "Don't tell me the minister is the
Reverend Albemarle?"

"Yeah."

We poked along behind them, down the valley and up
around the long, bare hill. Having got my wish and seen
these three odd individuals, I could not make up my mind
what to do about it, if anything. It was a toss-up whether
the girl would want me to uncover myself to them or not.

The judge's car was stopped at the gray stone prison gates when we pulled up behind. Two rifled-armed guards were just stepping back from the car and the gates were swinging open. The youth beside me slumped back and wriggled his shoulders.

"Well, come on," I suggested.

"I can't go in. They won't let me. You got to hoof it."

I damned him wearily, climbed out. By the time I had made my peace with the guards at the cost of giving up my gun and had been assigned one to accompany me across the prison yard, the big limousine was drawn up before the warden's house. Its occupants were out on the sidewalk, talking to a gray-haired man on the steps and a girl in a blue dress.

The prison was absurdly small and ramshackle. Two sides of the hollow square were plain stone walls—the one I had just come through and the one at its right-hand end. The other flanks of the enclosure were cell blocks and administration buildings, shops. The warden's house was in the corner between the administration buildings and the first cell block—sort of tucked into the left-hand corner of the little finger of precipice on which the whole prison stood.

We walked across the rubbly prison yard and up onto the sidewalk. The little group was still clustered around the steps of the warden's house. The girl was hidden from me by the broad backs of the tall man in ecclesiastical clothes and the bony, bald-headed Judge Hawkins, but I could hear her conversation.

I hung back as the short, rotund little Senator Nuys was saying in a pleading, almost tearful voice: "But my dear, why cannot you tell us why you want to see this criminal?

We, after all, are the victims of his crime, as well as having a civic interest…"

Her voice was cool, clipped, defiant. "By tomorrow morning you'll know all about it. Right now I haven't anything to say. You'd think I was asking you to do something awful. As a matter of fact, if I hadn't been delayed I would have been here by five o'clock and had an interview with this man without having to call on you at all. Because it's after hours, the warden seems nervous about it."

THE WARDEN was chubby, blond, with upcurling golden curls on either side of his bald spot. His blue eyes were bloodshot and anxious and the lines of his face deeply drawn. He said hastily: "I—in view of the criticism which is rife about my prison, I thought if you, Senator, or you, Judge, would just make the request…."

The Reverend Albemarle said in a voice like soft chalk, "Can't we go inside and discuss it, Warden, out of the heat?" and they moved to go up the steps. Then, for the first time, I saw the girl.

She was a dainty, earnest, lovely little child, not a day over twenty, I guessed, and afire with crusading zeal. Just from seeing her, the whole set-up suddenly changed complexion.

She did not belong in this sort of game. Messing with crooks is a mean, ugly business—and this mess looked about as deadly as they come. She wasn't the type to be in it and I was suddenly worried, suddenly anxious to get it cleaned up, kicked to pieces, before anything happened and she got hurt.

She went up the steps, still talking. She wore a perky little red pancake hat. Golden curls tumbled out from under it. Her skin was glowing, golden, fresh, her eyes deep blue, her dainty little figure graceful, with quick little curves under the plain red tailored suit she wore. She had half-socks and crepe-soled shoes on her feet and she might have been a highschool girl. Just as she got to the top of the steps she caught sight of me, and her hand went to her mouth to conceal the little *"oh!"*

She stepped around the others, caught the warden's sleeve as they went inside and nodded to me, said something quickly in his ear, then left him alone on the steps to welcome me.

He ran a finger inside his collar uncomfortably as I came up, shot a reproachful look over his shoulder after her. "You—you are the insurance man?" His bloodshot little eyes looked at me uneasily.

"Yeah."

"Will—will you please wait here a few moments? Miss Trent will be out presently." He vanished up the steps hastily, went into a dark hall down whose length I could dimly see figures moving. He turned off through a door at the left.

I was left alone with my escort, the guard. He looked at me gloomily and concluded, "I guess you don't need me any more," and took himself off.

I was disconcerted. I had never seen a prison run on such casual lines before.

The spectacled youth who had been driving the judge's car was sitting behind the wheel making notes in a tiny notebook. I went over and made him jump a foot by asking: "You mind telling me what church the Reverend Albemarle is connected with?"

His scared little eyes crawled over and inspected me from behind the spectacles till he was sure I wasn't going to bite him. Then he told me in a precise, tenor voice: "I do not believe he is connected with any. He is the president of the county Temperance Union."

I said, "Oh," as though I cared and leaned an elbow on his car. When he had refused my cigarette, I tried: "Haven't they cleaned up that holdup at the senator's yet?"

I got nowhere. His pinched little eyes looked fearfully at me and he said: "Really—I think you had better speak to the senator if you wish any information."

THE HAPLESS-LOOKING little senator suddenly appeared on the steps again, looking as though he were about to cry. "Frederick! Have you seen my spectacles?"

The youth looked over into the back of the limousine, climbed out, rescued a pair of eyeglasses from the cushions of the tonneau, and carried them wearily up.

The senator mumbled thanks, vanished inside again.

Two minutes later, he was out once more. "Frederick! Have you a pen with a stub point?"

Again the secretary climbed out, furnished the missing article and the senator scurried back inside the prison. My urge to get at this thing was making me restless and impatient. I stood on the steps, peering down the dim hall.

A man in a P.K.'s uniform came out of the warden's office with a bunch of keys in his hand. He stepped across the hall to a door directly opposite, put a key in the lock and opened it, held it open. The girl in the red suit followed him out, making a stopping gesture with her palm toward the inside of the warden's office. She quickly closed the door, turned toward the P.K.

I said, "Miss Trent," and she flung me a quick glance, paused only long enough to say, "I'll be with you in just a few minutes," then vanished through the door the big, beady-eyed, walrus-mustached Latin was holding open.

There didn't seem to be any reason why I shouldn't step into the hall and my anxiety for her was, queerly, growing by leaps and bounds. It occurred to me that a prison where liquor and hop was let through and where an exposé was imminent, was no safe place for the girl who seemingly held the key to the situation.

I found myself by the door that had swallowed her. It was half ajar and I could see dimly the lettering, *Please Show Your Pass*, on a square of pasteboard at my eye level. Inside the door was a large room with benches and at the far end, another thick oak door through which the keeper was just allowing the girl to vanish.

He closed the door, locked it, stood looking at it a minute, palmed his chin, and came slowly back towards me. He looked at a turnip of a watch, stopped, and paced around a little.

It was while he was doing this that I had a thought.

It was sudden enough and startling enough so that I must have moved suddenly or made some exclamation. Anyway, the P.K.'s lowering, swarthy face jerked up and he saw me. He growled something, strode hastily toward me.

"Hey! What are you doing there? You can't…"

Then the scream came from behind the closed door at the other end of the room.

For a split second we were both frozen. Then the scream came again—and died away abruptly. I plunged through the open door and, as he still stood like a bump on a log, I straight-armed him furiously, sent him reeling toward the door beyond. "Move, you fool! Open that door!"

He mumbled something, dived for the keyhole with his ring of keys, jabbed ineffectually, till I drove the key in with the heel of my hand, wrenched his hand till I turned his hand, key and all.

I burst into a long, bare, narrow chamber. A sign on the wall said, *Visitors Room,* and it was a crude imitation of a modern prison conference gallery. Two-thirds of its width was divided from the other third by a thick wire mesh. Like most everything else in this place, it was the wrong kind—with two-inch squares between wires.

Before the grill, the girl was half hanging by her fingers to the mesh, sinking downward. Even as we jumped for her, her fingers slacked and she fell away, lay motionless where she fell. Behind the grill, the biggest, crudest-looking thug I had yet to see in convict clothes stood staring at her with eyes like saucers.

I roared at him as I dived to the girl's side: "What happened?"

He shook his head from side to side, gasping: "I dunno! I dunno! She was talking to me. All of a sudden she screamed and started doubling up...."

I FELT the girl's pulse. It was beating fast. Her face was not pale, but flushed.

I looked up as the warden and the three members of the Citizens' Committee ran in. I snapped at them: "Get the doctor—fast!" I tried to rouse the girl a little. "Miss Trent! Miss Trent!" But she was limp, insensible.

The doctor and a prison attendant came, while I was chafing her wrists. The others were barking questions at the ape-like convict behind the mesh. He was saying over and over: "I—I dunno what happened! I dunno!"

The doctor shoved me aside, made a quick examination, then snapped, "Stretcher!" and the attendant ran out.

I bawled at him, "What is it? What happened to her?" but he only shook his head.

I jumped up, faced the convict—nobody had to tell me this was Finch the ex-gardener and hold-up man—and roared at him: "Come clean! What happened?"

"I dunno! I dunno!"

"You're a liar!" I swung on the warden. "This lug may have killed her. You know who I am. I want to question him somewhere—and I mean question him."

Two white-coated attendants ran in with a stretcher. I grabbed the doctor's arm as they lifted her onto it. "Is she in danger? Is it anything that might kill her?"

He said, "I don't think so," irritably, wondering who the hell I was, no doubt.

I pounded at him, "I'm the Acme Insurance Company. There'll be trouble if that girl dies. I want to know every and any change!" and he seemed mildly impressed.

I TURNED back to find that two guards were wrestling the convict from behind the grill. I shot at the warden, "I want to talk to that thug alone," and the bewildered little blond man nodded giddily, told the guards behind the grill, "Take him to Number Four, boys," and they dragged him through a door.

I swung back on the warden and the three excited men and then checked myself, looked suddenly back at the grill. I bent down, snatched at a portion of it, about waist-high. Then I really got mad.

On a line about eight inches long, the black-enameled wires had been snipped, obviously by a keen wire cutter. In the position they were now, the break was almost invisible.

I yelled: "Look! Somebody cut this for him! With his fingers he could bend it back and make a little opening. He probably got the girl close, opened this, and grabbed her and then—did something to her! By God, I'll find out what it was. Come on, Warden—where is he?"

The big, bony-headed, bald Judge Hawkins—the only one of the three Citizens' Committeemen who had kept cool—suddenly caught my arm. "Wait a minute." His cold gray eyes were like ice. "You're from Acme? Your interest in this is the jewelry you insured?"

"It *was!*" I assured him. "Now it's grown. I'm going to clean up this whole stinking mess. I'm going to find out who killed your newspaper editor, too—and just what's going on here in this joint. This town has too many loose ends and I'm going to tie them all up. How do you like that?"

"I like it fine," he said in a mild voice.

I turned again on the warden. "I want a harness strap," I told him bluntly, "and a handful of tacks, and your two strongest guards. Now don't anybody go squeamish on me, or I'll bat you one. If there's the slightest change in the girl's condition while I'm doing this chore, somebody please tell me. All right, Warden, come on."

The warden looked desperately at the bald-headed, eagle-faced Hawkins. The judge nodded his head slowly.

Two uncomfortable guards trotted with me across the prison yard toward the dungeons. I was really on fire. I was determined to beat the truth out of this halfwitted monster if it killed him. I was positive now that he knew the truth.

TWO HOURS later, I gave up. That is, I gave up trying to force him to talk. I stood over him, my clothes wringing wet with sweat, my hands blistered from wielding the strap. He was a mess in the corner of the windowless cell—out—his breathing like that of an animal. But I had broken his formula of, "I don't know anything about it." To

one of my questions—the one about who had hired him—
he had slipped and said, "I ain't saying," and to another—
my asking what he was going to get out of it—he had
fumbled again with, "I ain't worryin'."

When I strode stiffly out of the cell, the two white-faced
guards came forward as if they thought I was going to fall
into their arms. I gave one the cat, and snarled: "What's
the matter? Think I can't take it? Has there been any word
from the infirmary?"

As though called, a white-coated attendant ran down
the corridor and shouted my name. When I answered, he
said: "Doctor Considine said to tell you the girl was apparently given a hypodermic in the arm—insulin. It doesn't
look as though she got enough to kill her, but she'll probably be unconscious for a good long time yet."

I caught my tongue in my teeth, cursed slowly and
savagely. I was in a mood to turn back and start in on
Finch's face—the one portion of his anatomy I had left
alone. That I didn't was because I thought suddenly of two
things. The first—that in spite of his seeming stupidity,
this big lout wasn't as dumb as I had thought—and that
meant plenty. For instance, he had had enough intelligence
to be taught how to seize the girl's arm through the hole
in the mesh and administer the hypo. The second—that I
was putting myself, when I came to think of it, practically
in the lion's mouth by remaining in this place. For that
hypodermic must have been on Finch's person when the
guards led him out to the visitors' room! Without conniv-
ance of someone—or everyone—in authority, that would
have been impossible.

And over and above that, there was the girl's telegram
to Preeker—... *must arrive before... night or it will be too
late.* Plus—and this was the real reason—that I suddenly

realized what I had and that I needed the answer to only one more question—an answer that I had to get from a spot away from here to blow the whole thing up.

When I got back to the warden's office, you'd think—from the pasty faces and sopping wet handkerchiefs of the others—that they'd been doing the work. There was a big pitcher of iced tea on the table and they were all gulping at it except the pudgy little senator. He had his hat off and his straggly gray locks and seamed face made him look like a bewildered little witch. He was waiting for his secretary to bring in some saccharine tablets.

The bony-faced, square-headed Nuys said: "Did he talk?"

"Enough," I said, and waited while the senator dropped pills into his drink. I looked at them all carefully and said: "I think somebody here has had a tough break, because of my coming to this town in such a hurry. You don't know what that means, and it isn't important, but I plan to open Carmay up by morning. In fact"—I looked up at the warden's clock which showed twenty minutes to nine—"by midnight, I'll promise you a surprise. The person who put that cretin Finch, up to his tricks and tried to kill Miss Trent made a bad mistake—because I know more than she did. I can use some help from some of you."

"Name it," the bald-headed judge snapped.

"A ride back to town, and some help hiring a car of my own in case I need it."

"What else?"

"A visit to the place where Hess, the editor, was murdered."

"You want to start now?"

Before I could answer, the chalky-soft voice of the dark-faced, Reverend Albemarle asked: "What are you planning to do?" It was the only time he had spoken to me.

"Finish up Editor Hess's work," I told him.

I STAVED off their questions one way or another while we raced back to town. Now that I had the key to the thing pounding in my mind, I was agonized at not having seen it earlier—and amazed that nobody else had either.

At the edge of town, the bald-headed, grim judge hired a coupé for me from a garage and I got rid of them—all but him. He even got me a police department license plate at the station house—all without asking, and rode with me to the one place I had to go—the death scene.

It took me just one minute inside the shabby office-living-room. It had been cleaned up, but enough time had elapsed to put a layer of dust over the whole apartment. Evidently the people who were carrying on with the *Courier* were not using the room. I saw what I wanted the first instant I stepped into the place.

The editor had evidently batched it in his own peculiar way. He had an oversize electric refrigerator directly beside his desk. The phone sat on a small drum table beside the other end of the desk and beyond that was a tall bookcase, six feet high.

I said: "That's all I wanted to know. If you want to be really helpful, get hold of the staff of Miss Trent's paper and tell them to get ready to run off an extra. You can either wait here, or go home. I'll be phoning you in the next hour or two."

He nodded slowly, and I backed out. I took my hand off my gun when I was in the little coupé and not before. I sent it scudding up Main Street.

I had to waste about ten minutes in making absolutely positive that I was not being tailed, and in finding my way about the unfamiliar town, but I figured I had that much leeway anyhow.

Then I was alone, pushing the little coupé back along the country road at the other end of town—the road that led to the station where I'd been potshotted at—the disused Carmay depot.

At last—the car hidden in the woods a quarter of a mile away—I was slipping back through the woods and into the clearing that held the lonely little wooden building with its T-shaped platform.

There wasn't a sound. Even the bullfrogs and insects in the swamp opposite were absolutely hushed. I am not much of a ruralite but that, of course, told me the story.

I knew I had not much time to spare, at best, so I did the only thing I could possibly do. I stole away from the edge of the trees, half rounded the clearing and knelt down. Somewhere I had heard that it is harder to locate the direction of a voice when it comes from close to the ground.

I put my face down and said: "Clyde Daniels."

Naturally, I didn't get any joyous reply. I gave it time to sink in, then I said: "I'm not a dope. The frogs went silent That means somebody came out of that station shack. That means you—the guy who was trying to draw me away from the shack this morning when I threatened to go in. What have you got in there? A supply of grub?"

That drew nothing so I went on—a little faster now—as the fear gnawed at me that my remarks back in the prison in the presence of the guilty man might have sunk in quicker than I expected they would and that he might be along any minute. "I'm Acme Insurance," I continued. "You're a rat and a dope-peddling heel, but I'll give you a break to get your top man. I've got it figured like this—

"When the scandal broke about the prison, your top man paid you to duck out, in hopes it would keep him from being suspected. You didn't see what you were letting yourself in for and, being a green hand, you were scared enough to be glad to do it. Then, when you were gone, they started laying the whole thing up to you and you got even scareder. You were just a punk along the line, like the P.K. up at the prison. Right?"

I WENT right on as though he had fervently endorsed what I said. "It began to look better to you to come back and give up, confess what you'd done, rather than have ten times as much pile up against you. You got in touch with Hess.

"Hess promised to play ball with you—just as I'm promising now—to get the top man and the others. He had certain affidavits, let's say, and he needed yours to round out the evidence. Or maybe you had to go and dig them up. I don't know. Anyway, your evidence was the key to the whole picture. None of the others knew the top man. So you sneaked into town—six weeks ago. You went to his office—and found him murdered—and you were sewed up in the burg, with every highway watched.

"You thought of this shack and came here to hole up, all ready to take to the woods if anybody came. You must have had a time keeping yourself in supplies, but you were born here and maybe somebody helped you out. That it?"

There was still no answer and I began to sweat, my ears strained for sound of a motor hum along the road behind me.

"There'll be somebody along here any time now—your top man. I practically told him where you were, an hour or two ago. Here's my proposition. Give me the evidence you were going to give Hess and I'll let you take my car and make a getaway. They won't stop you, because there's a police department license on it and you can get out of the dragnet. It's about your only chance, so you'd better speak up. I know you're there and if you stall any longer, we'll both be sunk."

That was all I had. If it flopped—

It didn't. There was a rustling from the edge of the clearing above the shack and a frightened, husky voice said: "All right, mister. I'll take a chance on you. Hess sent me three other affidavits he had and asked me to round them out. I got them all. I was taking them back to him—with my own—that night. They're in a little oil-silk pouch under the floor of the station shack. You can get them by crawling under the plat—"

And I saw where I had made my mistake.

A flashlight's beam blazed out for one second—from a spot just about halfway between me and the shrinking figure emerging from the woods' edge. For one instant, it spotlighted the shabby, furtive figure of the ex-druggist. The harsh, snarling spurt of flame leaped instantly from behind the flashlight. Clyde Daniels screamed, clutched at his throat as he was blasted backwards—and the light was gone.

I had underestimated the quickness of thought—and movement—of my murderer. He had outdistanced me, beaten me here—and now shot my key witness out of the picture. But he had had to expose himself to do it. I was only a split second behind him. I had my gun kicking in my hand, almost as the echo came from his shot. I was furious—I don't know why. Clyde Daniels had nothing better coming to him—but I was wild that I had, by my promise, baited him out to be shot down. But I had the edge and I knew it. My first shot drew a gasp. I pounded lead viciously into the spot where the flash-beam had showed and I got a queer break.

The other's gun had just started to answer me with two sharp spurts of flame—and when I returned the fire I heard a *zing* and the flashlight suddenly came to life, arcing through the air, its beam alight, whirling and twisting— to fall and lie, still burning, in the patch of gravel.

Plainly trapped, I saw the diving figure of Frederick, the senator's secretary, as he tried wildly to cross the clearing. I pumped two shots slowly and coldly into his head and he slammed up against the platform and lay there, dying.

I WAS sitting by the girl's hospital bed. "He was in position to run the prison racket," I said. "As the senator's secretary, everything that dim-witted old bird did went through Frederick's hands. He could speak for the senator whenever he wanted to and everybody knew it. When he saw a chance for easy money, he took it. When Hess got on his trail, he had to bump him. Also, he had to kill Daniels. He was a shrewd little rat and he kept closer to what Hess was doing than Hess thought. He found out, somehow, about the night Daniels was to sneak back in and meet Hess at the *Courier* offices.

"He isn't much himself physically, but he was able to talk this giant, Finch, into working for him. At that, forty thousand dollars was probably more than Finch would ever see in two lifetimes. That was what he was supposed to get—the loot from the robbery was to be his. He was to serve some time for it, of course. The gag was that when he gathered in the swag at Hawkins' place, he dropped it right outside the door and then went and got pinched. Evidently he had enough faith in Frederick to believe that he would keep it for him till he got out.

"Anyway, the idea was for Finch to go to the *Courier* office at a certain time. He was supposed to find both Hess and Daniels there and he was supposed to be a match for them both. At that, I don't doubt he would have been, but Daniels was late. Finch can be told how to do pretty involved things and will do as he's told, up to a certain point, but he can't think for himself. He went there and found only one man. He killed him, and left the spare noose on the floor. Then he took the telephone and set it on top of the bookcase, near the edge, with one edge of the phone on a book, the other on an ice cube.

"Then he beat it for Hawkins'. From a store right across the street, he dialed the judge's number. Frederick, in the house, made sure he answered the phone and he asserted it was Hess, who was now dead, talking. Then Finch hung up his end of the phone, ran across the street and pulled the holdup. Along about then the ice cube melted back in Hess's apartment, tipped the phone off onto the floor, bouncing off the drum table and so forth. That gave Finch an ironclad alibi. And it would have worked, at that, if you hadn't somehow doped out most of all this yourself. How did you get on to it?"

She blushed. Lying in bed, with her creamy shoulders and arms bare, she made my throat dry. She looked down at her hands and admitted: "Mr. Hess told me he was going to meet Clyde Daniels that night. He—he didn't want his paper to beat mine out and make me look foolish. I—it took me weeks to figure out even part of what you have. I—I think you're wonderful."

And Preeker beefed at paying a two-weeks hotel bill for me at the Holland House! Incidentally, she wasn't nearly as young as I'd thought she was the first time I saw her.

STORM SIGNAL

IF THE BUSYBODY OLD LADY WITH THE UMBRELLA HADN'T PICKED THE WRONG MINUTE TO WHACK THAT HARD-AS-NAILS INSURANCE DICK ACROSS THE LEGS, THE MAD MR. MOON MIGHT HAVE FOUND HIMSELF SAFE IN THE CAN, INSTEAD OF LYING DEAD IN A MUD PUDDLE BESIDE A BLACKJACKED GREAT DANE WHO FORGOT TO BARK LOUD ENOUGH.

CHAPTER ONE
THE MADNESS OF
MR. MOON

M AYBE IT was the storm that made me touchy and nervous. Maybe the unfamiliar realms of banking through which I was groping. Maybe just plain exasperation at my three-months-old, grueling assignment. Or maybe the irritating, unreasonable, stiff-necked attitude of this vice-president, McGrath, that threatened to blank out what faint progress I *had* made. But mostly, the storm.

It was a museum piece. At one o'clock the skies had suddenly opened and flung water down. For a fifteen-minute cloudburst, it might have been normal. After half an hour, it was startling. After an hour, it was unbelievable. The wind came up then. So did the storm signals outside New York harbor.

It was two hours old when I stood in McGrath's elaborate, ground-floor office in the luxurious private banking house, and there was no abatement. Rain thundered and lashed on Wall Street outside, racketing the windows so that he had to raise his voice to tell me impatiently: "We'll do nothing of the sort. Your request is preposterous."

He looked like a fanatic—tall and bony in his morning coat, with a razor face and small, shining gray eyes. Irongray hair waved thickly back from his high forehead, and his long lips were thin, bloodless—and tight now with finality.

I struggled once more. "This matter cost Acme Indemnity eighty thousand dollars, Mr. McGrath. If you refuse us, you block our only lead toward getting it back. This is about the only way we ever recover on stolen securities—one of the certificates crops up and we trace it back and back to where it came from. Most banks cooperate with us. These eighty thousand of Algoma bonds were stolen over three years ago. It's a miracle that we get a lead at all,

The screaming woman suddenly whacked at my legs with her umbrella.

after this lapse of time. What I'm asking you isn't so much. Don't tell me it's impossible."

"I didn't say it was impossible. I said it was preposterous. Morgan and Haley will always cooperate—if the situation makes sense. Your hypothesis makes no sense."

"I'll admit it isn't enough to get a court order on, but it's all we've got. Appreciate our position. I've struggled three months, pounding away at this Murray Moon on the strength of a thin tip. We've known him as a receiver for some time, but he was crafty and—prosperous. I was told he had the Algoma bonds tucked away. I tried to make him not so prosperous—in fact I damned near ruined his business—in hopes that he'd bring out the Algomas. It didn't work just that way, as I've told you. But when I did finally convince the police to take a chance and raid his office, we surprised him. He didn't have quite enough time to get everything cleaned up before he lit out and we found this one Algoma bond, with a notation on it to *Try the trust department of Morgan & Haley.*"

"What of it? A thief's reasonless scribbling. Are we to turn the firm upside down—"

"Murray Moon didn't do many reasonless things. If he planned to try and slip that bond past an old, established, top-line firm like yours, he had a reason. The obvious reason was that he—or some other sharpshooter—had caught you napping before."

"Preposterous—as I said before."

"At any rate, won't you take a look at what you've got on hand. You might find almost anything—"

"A look! A look! Great Jupiter! Come here!"

HE BOUNCED out of the chair and led me from the office into the empty—it was Saturday afternoon and most of the tellers had long gone—marble-and-brass-grille banking rooms. He led me to the far end and down a little marble stairs to a barred door. A special cop let us through this and another—its twin—and then there was business with signing a register and at last we were in front of a massive, open time vault. We stepped through its circular, foot-thick entrance and were inside a square safe. The faces of row upon row upon row of chased steel drawers surrounded us solidly.

"This is the vault belonging to the trust department of the firm—entirely separate from the banking part. Each of those drawers is filled with securities. There are upwards of forty million dollars' worth of certificates in here. Some of them have been here for years. We rarely change them."

"Why?"

"Do you know anything at all about trust business?"

"Not much."

"People sometimes wish to put certain money into trust funds. You've heard of that?"

I said I had.

"They entrust the money to us. We put it into securities, within legal limits, buy and sell occasionally, using our best judgment to keep the principal intact for the number of years that the trust exists. We pay the income to the beneficiary of the trust, turn over the principal when the trust is closed out. Naturally, our investments are very conservative. They do not vary much from year to year. Is that clear?"

"Yes."

"These securities represent what we have on hand at present. There are thousands and thousands of certificates. And you say: *Take a look!* What you mean is, take an inventory of this whole department, check over every one of those thousands of certificates, because some thief has an idle notion to jot our name on a piece of paper!"

"If you found so much as one sour item in the lot, wouldn't it be worth it?"

"If! Yes—*if* we did. But I see not the slightest indication that we would. Every one of those certificates was checked when it came in here. It will be checked again when it goes out. I can see nothing—absolutely nothing—in your suppositions. Because a thief may plan to sell us a stolen security does not, in my mind, prove that he has bilked us in the past."

"It's happened to the best banks—"

"Not to Morgan and Haley. Our tellers keep files—lists of all the certificate numbers of securities which have been reported stolen—on spindles beside their windows. They check the serial numbers of all deliveries before accepting them."

I said bluntly: "Nonsense."

"Non…? What the devil do you mean nonsense? They do!"

"In theory. Not in practice. In three years time, the quantity of circulars reaching your cashiers would overflow their cages. If they were to check every delivery, it would take two hours to accept a single bond. They have to depend on memory. A three-year old number just doesn't stick in anybody's memory and you know it."

The special cop outside the grilled door declared himself in. "They took an inventory of all the trust securities only last month, Mr. McGrath."

"Yes. Yes, of course they did. It had slipped—"

"That doesn't help. I spoke to your cashier. Only the names of the securities and the amounts were checked. Not the certificate numbers."

A voice called from outside the outer grilled-iron door: "Mr. Dan Odium to see you, Mr. McGrath."

He snatched out his watch. "Yes, yes. I am ready now." He drew himself up and told me in an irritated prim tone: "I think you must have just rushed in here on impulse—without thinking the thing through. On reflection, I am sure you will see how bizarre your request really is—on the basis you offer. Now you will have to excuse me."

Morgan and Haley were sound, conservative, rich bankers, beyond any kind of criticism. Their rating was the very highest. It is forbidden for Acme's sleuths to call their vice-presidents pinheaded incompetents and I couldn't think of anything else.

I gave up. "O.K. It's your bank." I followed him out. "However—"

HE RAN away from me up the stairs. When I reached the top he was halfway to his office. A pasty-faced youth with a spoiled, moist mouth was waiting for him in a black leather slicker, slapping his hat against his leg, pushing a snaky lock of black hair impatiently out of his sullen dark eyes.

The blond cashier who had been friendly to me was leaning, amused, in the vestibule, his arms folded. "I told you to wait and see General Haley, didn't I? When the general's here, McGrath's just another office boy."

"All right. You told me. Pick up the marbles."

That was uncalled-for. He had been very decent. It was just that I was disgruntled and ugly.

Remember—up to this point the three-months' job was as bitter as gall. I had got nowhere, by inches. I was putting in fourteen, eighteen hours a day, with only the flimsiest results. I was fed up, discouraged, nervous. I didn't even take satisfaction from having torn down the crafty, deadly little Murray Moon. It was mainly accident that my vicious close-checking on him night and day had hit him at a disastrous time. It had blown up a couple of deals under him, frightened away some of his important contacts just when he needed them. We had even picked up two wanted men when they tried to visit him. His standing in the underworld had gone to pot—but it hadn't got us a thing on him, nor the bonds. Up till here—up till the storm—up till the minute when I left the bank in the storm—the situation seemed dead, stuck, immovable.

It was the storm that jerked it to explosive life.

I WASN'T fully licked when I left the bank. I headed grimly for the subway that took me uptown to Acme's offices. It was already in my mind to try and go over McGrath's head. Mostly, however, I had to concentrate on picking my way in the lashing, blinding rain.

It was like black twilight, with the rain a thick curtain. Hurrying figures—what few there were here at this hour—burst suddenly out of the cloying murk, skidded around each other, were swallowed up again.

I plowed up William Street to Perry Lane, stumbling and sliding. The black pavements were as slippery as ice, footing a matter of prayer.

I saw occasional, dark, fuzzy figures in the black haze ahead of me, of course, but that someone might be tracking me from in front, or laying for me, never entered my head. Why it didn't, I don't know. Or why I was stupid enough not to have thought of Murray Moon as having feelings—feelings that, by now, would reasonably be murderous toward me.

I came abreast of the narrow lighted entrance of the Considine Building, bent into the storm, one hand holding my hat on, the other in my slash pocket—and I saw him instantly.

I don't scare too easily, but I was scared in that instant because I was caught flatfooted. I couldn't mistake his monstrous oversize head and flabby white face, his gleaming little, pinpoint black eyes and frail spidery body. He was crouched, low down, and his teeth were bared. The knife was held low in front of him, thumb and forefinger pinching the blade.

He almost sobbed, "You — —— ——! *Try this!*" as he dived for me.

He would have opened me from navel to jowl if it hadn't been for the storm. I was caught cold—except that he skidded sideways a little and I had time to eel my belly forward. I had no time to start a punch. All I could do was take a wild, backhanded swipe at him as I skidded.

We were like two men on ice. My knuckles caught him in the teeth, knocked him off balance and his feet got tangled. He slammed down as I clawed frantically for balance. I flung back at him, kicked hastily at his knife hand, missed it, hit his shoulder.

An old woman ran out of the building and started screaming in my ear. I didn't hear her. I was in a frenzy to kick the murderous knife out of the little madman's hand. He ducked, tried to come at me on his knees, his flabby face crazy with fury. I lashed out a foot again, missed the knife once more, caught him in the short ribs with all the force I had—and literally kicked him out into the street, skidding and rolling, between two of the curb's solidly parked cars—and directly under the wheels of an oncoming taxi.

His mouth opened as he saw it over his shoulder—maybe he screamed—and he tried madly to scramble away. The taxi whacked into him as the driver jammed on brakes and whirled completely around, sent him catapulting crazily ahead, head over heels, barely hurt at all.

For one second, the hot electrifying thought went through my mind that the prize had been flung into my lap. The fright, fury at the lethal little rat, were secondary to the explosive miracle that he was almost in my hands—the solution to every trouble I had. I was beside myself with sudden frenzy. I no more heard the shrieking woman at my side than I felt the blows she was lashing at me with her umbrella. I had my gun out, was throwing myself desperately for the next gap in the parked-car line—and then fate coolly whipped it all away and left me in the most ironic spot of my career.

The screaming woman suddenly lashed at my legs with the umbrella. On a dry pavement I would not have felt it. Now, it crossed my legs, I tripped—and went diving, flopping headlong into the rear mudguard of a parked car, sprawled all over the streaming pavement, the wind half knocked out of me.

BY THE time I had wrenched myself flailingly erect, two black hulks were diving at me, and as I plunged around a limousine they slid furiously into me and a gun pounded my stomach.

For the first time I heard the wretched woman's screaming: "... tried to kill the little man! Knocked him down—tried to kick him in the head—kicked him under that yellow taxi—the murderer!"

A hoarse voice roared in my ear: "Drop that gun! Get your hands...."

I mouthed, "Don't be a fool! Acme Indemnity—Murray Moon—tried to knife me—" and wrestled my way frantically out into the street with the two of them hanging on to my shoulders, roaring at me to stop.

I don't know if I saw Murray Moon or not. He was not down, anyway. A dozen curious forms were running in the road, from various directions, rain or no rain, and in the split second that I had to rake the murk, I could not pick him out. The rain swallowed him up.

Then I was yanked backwards and a fist slammed under my ear, knocked me giddy and I reeled as a ton of beef at my left shoulder snarled: "What the hell do you think you're pulling off here?"

I tried to yell at them, but a hand like a ham slapped across my mouth and a clipped voice said, "Get in out of this rain—that building," and I recognized Chambers' voice. That meant the ton of beef was his partner Myers. The cops had me and I was licked.

I shook the giddiness—but not the sick fury of defeat—out of my head as I was slammed up against the building-entrance wall. The woman was shouting her piece again: "Tried to kill the little man! I saw him do it! I'll be a witness!"

The thick-headed Myers blurted: "Hey! It's the insurance snoop!"

I knew, of course, that it was pure luck that put this pair in my way but I had a moment of unreason. Myers was nothing, but Chambers was, positively, the one crook on the Wall Street Squad that I was certain of. I shut my teeth on the raving I wanted to do. It would do me no good here. For a minute, I had a wild wonder if Chambers were working in with Moon. I knew it was wrong the minute I thought it, though he hated me nearly enough to try to have me killed, at that.

I saw the excited, yelling woman for the first time now—a scrawny bespectacled old maid—somebody's secretary, no doubt, with a long, thin horse face and blazing eyes. She was fumbling with her purse, staring me down furiously as she got out a card. "You needn't look at me that way!" she shrieked. "You can't frighten me. I'll come into court. I'll tell just what I saw! Here, officer—this is who I am."

For just a second, in Chambers' fat, shining little face and beaming blue eyes, I saw comprehension and a quick, half-amused measuring. He took the card without taking his eyes from my face. For one minute, I think he actually considered taking a chance on the crazy old maid's yipping and jugging me. It would have been a banner day in his life if he could have concocted a frame out of it. I had killed more than one deal Chambers had been in on.

He drawled: "Well, well, Acme's wonder boy. I heard you were having some trouble with Moon, but I didn't think you'd assassinate him."

"Behave," I growled. "The rat was trying to stick a knife in me."

"He was not," the old maid shrilled. "I didn't see any knife."

"Lady," I told her through set teeth as I tried to wipe the mud and water from my face, "your little friend was a notorious criminal. I am an insurance company detective. He was annoyed because I've practically ruined him."

Her mouth and eyes oh'd.

Chambers drawled maddeningly: "So Moon is a criminal! What was he ever arrested for, Acme?"

"He wasn't ever arrested," I snarled. "He works in Wall Street where he has only the Wall Street Squad to contend with. They never arrest anybody—just interfere with honest sleuths who do."

"Then how dare you call him a criminal?" the old maid started in all over again. "I know you insurance detectives! You're all grafters! You were probably trying to extort—"

I swung on my heel, growling in my throat. I had to do that or throttle her. They made no move to stop me. As I plowed into the crowd of curious that had gathered, I heard her yowl, "Aren't you going to arrest him?" and Chambers reassuring her, "We always know where to get him when we want him, ma'am."

CHAPTER TWO
THE BLACKJACKED
DANE

PREEKER, **MY** boss, paced the office wildly, excitedly, as I peeled wet clothes. "You had Moon—right in the palm of your hand—and you let him get away! That's fine! That's marvelous! That's—"

I opened my bag and bit at him: "Sure—I had him right in my hand. Nothing but two cops that knocked me around till he could vanish stood in my way. Cut the noise and get me an appointment with General Haley!"

"Haley! What for?"

"Because I say so. It's suddenly occurred to me that maybe Moon didn't try to knife me just for personal reasons. Maybe it's because he doesn't want me to get that information from the bank."

"Eh? Why? What inf—"

"How do I know? Maybe he's put other certificates in there whose delivery we can trace to some of his stooges. Maybe we can dig out his whole ring. How do I know? All I know is that now I'm going to get that trust department checked from stem to stern, if I have to kidnap this General Haley and hold him for ransom!"

Preeker snatched up a phone, his long nose sharper than ever, his gleaming spectacles shimmering as he told the operator what he wanted.

Then we waited.

We waited fifteen minutes before he finally started yelling "Hello! Hello!" into the transmitter. Even from where I stood, I could hear the crackling and snapping sounds that were battering his eardrums. Finally he yelled, "Who? Mr. Acton?…Yeah. Acme Indemnity…" and then a crazy argument at the top of his voice trying to straighten out the confusion of names. Finally, "It's most important that we see the general as soon as possible…What? My God, when?"

He clapped the mouthpiece against his bony chest and croaked wildly: "The general's leaving at dawn tomorrow with his niece for three-months in Honolulu." Then back to the transmitter. "Hello! Well, one of our men is coming out tonight. Could the general…Yes, I know, but it's most impor…Yes, of course, I know, but we would rather see the general hims— But damn it, it's urgent! Hello? Hey, hello!"

He swore roundly, slowly hung up the receiver. "He says the general is not available for business for three months. You should see McGrath."

I walked over to the window, pulling on a shirt. The skies were still dark-gray lead, the wind and rain mounting, if anything. I said grimly: "If this damned thing would let up, I'd go out and brace him anyway. There's something funny here."

"It can't last much longer."

It did, of course. When an hour had gone by, then two, without any let-up, I said, "Damn it, there's no use waiting any longer. It's not going to let up," and phoned for my convertible.

THE TRIP was a nightmare. The highway was an inch under racing water. My windshield wipers just weren't adequate. My convertible roof leaked. It took me an hour and forty minutes to get to Maidbank where I gassed up and inquired my way.

The attendant pointed to a fork not twenty yards ahead. A gravel road V'd off the highway. "The island widens out right here," he yelled at me. "The general's right out on the tip. You can either stay on the highway eight miles more, then take a chance on cutting back about six miles, or you can take that gravel road about twelve miles and get right to his gates."

"What's wrong with the gravel road?"

"Nothing—ordinarily. It's a good road. But in this—I dunno."

So I chose the highway. Maybe it would have been the same either way. I thundered through the dark. That is, I thundered to the turnoff from the highway eight miles further on, and I thundered along the sopping, loose country crossroad for about a mile and a half, bucking and skidding. I knew I'd pulled a bloomer before I even saw the hill ahead of me, but it was impossible to go back. I had to keep my foot to the floorboards and pray.

My prayers gave out when I hit the bottom of the hill. The rushing torrent pouring down the hill came up mudguard high. The car spluttered once, caught again, spluttered and died permanently. I slid slowly backwards down the hill and came to a stop.

I reached the general's estate—don't ask me how, or how many hours later. My legs were numb from the knees down, but I reached it and swore with relief as I unbuckled the tall, spiked iron gate in the high walls! I had no idea how I was going to get back—ever—but I was there. The general was there. He could hardly refuse to see me now, and if he were one tenth the mind that Wall Street said he was, I was going to get my nose into that bank. I thought I had actually topped my main problem.

Instead, it really started here—beginning with the dog.

The dog had been blackjacked.

It lay, five yards inside the gates, a foot from the oversized kennel. In the pelting rain the length of chain round its neck glittered in the beam of my torch. A huge, coal-black Dane, its head was almost mashed flat. It was stretched out, stiffened on its side, its coat gleaming in the hammering downpour, little drops bouncing in and out of its eyes without disturbing their hushed, glassy look. I knew it had been blackjacked because the blackjack lay within reach—the sawed-off, twelve-inch end of a weighted black riding crop.

I sat there on my heels in the dark, bracing myself against a dripping tree bole, astounded, for all of three minutes.

Naturally, I thought of an intruder, a prowler, but my thick head would not, could not, think it through any further than that.

I stood up, scrambling my brains to try and grope out some connection between my visit here and this.

I couldn't. I stared into the black belt of woods directly ahead. Finally, I stumbled cautiously on, my torch out in one hand, my other on my gun, in my pocket. I had to skirt the ankle-deep, rushing torrent that was the road. The wind whipped the tall trees into tossing plumes. Once I got into them, I got a little less wind, but two or three times I winced at a long, wrenching *cr-r-r-ack* as a limb was ripped from one of the trees overhead. The storm was a hurricane now.

Presently lights twinkled, far ahead and high up—seemingly above the tops of the threshing trees, informing me that a heavy climb was waiting. I stopped to listen, to mop the rain out of my eyes, stumbled on again, breasting the hill.

It was not really a hill but a succession of rises, with dips and hollows in between. The water in some of them was six feet deep. It was in the second hollow from the top that I ran into the mired car.

It was invisible, being shaded from the lights of the house by the brow of the hill. I squirted light, saw that it stood, half slanting sideways, water higher than its running boards. And then the edge of my beam of light caught the thing beside it and my stomach jerked.

The spidery little body of Murray Moon floated, face up in the water beside it, his beady, little black eyes staring straight up into the lashing rain. Something had hit him hard, obliquely against the side of the head, and his skull was quite obviously crushed. He was, just as obviously, quite dead, and had been for some time.

FOR A moment I was shocked numb. Then the fantastic, incredible possibility leaped into my brain. My head snapped upwards toward the hilltop and I ran up the rest of the way, my torch on the ground.

At the very lip of the hill I found deep indentations—the tire marks of a car that had been parked there. Most of the gravel had been washed off the road and it was down to clay.

It was a mad impossibility but it pounded through my mind insistently. Murray Moon—divining that I would probably come here, in the light of what had happened at the bank—sneaking in, lying in ambush for me—and a parked car, loosened by the streaming torrent above, sliding down on him by pure accident, silent, murderous....

I ran back down to the car, splashed light on the interior, yanked open a door.

In the glove compartment I found the registration certificate. It belonged to one Rene Leboutillier. I glanced at the rubber floor mat. The emergency brake was in the forward position and water pulsed gently through the opening thus left in the floor boards. There was a quarter-inch of water in the car.

I let the torch go dark, stood there in the lashing rain with thoughts cascading in my head. Why? Why was Murray Moon so desperate that I should not see into the vaults of the bank? Assume that he *had* managed to get some hot securities past the exclusive institution? It was no major catastrophe if I should get to them—at least not major enough to attempt to kill me. Or had his tries at me been, after all, simply because he had gone berserk at me for torpedoing him?

Naturally, a vaguely uneasy feeling crossed my mind at thought of the Wall Street Squad detective, Chambers. Coupled with the fantastic trick that fate had played me five hours ago in Wall Street, that crooked rat would naturally cock his ears at hearing that I had shown up beside Moon's dead body. If a frame were possible, he would be there with both feet—not that it seemed any way possible here. Nevertheless, even of that I could not be sure without getting to the bottom of things.

The agonizing part was that there hardly seemed to be any mystery. Everything would have been clear enough save for that wretched emergency brake. It was in the forward position—the off position. The car had not been washed accidentally down the hill. Somebody had let the brake off and let it roll down.

I circled quickly to stand in front of the sprawling vast house and for the first time heard the music, filtering faintly from inside. Also, for the first time, I saw the huddle of parked, shining cars at the other side of the house, on the main drive. I looked at my watch, and it was eleven twenty. A party was in progress—a party, presumably, that had started some time ago, for I knew that the driveways here must have been impassable for at least two hours.

The house was of ivy-grown brick. Glassed-in terraces winged out on each side. Blue canopies hung low over the terraces, matching the blue awnings on the blazing windows. The front door was a little, porticoed white island.

I knocked—and then I was inside a white-and-polished-oak Colonial entrance hall. I knew it must be Acton who had admitted me—an overgrown, self-conscious youth with corrugated blond hair, oversize blue eyes, and a big, rounded face whose youngness and splotchy pinkness must have been a constant embarrassment to him. His mouth fell open as he hastily shut the door behind me. "You—how—" he gulped. "Did—did you drive in in this…?"

I didn't want any conversation with him. Instead of a card, I flashed the little silver badge they give us and said: "I want to see the general—in a hurry."

His throat worked and he sort of backed away, still looking at me in incredulous indecision.

I snapped, "Hurry it up," and he finally bobbed his head.

"Yes, yes, of course," he said and turned to stumble into a room from which music and dancing sounds emanated.

AT THE door he bumped into a tawny-haired, peaches-and-cream, slim girl who was hurrying out and a white pique bag flew out of her hand, hit the floor and burst open almost at my feet.

The secretary's blush was crimson. "Oh, I'm terribly sorry, Miss Priscilla… terribly sorry.…"

She ignored him. Her startlingly deep eyes were on mine, incredulous, intent as she sailed on. "You—how did you get in? Can you drive through…?"

I stooped and picked up her trinkets. "Not in a car, ma'am. And it's no fun walking."

Among the spilled objects on the floor was a brand-new passport. I knew it by feel. She would be Priscilla Haley, the general's niece, who was leaving on the trip with him tomorrow. Her white pique suit and blue silk blouse were nice, her too-dark lipstick amateurish.

"But *could* a car…" she insisted.

"Not tonight." I nudged her with the bag. To the yammering secretary. I snapped, "Please hurry," and he mumbled another apology to the girl, darted on into the dancing room.

The girl looked down at her bag, startled. "Oh—oh, thank you." She took it, turned away and hurried up a long, curving, white-railed staircase.

In the moment that she disappeared a door unlocked down the long hall ahead of me and a short, ruddy-faced, white-haired man marched out from under the stairs, buttoning his dinner jacket. He shot his cuffs, checked himself and gave me a quick, appraising look from startlingly bright, pale-blue eyes. He closed his bushy eyebrows over them and I knew I was looking at a big-wig—the one banker who, according to report, had outwitted the Big Crash, and the Big Depression. His ruddy face was as smooth and clear as a tomato, his oversize white mustache bristling. "Who are you?" he wanted to know.

"Acme Indemnity, General. It was highly important that we get ten minutes of your time before you sailed in the morning."

He looked at me curiously. "It must be to bring you out on a night like this. What is it?"

"We have reason to believe that some stolen securities have been slipped past your tellers in the trust department of Morgan and Haley. I asked Mr. McGrath to check up and he refused."

"What—where did you get this idea?"

I told him, and added, when he hesitated: "Incidentally an attempt was made on my life to prevent my getting an inventory made of your trust securities."

His eyes jumped up. "Great Scott! Then you really think...?"

"I think there's something odd to be found in that inventory. Naturally, knowing how touchy banking reputation is, we wouldn't think of trying to get a court order."

That bluff fizzled and I decided he was no man to bluff at any time. He said, almost absently: "You couldn't get a court order. Just what *do* you think might turn up? Damn it, this strikes me as serious."

"I don't know what might turn up. I think it's more serious than just a few stolen securities, to tell you the truth."

He was troubled, intent. "Dash it, I run that department. I can't see how anything..." He rubbed his short, blunt chin vigorously. "All right, young man, I'll take an inventory for you—myself." Then he blinked suddenly and blew out a breath. "Hell and damnation! I'm supposed to sail with my niece for Honolulu tomorrow morning." He chewed his mustaches a second in hot debate.

While he was doing it a youth lounged indolently out of the dancing room, stared sullenly at me with insolent dark eyes. A lock of snaky, black hair fell down over his forehead and his mouth was spoiled and moist. With somewhat of a shock, I recognized him as the youth McGrath had been hurrying to join in the bank. If he recognized me, he made no sign of it. He looked round the hall, turned and idled back inside.

The general said suddenly: "I'll tell you what I'll do. I'll order McGrath to do it and keep in touch with me hourly. Come in here."

He turned and I asked: "Who was that young man who just came out?"

"What? Dan Odium. Going to marry Priscilla as soon as we get back from the trip—one of our biggest trust clients."

CHAPTER THREE
THE DUTCHMAN WHO
SAW DEATH

I **FOLLOWED** the general's short, rattling steps down the hall to a point where two doors faced each other. He opened the left-hand one and I almost bumped him as he stopped short inside the door before going on in.

A throaty feminine voice said: "You don't mind us using your office, General?"

"Not at all, Rene, not at all."

A tall, cavernous-cheeked thin man with piercing, glowing dark eyes and rippling black hair stood smoking moodily at one end of a huge flat-topped oak desk. He looked dark and Gallic. But my eyes, were for the ripe, vivid young woman who sat at the desk. She had evidently been writing a check. The checkbook she held out to the thin Frenchman and the check she waved at the gloom—the only light in the office was the green-shaded desk lamp. She had amazing plum-blue eyes, short-lashed, and they were utterly, absorbedly shameless—the eyes of a cold-blooded voluptuary-if that means anything—who knew all the facts of life and some of the fancies. The red-jacketed black skirted evening clothes she wore barely held her ivory-smooth, perfect, full figure. Her costume was the absolute minimum above the waist and I did not see how she could dare lean sideways. I placed her as Rene Leboutillier, the owner of the coupé outside—the coupé beside which Murray Moon's battered body was floating.

I was so intent on her that I almost missed seeing Harry Joesting. His painfully thin, stringy mahogany body was in evening dress. He wore a straggly black beard and a turban. He bobbed out of the gloom to receive the check she was holding out. His strange topaz eyes jumped as she caught sight of me and he almost missed the check.

He quickly didn't look at me. A Dutchman—don't ask me about his coloring, I don't know how he got it any more than you do, but it was a natural for the fortune-telling racket—he had been playing tag with the police for years. Nothing serious. Lately I had heard that he had achieved a high-class agent, was no longer a fortunte teller, but an "astralist," whatever that may be.

The general said: "This is ridiculous, Rene—your paying for my entertainment."

"Not at all, General. I insisted on bringing Mr. Rahmanna."

There was a moment of silence. I was aware suddenly of the luscious, dark-skinned French girl's eyes, coolly on me through cigarette smoke. She literally forced the general to make introductions, and I found that the tall, glowing-eyed thin man was her husband, and that I was a "business associate." I also found that Joesting was "Mr. Rahmanna, who will entertain us presently."

The girl's eyes were dark, searching, on mine as she got up with the slow grace of a cat and strolled to the door. "Immediately, in fact. I hope you two don't think we're going to allow you to talk business."

"We'll be just a moment, Rene—just a moment."

THE DOOR closed and the general sat in the desk chair and picked up the phone. "McGrath is a good man," he assured me. "He will cooperate if I tell him to." He sat there for a full minute with the instrument at his ear, while a scowl gathered on his face. He suddenly looked at the handset, rattled and banged the hook, restored it to his ear, rattled and banged some more.

"Damn," he said finally. "The wires are down, I guess." He sat a minute in further, quick thought, then said abruptly: "Maybe it's just as well. The more I think of it, the more I think I'll stay and do it myself. Priscilla can wait for a few days." He leaned back and relaxed.

It was on the tip of my tongue to tell him what was just outside his door, but I refrained. After all, we couldn't even notify the law, much less bring it in. And I knew that, if I showed him the dead man, this little czar would be giving orders from now on, not me. Instead, I hastily cast about for some logical excuse to remain in the house.

He saved me the trouble. "You'll stay all night, of course," he announced. "A mouse couldn't reach the highway now." He went over and peered out at the lashing, thundering storm. "Well? What do you say? Want to see this Indian perform? They say he's very clever."

I said that sounded fine and we went in to the comfortable, large living room, through the door opposite the general's office. Just inside the door he introduced me to a white-haired old lady and a man with a pinkish fringe of hair around a square bald head—a Doctor and Mrs. Hagedorn. The room was bathed in orange glow and there were no other lights. Harry Joesting had his crystal ball set up on a table covered with a green velvet scarf and the orange light came from the crystal ball. He had some sort of flowing robe on now. A velvet bag beside him held little green capsules—questions written by the guests which he divined and answered without opening—an old act but a good one. His dark face and yellow eyes were impressive above the light—and the raging of the storm outside didn't hurt him any.

TWO REDHEADED young men sat in a group of four clustered in the center of the room. They were obviously twins and the girls with them were obviously their wives. I didn't get to meet them, either then or later. The rest I knew. Odium, the sullen-faced, surly youth—the fiancé of the tawny-haired Priscilla Haley—was sprawled on a settee at the very end of the room. Acton, the pinkish-blond secretary fiddled with his hands just inside the now closed door that led into the entrance hall. The Leboutilliers were sitting on adjoining chairs across the room, their backs to the slightly opened doors of the screened-in terrace.

I didn't see Priscilla Haley.

There was a bar at one end of the room and I could have done with a drink but I didn't know how to ask for it. I slid around the room to the back with the general, and he stopped to conduct a whispered conversation with young Odium. I spotted a love seat, a few feet away from where the sulphurous Rene Leboutillier was seated and I saw her eyes turned toward me. I had been conscious of them ever since I entered the room.

Joesting droned on, reading questions, answering them. An occasional titter came from one or the other of the room's occupants. I eased down in the love seat.

I wasn't very surprised when, after a few minutes, the glowing dark Rene suddenly stood up and tiptoed over to me.

"Would you like a drink?" she whispered. "The general is a very poor host."

I said I would and she slipped away to the bar. I had shed hat and coat in the general's office and I was not as cold as I had been but I needed the drink.

When she brought it back to me, she looked down at the narrow love seat expectantly and I had to move over as best I could. She sat down—and I was suddenly uncomfortable. That was not all from worry as to how her husband might react to this, either. Some of it was from the amazing warmth of her soft body, some of it from the heavy scent she used—and some was because she had nudged the gun now on my hip and looked quickly down. I kept my eyes on Joesting while I downed the drink.

She said, too loudly, "Tell me about the banking business. Is it true that the government'as…?" and stopped, as several faces turned reprovingly towards us.

Surprisingly, even her gaunt-faced husband scowled—and made head motions toward the open door of the terrace behind us.

Her warm, moist hand caught mine and she whispered: "Do you care for this particularly?"

"Not particularly."

"Come on, then."

Nobody seemed to pay much attention to our casual, semifurtive escape onto the terrace. She kept my hand and led me to the darkest, most secluded corner of the porch. She cleared a solitary wine glass from a deep club chair and fairly pushed me into it. She put the wine glass on the railing of the porch and seated herself lazily on the arm of my chair, facing me. Her eyes glowed in the darkness.

"Now we can talk."

It was too fast for me. I was getting uneasy.

"Have you been in the banking business long?"

"Off and on for some years."

She suddenly leaned forward and her hand slid smoothly inside my coat to the butt of my gun. "Do all bankers carry those?"

"Well, uh…"

Her face was close to mine in the gloom. She laughed softly, took her hand away from the gun and put it, warm, on my side. Then she put her hot mouth slowly over mine.

"Who are you, really?" she whispered eagerly when she got some breath.

"Look, lady—your husband—"

"Paul? Bah! Do not think of 'im. He has los' his fire…"

Joesting stopped then. His drone had been so continuous, and so monotonous that its ceasing was like a sharp sound.

LIGHTS WENT on in the living room. Rene's dark eyes were shining and she was smiling tightly. She did not draw away from me, although she trailed her fingers slowly out from under my coat. Talk started in the living room.

Then a hesitant voice suddenly spoke my name huskily and I looked over and saw Joesting in the doorway, mopping at his neck with a yellow silk handkerchief.

I said, "Excuse me," and got up, as she muttered under her breath in French.

Joesting's dark face was shining and his yellow eyes were gaunt. He said, "Come—come here," and led me across the living room and out into the hall before the general's office. When he closed the door, the sounds in the living room were blotted out. The place was soundproofed.

"I—I'm sorry," he gulped desperately, and ran a finger inside his collar. "Look, pally," he said hoarsely. "There's something wrong in this house."

"Yeah? What?"

He swallowed and his topaz eyes squirmed on my tie. "You'll—you'll think I'm bats, but I don't care. I—I seen something in that crystal ball."

I blinked at him. "Dear God. Are you seriously trying to run a racket on me?"

"No, no—I swear I ain't. I—I been handling them things a long time, like you know. There—there—I don't know what happened. I— Judas, guy, you know I ain't a sucker! I swear I seen something."

"What did you see?"

"I—I didn't actually *see* anything—I couldn't describe it—but it—it was like somebody was dead. A—a skull and crossbones. It—just come in the thing, and drifted off again."

From the front of the hall came a sudden, choked sob. Then a sucking, grating sound, as of somebody unable to get their breath. I jerked round.

Joesting gasped: "My God, what—"

I ran back along the hall to the foot of the wide, curling, white-railed stairs. The sound was suddenly continuous, horrible, right above me.

I reached the foot of the stairs in time to see Priscilla Haley sway, four steps from the top. She was crouching over, her face contorted, suffused with a purple flush. Both her hands were at her throat and her eyes were frantic, tortured. She was shaking like a leaf, her mouth gulping, making that terrible: "Uh-uh—uh-uh…"

She tried to take a step downward, stumbled. One hand reached out for the banister as she fell forward. I dived for her. She crashed once, on her knees, halfway down, before she pitched headlong into my arms, driving me back into the banister, her body writhing, whipping in my arms like a snake, the terrible gulping gasping rising in choking crescendo in her throat. I had to clutch her madly to keep her from flinging herself out of my arms. I flung at the stupefied Joesting, "That doctor—Hagedorn—in there! Get him fast! Tell nobody else!" and he came out of his trance, flung back along the hall.

The girl's frantic contortions reached their peak and she suddenly sobbed, went limp. Her face was still suffused and her throat was constricted, as though she could not suck breath through it, but her strength was gone. She was strangling.

When the man with the red fringe of hair round his baldness ran out, I heard a snatch of music from the opened door, instantly shut off. The guests were playing the phonograph again.

The doctor said: "My God, what—?"

"She's strangling," I clipped hoarsely. "Don't ask me how." Then I said, because it popped into my head: "Poisoned maybe."

He moved fast for a bandy-legged old man, dived back to a clothes cupboard under the stairs for his bag, jabbing at me: "Take her up to a bedroom, quickly."

CHAPTER FOUR
MURDER IN TRUST

TEN MINUTES later the closed door of the bedroom opened and the doctor came out. His face was drawn and he said: "Get the general."

Joesting blurted: "Was—is she…?"

"She's not dead, yet. She may be any minute—I don't know. She shows all the symptoms of aconite poisoning."

I ran down into the silent hall, opened the door and let music blare out, beckoned the sturdy little general urgently. He was still talking to the mean-looking Dan Odium, Priscilla's fiancé. He excused himself, came out looking a little impatient.

I closed the door behind him. "Upstairs, quickly."

"But—but what…?"

I did not tell him till we were in front of the closed bedroom door.

"Priscilla has been poisoned."

There was nothing affected about his gasp, about the sudden draining of color from his face, nor about the sudden slackness of his knees. Terror peeped out of his brilliant pale-blue eyes for just an instant as he jerked his head toward the door. "God Almighty, how?" He dived through as I pushed it open.

I followed in at his heels. The doctor was in his shirt-sleeves, bent over the bed. I could see only the girl's legs and the torn knees of her stockings. He flung over his shoulder: "Not you, young man! Just the gen—"

The general blurted hoarsely: "He's a detective, Tom. What in God's name…?"

The strawberry-faced doctor's brown eyes were suddenly amazed. "A detective! Did you expect this…?"

"Never mind, for God's sake! No, we didn't," the general blurted. "Is she—is it serious? Tom—she—how badly…?"

"I don't know. She's been poisoned with aconite. She must have gotten just short of a lethal dose—usually it kills instantly. Some amateur must have done it—given her not quite enough."

"Given?" I said quickly. "How do you know it was given? Why not an accident?"

"Aconite is not used for anything any more. You didn't have any in the house, did you, General?"

"No, no, my God, no! I never heard of it." The general's ruddy forehead was covered with damp sweat, its vein standing out. He was wringing his hands. Suddenly, his piercing blue eyes jumped at me, and his lips were like short, straight lines. "You—you find out who gave it to her. I'll pay you anything!"

The doctor said hesitantly: "General—the sheriff—"

"Sheriff!" The old man's voice was like sandpaper. "Don't be a fool. We can't phone. We can't get out. This young man is a detective. Can you—can you," he fired at me, "find out who did it?"

"If the person is in this house I can," I said. "Doctor…?"

He anticipated my question. "She was given this within the hour, at the outside."

I LOOKED at the girl. She lay limp, her eyes closed. Her breath still rattled. Her complexion—even her bare thighs, where her dress was twisted up under her—was sort of a purplish white.

The doctor straightened up, asked suddenly: "Do you suppose that young paranoiac, Dan Odium, could have…?"

"Dear Heaven, are you crazy? He's going to marry her in—"

"Maybe he decided not to. Remember, you were pretty strong for the match. Maybe he had some reason why he didn't want to, and couldn't think of any other way out."

"You're mad, Tom! I was in favor of the match, but he—as late as yesterday—urged me to call the cruise off so they could be married at once."

I asked: "Did she jilt anybody lately? Are any of the people downstairs former sweethearts of hers—or of Odium's?"

"No, no!" the general said wildly. "She had little to do with young men."

"How about money? Has she any—?"

"Not a penny of her own. I—there's mine, which she'll have some day."

"Your secretary, Acton," I asked the general suddenly. "Is he at the bank with you every day, or is he just here at home?"

"What? He's with me both places, of course. You surely don't accuse…?"

Then strangely, I saw the first half of the stunning little drama, plain and clear.

I asked quickly: "What condition is she in now, Doctor?"

"I wish I knew. I've given her everything I can. In an hour she'll be dead, or safe, I think."

"Can you leave her with a maid for a few minutes?"

He looked anxious.

"None of the people downstairs are supposed to know what's happened," I said. "I want Joesting to go ahead with his entertainment and I don't want you two tipping it by staying away."

"I—well, I guess so, for a few minutes, if you—if there's an intelligent girl I can count on to call me if anything—"

I looked at the general.

"Yes, yes. Priscilla's own maid is a fine girl."

I went out and took the terrified Joesting down into the lower hall again.

"You're in a tough hole," I told him. "If the local law ever gets here before I find out what's what, you'll get some nice attention—not to mention ruining your racket."

"I know it," he moaned. "I know it."

"Do what I tell you and I'll give you a break," I said. "Go back in and do your act. Only—read off what I tell you. Come here." In a corner, I clipped words at him for ten minutes.

He gasped: "God, pally—I won't do it, unless you give me a gun or something. If the guy—somebody might go bats and—and jump me."

I said all right and gave him the one from the car. Then I went back in ahead of him, with the general and the doctor. We managed to laugh among the three of us, so that no one started asking questions. I spied Rene Leboutillier out on the sunporch, with her husband, Paul. I strolled over as the general signaled for the phonograph to be turned off and, in the ensuing silence announced that "Rahmanna would complete his reading."

Everybody wound up about where they had been before. The girl, Rene, stayed on the porch and I went back out to her.

"Don't you and your husband ever get on any better together?"

Her eyes were startled, uncertain in the gloom. "We—get on well enough together. Only—I—ah, what does it matter about Paul? We simply do not love as we did, and you…"

I kept my eyes away from her, stared at the wineglass I had picked from the railing. "Let's go in and listen to this for a moment." Puzzled, she reluctantly accepted my urging.

I said, "Excuse me," once I had her set and slid away to the back of the room. I set the wineglass carefully in a flower pot. I didn't want anything in my hands.

THE LIGHTS all went out, save the orange glow from the crystal. The atmosphere was again exactly right. I looked at the faces around. Odium's, where he sprawled on the settee at the rear of the room, was bored, sulky. He looked drunk.

The pinkish-blond secretary, Acton, fussed with his ring, inside the hall door nearest me. The white-haired general and the bald-pated Doctor Hagedorn sat with his wife, close to the small door opposite the general's office.

Joesting began to drone off the questions he had left over when his queer hallucination had suddenly frightened the wits out of him and he'd come looking for me. His voice went on, and on, and on.

Finally I could not wait any longer. I had to gamble all I had. I coughed.

Joesting did not betray his reception of my signal, except that when he finished the current question, he did not reach for another. Instead, he suddenly looked startled. He was a good actor.

He said in his droning, resonant voice: "Wait! Something seems to be coming into the crystal—something strange."

He let that stand a minute, while he widened and thinned his eyes. A concerned expression spread over his face and his voice became quick, startled.

"I see a girl—a girl with golden hair. I see a man—a tall man. I see a—a passport. Yes, a passport. They are going somewhere together."

There was suddenly curious silence in the room.

Joesting's face became alive with intentness. "I see a car—a car that runs without noise. They are in the car. They are going silently somewhere—away from a house—*this* house! They are going down a hill—there is a great dog—but the dog is silent, too. He does not bark, though he seems to be trying to give the alarm—to tell that these two are going away. And then I see a great storm."

His little eyes seemed to swell over the orange-lighted ball and he crouched closer. "It is a terrible storm—it stops the car—it sweeps it back to the house—it forms a great wall—they cannot go." He hesitated, then, "They are quarreling. She shakes her head. Now he grabs her hand. Now—wait! She breaks away from him." He sank his voice. "Now it is fading—no! I see them again—they are in a dark corner of a room. I see a wineglass!" He caught his breath suddenly. "There is a white powder in the wine glass! He is urging her to drink it! I see hate in his eyes… His face is dark, gaunt…."

Too late I realized the terrific blunder I had made. And in realizing it, I saw the truth that I had missed completely.

Even as I saw it, Joesting's voice rose to a crescendo. "I see death—and I see the man—he is French…."

I snapped up all the lights.

"No! No! It's a lie!" Paul Leboutillier was suddenly on his feet, his hand clapping to his mouth, his dark eyes frantic, staring. And then the amazing timing of the thing twisted it ironically. Even as I jumped for him, his hands suddenly crawled to his throat and he began to crumple.

I yelled: "Doctor! Quick! The same poison that got Miss Haley."

Someone shrieked: "My God—Priscilla—poisoned?"

SUDDENLY THERE was a screaming red-and-black wildcat in my path. Rene Leboutillier, her face contorted, her eyes shining crazily, flung herself in my path. "No! No! You shall not touch him! Let him die. The *canaille!* I see it now—see his mysterious absences— his cooling toward me! Ah, he was sly, that one! No one knew—but look at him now! He is discovered—and he cannot face it. Ah, the dog! The dog! Let him die!"

I flung her, sobbing, onto a divan and the doctor and I reached the Frenchman, just as he crashed down.

After one minute, the doctor snapped: "Get him upstairs, too. He'll be all right. He's only taken a mild dose!"

I bit at Joesting: "Here! Grab him!" And at one of the two young couples in the room's center, "You—redhead! His feet! Doctor—show them where to take him! Nobody else!" I thundered, as the pinkish-blond secretary tried to slide out into the hall. He stopped, blushing.

The general croaked: "Has she—is it possible that she has—that she and Leboutillier have been carrying on under our noses—with no one suspecting—"

"No," I said. "It isn't."

The general stared.

In the silence, I continued: "One person found out." Then I threw it at him.

"One person found out—found out the whole scheme. Maybe this person suspected from seeing what I saw—a passport. The girl was supposed to be going to Honolulu and you don't need a passport for Honolulu. That person found it out—found your daughter was going to run away with Paul Leboutillier—going to ditch young Mr. Dan Odium there. So that person turned to poison."

I looked over at the sullen face, the venomous eyes of the young multi-millionaire. He licked his lips and said nothing.

"Mr. Odium is accustomed to having his own way," I clipped. "He is not used to being balked, to being made a fool of. Having his fiancée run away just before the scheduled wedding would be likely to make him furious. Being furious, he would be likely to lose his head—"

His mouth was vicious and twitching as he jumped to his feet. "Damn you—are you accusing me of poisoning them?"

"No," I said. "No. You didn't poison them. You weren't likely to be that furious, Just—oh, let's say that you would be just furious enough to have your business taken away from the general."

The general's eyes were on mine. He said: "Wait a minute!"

I waited.

He said: "Come out here a minute."

I couldn't figure it. "The rest of you—don't move," I said after a second.

He faced me in the hall, his hands in his dinner-coat pockets. His face was stolid, expressionless, dark.

"I could use a man like you in my business—a five-year contract at fifty thousand dollars a year."

"What business? You've got no business. You think I'm sap enough not to realize that it was you—the boss—who salted all your trust accounts with stolen securities, bought at thieves' prices from Murray Moon? I'm not a fool. Murray Moon nearly went crazy trying to protect you from my nosing—and he'd only do that if you were a big market. You must have switched millions. What happened? Did you lose your own fortune in the crash just like everybody else and decide to recoup this way?"

"The offer still stands."

I sneered. "I should do business with you. You're done. You were too big. You've cracked—and you're in a panic. Murray Moon comes here to try and warn you and the only thing you can think to do is close his mouth. It didn't even *look* like an accident. Your daughter threatens to jilt one of your big customers. You're afraid to have his account transferred to some other bank where they'll find the stolen stuff in it—so you try to poison her boy-friend."

I hesitated and our eyes blazed into each other. "It was tough that you miscalculated on the pretty little tricks these lovers go for—that you didn't expect them to make a loving cup of...."

He shot me through his pocket.

Whether it was good luck or bad shooting, or what, God knows, but the bullet plowed into my side inside of my heart, doubling me over as though a mule had kicked me. It was the one thing I didn't expect.

When I jackknifed down, blood roaring in my ears, he didn't even give me a backward glance as he leaped over me and flung open the door. He was sure I was done. "Nobody move!" he snapped.

The room was swaying in front of me and there was a red haze, but I had my hand on my gun and I managed to get it up and lay a row of buttons down his side. I heard him cry out and crash down before I faded out of the picture.

TOO WEAK TO KILL

I'D HEARD OF NURSES
PROPPING THEIR PATIENTS
UP IN BED TO DO ALL SORTS
OF THINGS, BUT NOT UNTIL
THE MACWHINNEY CASE
BROKE HAD I EVER RUN
ACROSS ONE WHO FELT IT
HER DUTY TO SUPPORT THE
GUN-HAND OF AN INVALID IN
AN OXYGEN TENT WHILE HE
BUMPED OFF HIS VICTIM!

I **SEEMED** to have known this Dunphy—in a vague way—a long time. He hung around Tenth Avenue cafes—a tough, dumb thug. I had an impression he was part Indian because of his cap of straight black hair, but there was nothing Indian about his thick, long-armed body, nor his stupid, mean, little red eyes. I couldn't recall much about him—a few arrests for labor slugging, one stretch for mayhem. I had heard he worked a while for a Harlem witch doctor who ran a love-charm racket plus a beating-up service.

He was at the elbow of the hall ahead of me, craning stupidly at the lettering on a door's ground-glass panel: *Acme Indemnity Co.—Private,* when I came from the elevator. I had an impression of troubled question in his meager mind—and then he saw me and faded. Thickheaded and thick-handed he may have been, but he moved like a wraith when he saw me. One minute he was there. The next he had melted down the side corridor without a sound.

By the time I reached the corner he had vanished, nor did peeping down the stairwell a few yards along the cross-hall give either sight or sound of him.

PREEKER'S BONY, pointed-nosed little face was flushed and his glasses glittered wildly when I walked

Just then I got shot in the back.

into the office. That did not impress me. Anything that threatens so much as a thin dime of Acme's money sends Preeker into a spasm. I'm not knocking him, mind— after twelve years working under him in the investigation department, I rate him a genius—but I was more curious about Dunphy than his immediate problem.

"Don't frown at me!" he exploded. "Does it take you twenty minutes to get from the ninth floor to the nine-teenth? Did you crawl up on your hands and kn…?"

I told him the truth. "I got lost, chum." Acme has nine solid floors in its own skyscraper plus endless little suites scattered through the rest of it. Even after twelve years, I was still finding new ones. "What department is this?"

He cursed fretfully. "Ames and Holden—our so-called star salesmen. A pair of vultures! They'd sell a policy in the death house—and leave me to worry about it. Come in here—quick, before the guy leaves."

We were in a suite of two offices and reception room. One office was empty and dark, the other lighted and exuding a rumble of voices. He dragged me into the dark one, jabbing a sheet of paper at me, whimpering: "MacWhinney! They want to sell a fifty-thousand joint-coverage life to James MacWhinney and his new wife. Look!"

The partition between the two offices was mostly plate-glass, with a strung green curtain head-high on our side. He lifted a corner of it to let me peek through. If you can sob in a whisper, he sobbed now.

"Six years ago, he collects five thousand on the same kind of policy, on his first wife. Now—*now* they want to hang a fifty-thousand one on us."

"Why not?" I asked. "A satisfied customer and all that."

"Satisfied! I'll say! This guy murdered his first wife for five thousand. What'll he do for fifty?"

I didn't have to believe it to be interested. I applied my eye to the chink. The man behind the desk in the next office I knew, of course—Ames, white-haired, ascetic, distinguished, pale. He had almost gone to the pen in thirty-three for income-tax evasion.

One of the other two men was drunk. If I was any judge, he had been drunk for about twenty years. His bright little blue eyes, behind gold-rimmed glasses, were reddened and muddy with alcohol, not quite concealing the merry twinkle in them. His button of a nose was red, and his cheeks, where they showed above his ragged gray-black vandyke and mustache. He had on black clothes and a bat-wing collar. He lay back in his chair, his fingertips pressed together in a judicial steeple, almost cross-eyed trying to focus on them.

"Not the little lush?" I whispered to Preeker. "Is he…?"

"No. No. That's his lawyer, Byron. The other…."

MacWhinney had a head as round as a billiard ball, cut away under his thin black eyebrows to make hollows for his intimate, naive little grape-blue eyes. He had no chin and a little wet, red mouth that perpetually hung open as though getting ready to smile. Either he wore a toupée or he combed his scant black hair to resemble one—plastered down, parted in the middle, two flat ovals above his round little red forehead.

I could not hear what they were saying, but I saw our demon salesman, Ames, take out his watch, frown at it, mumble something and get up. He came out into the reception room. Preeker whispered, "All right, just a minute, just a minute," and Ames snarled, "You —— —— louse, if you queer this sale you'll explain to the board of directors."

"Go on back," Preeker bit. "We'll be right in."

"What the hell is this?" I complained. "If he killed one wife…."

"It wasn't proved—legally," Preeker whispered hastily. "Here" —he pressed the sheet of paper into my hand— "this is the way they sent it to me from the records bureau. He—he *had* it done. I'm going to introduce you as a supervisor…"

"Wait a minute. What am I supposed to be doing?"

"You get me something on which to refuse that policy, that's all. I've got a forty-eight-hour block on it."

"This doesn't say he murdered her," I objected.

"My God, you're supposed to be a sleuth, aren't you?" he almost screamed. "Come on…"

"Wait a minute," I fended him off.

I READ the report over again. The gist of it was that this MacWhinney had been a dry-goods clerk in Grimsby, Maine. He'd married a local haberdasher's orphaned daughter, one Kay Guiness, Oct. 11, 1933, insured Oct. 15, 1933 joint coverage $5000. On Dec. 29, 1933, she circulated a report that she planned a trip to New York, expected to meet an unnamed friend (presumably either fictitious entirely or one Sue Brandt, chorus girl, with whom she was known previously to be in correspondence, but whose address was unascertainable. In either case no basis was found to believe there was such actual appointment. The announcement of her impending trip followed closely on violent disagreement with beneficiary, to whom she had long made known her wish to leave Grimsby and take up residence in New York.) This meeting was to be on Suspension Bridge over the Blythe River at the east end of town, within a half-mile of the railroad station at Woolwich. (Grimsby has no railroad station.) She was known to have drawn her savings ($236.43) from the local bank and believed to have same in her handbag when she set out with a small suitcase, at eight o'clock at night.

Her body, battered almost beyond recognition but identified by husband and neighbors, was found at the mouth of the Blythe River two days later. Neither bag nor suitcase was ever found.

On the basis that he had been seen following the girl the night of her disappearance, the brother of a local tavern-keeper, one Harry Mehr, was arrested. Attempt was made at trial to draw admission from him that he had been paid by the husband of the girl to prevent her departure. He admitted having gone in search of her, but claimed he had failed to find her, being prevented by the unusual severity of the storm from reaching the railroad station before the arrival of the night train, on which he assumed she had departed.

Defense counsel theorized that, owing to unusual wind and rain the girl might have lost her footing on the bridge and dropped to the rocky riverbed below. No satisfactory statement could be secured from the conductor of the night train, save that his passenger count was the same at stations each side of Grimsby and that he believes no one got on or off at Grimsby. The defendant was acquitted by direction of the presiding judge and further efforts to connect Henry MacWhinney with any criminal act were unavailing. The policy was paid Mar. 11, 1934.

"I still don't know what I'm supposed to do," I complained as he hurried me out.

"Do? Do? How do I know? I don't care so long as you expose this murderer."

I was about to sneer in his face, till I recalled Dunphy.

As we went into Ames' office, Preeker biting his nails, the ascetic-looking, lofty Ames whispered to me out of the side of his mouth: "There's a yard in it for you if the policy goes through. Damn that old sourpuss anyway."

Then he was all urbane affability as he closed us in and introduced me.

FORTUNATELY THEY had left me an out— or an in—by not bringing MacWhinney's new wife with them. I guess they hadn't expected really to get down to business until Ames got his claws in them. I was introduced as a supervisor who would accompany them to the hotel and get Mrs. MacWhinney's signature to the application and make an appointment for her examination. The little, round-headed dry goods clerk jumped up and bowed jerkily, his little grape-blue eyes beaming ingratiatingly, his mouth open ready to smile. He almost forgot to shake hands, belatedly stabbed out a soft, warm red paw. When the little lawyer finally came to and scrambled out of the chair, he made me a bow that was too low to be safe and told me in a sonorous, whisky-tinged voice that he was proud to know me.

"Well," I suggested in my best salesman's manner, "it's getting on toward dinner time. You folks probably have plans, so suppose we run right down to your hotel and get this over with."

I saw no more signs of Joe Dunphy in the building as we went out, nor any sign of a tail as we went downtown in a taxi. The lawyer, Byron, lay back in a corner of the hack, his hands folded over his round tummy, his eyes shining merrily while MacWhinney fumbled with his hands between his knees and tried to please me.

I groped. "A pretty nice-sized policy you're taking out, Mr. MacWhinney."

He assured me hastily: "Yes, but I can afford it, you know. I—well, I've made a good piece of mon—"

The lawyer's, *"Harr-ump,"* and his stern, if glassy, eye checked him. MacWhinney gave me a sick smile.

"I—well, I can afford it," he repeated lamely.

We rode a block or two, then he caught me looking out the rear window. "What—are you watching for something?" he asked innocently. "I've noticed you several times...."

I had an urge that I couldn't explain. I looked at his eyes and asked: "You don't happen to know anybody named Joe Dunphy, do you?"

He said, "No," wonderingly.

The lawyer's resonant voice creaked into booming activity. "Who is Joe Dunphy?"

"Just a thug I'm curious about," I said. "Pay no attention. How old did you say Mrs. MacWhinney was?"

"Valda? Twenty-nine," the round-headed man told me eagerly, "and I'm thirty-nine."

"She's a Grimsby girl, too?"

"Yes, she—you see my first wife didn't have any relatives and she lived with Valda's grandparents. I met Valda when I was calling on Kay and—well, after Kay's death, I used to talk to her and we—well, fell in love."

"You've been married—how long?"

"Oh, just a month. This is sort of our honeymoon. Mr. Byron had to come to New York on business and he suggested we come when he did and—well, see the World's Fair and all like that. We saw the Acme building from a sightseeing bus and—well, I thought I'd take out the policy while I was here. It—you see, the folks back in Grimsby don't know about the deal. The man wanted it kept quiet till the title was searched and if I took out a—"

The lawyer's weary drone said: "Henry, I'm sure this gentleman is not interested in your private affairs."

"Sure I am," I said quickly. "What are you selling? A piece of real estate?"

The lawyer frowned owlishly. "It's a matter on which any discussion would be premature," he said, with relish at finding the right words coming out, and lapsed into silence.

Two things only kept me from declaring then and there that this whole situation was a farce. One was the still-provoking recollection of Joe Dunphy hanging around Ames' and Holden's office. The second was Preeker's hunch.

As we climbed out in front of one of Broadway's gaudier and more expensive hotels—the Hammond—the idea that this babe-in-the-wood was a wife-killer seemed fantastic. They were just a couple of yokels. Yet long experience had taught me that Preeker never missed. If he smelled something wrong, there was something wrong. That his first guess was haywire didn't change anything. There was *still* something wrong. Maybe my own growing feeling of uneasiness was based on his—I wouldn't be ashamed if it were—but now I was beginning to expect trouble.

We got trouble—of a sort. MacWhinney said over his shoulder, "She doesn't expect us. I'll give her a ring," and paddled over to the house phones. The lawyer and I stood waiting.

Then he came back, his chinless face aghast. "I—I'm terribly sorry," he stammered. "She doesn't—doesn't seem to be in. I—would you care to come up and wait? I'm sure she won't be...."

I said: "No. I have one or two things to do in the neighborhood. I'll give you a call in an hour and if it's convenient, I'll drop over then. If not, we can let it go till morning."

He moaned how sorry he was, and I assured him it was all right.

I WATCHED them to the elevator, then went over to the row of phone booths and did some telephoning. The next to the last call I put in was to one of the boys in the Acme investigation department, asking him to see if he could get a line on what Joe Dunphy was doing or had been doing lately—who he was connected with. The last one I made was to Preeker, still in the office.

"This MacWhinney has some real estate deal on," I said. "He's selling some property or something. Might find out exactly what, if you can, but it's apparently secret so don't go letting the cat out of the bag… No, I haven't seen the woman yet."

I hung up on his yammered questions.

I thought the woman who stepped out of the booth adjoining mine looked at me queerly. She was striking, young, slender, with finely drawn, yet electric features, white skin and eyes so deep a blue as to be almost black. We stepped out exactly together. She gave me a sidelong glance, hurried on over to the desk.

I was not following her. I just happened to spot Charlie Dumart on duty behind the desk and wandered over, hoping maybe to pry out some information about the MacWhinneys. I got to the desk, just in time to hear Charlie say, "I'll tell him, Mrs. MacWhinney," and to see the dark girl of the phone booth sail off toward the Broadway exit.

On impulse, I did follow her then. It occurred to me that there might be a chance to catch a few minutes talk with her alone—if I could think of anything to say.

She took a cab outside the hotel, and I sifted thoughtfully along behind her in another. We drove straight downtown to the Nightingale Club, one of Greenwich Village's more pretentious night clubs. They did a dinner business as well, so the place was in full blast. Neither her entrance, nor mine behind her, got any attention. The floor show was on.

I got in just in time to see her talking to the headwaiter at the entrance to the supper room. I saw her slip him a bill. Then he went away, down the side corridor outside the supper room and, a minute later, came back, bowed and said something to the dark-haired girl. She waited. Presently, a luscious little blonde in a strapless evening gown emerged from the hall. I recognized her—from the billboards outside the place—as Gloria Lee, a featured singer in the show. I seemed to have seen her around. She was cuddly, blue-eyed—but she had quite a few years on the eighteen that she affected. She was made up for the show and when the dark-haired girl ran over eagerly and tried to put her arms around her, she backed away smiling, holding out her powdered arms.

They talked eagerly to each other, like old friends, for a few minutes. The dark-haired girl got a little book from her bag and scribbled down something that the blond girl told her. Then the callboy came down the hall and spoke to Gloria Lee and she had to go. The dark-haired Valda MacWhinney blew her a kiss and then hurried out of the place. I decided to stick around a bit.

Presently the blond girl did a turn—a couple of torch songs—and bowed off. I sought out the headwaiter myself and gave him my card and a five-dollar note.

That got me nowhere. The headwaiter returned, all apologies, and told me: "Miss Lee says that she does not care to see any detectives of any sort, shape, or order. If you want her in court for anything, serve her a subpoena, she says. If you don't want her in court, go—er—fly a kite."

I wasted no tears over the tactical blunder. Gloria Lee would be there for some time, till I thought up a way to get around her. The MacWhinneys, on the other hand, might go out to eat or something.

This time, when I called on the room phone at the Hammond, MacWhinney's eager voice urged me to come right up.

HE MET me at the elevator on the sixteenth floor and walked through vast mazes of corridor with me. He assured me, *sotto voce*, that this was a very strict hotel—that they had had to show their marriage license in order to get a double room. I could picture Charlie Humart getting that one off with a straight face.

Only the girl was in the room—more striking than ever in a plain gown. After one glance, she kept her eyes down from mine, as though aware but not caring to concede, that the round-headed, little, red-faced dry-goods clerk was no great catch. He bounced around introducing me. By the time he had finished, Byron, the lawyer walked in, rocking a little and preceded by a fresh cloud of rye whisky, the merry twinkle still in his foggy eyes.

We gabbled around and then I got down to business. I got the forms out and said: "If you'll just read it over and sign here—and maybe you could drop in at the office some time tomorrow...."

Apparently the policy-taking-out was news to her, for MacWhinney hurried out: "You know...? The policy we discussed before we left home. Thought I'd get it over and done with and all that, dear—just a matter of form."

I couldn't read the single sharp look she gave him. Maybe it was anger. Maybe, for all I know, she was wondering about the first Mrs. MacWhinney and her signing an identical application. For an instant, I thought she was going to refuse to sign it, but she only said in a soft voice, "Are you sure we can afford it, Henry?" and sat down. She sat down with a country-bred woman's movement, for all her looks and apparent sophistication, took my pen and the forms.

When he said, "Yes, dear, of course," she signed where I pointed out.

I had the forms in my pocket, the appointment made, was out in the hall, trying to say goodbye. Hunch or no hunch—mine or Preeker's—there was simply no opportunity to ask any more questions, nor were there any more that I *could* ask.

MacWhinney, still fumbling with his hands, accompanied me a step or two. "Everything is all right now, isn't it, Mr.—"

I was shot in the back!

I had turned round to bow to the woman and the lawyer still in the doorway, and I was saying, "Yes, of course. Tomorrow…" when the gun thundered from the cross corridor.

Something like a ten-ton truck hit me just behind the right armpit, exploded fire inside me and slammed me against the wall as though I had been flung there. I went down like a pile of brick, half spinning around. My right side was paralyzed and there was a lancing hell from neck to ankle.

I saw Joe Dunphy, saw the gun in his big hand fling down on me again. Then—almost a split second after the first—the second shot came. But Joe Dunphy did not fire it.

I had no time to choose which way I would dive. My tangled feet decided that for me. I was reeling. As agonizing feeling shot back into my right leg, I plunged—almost straight toward Dunphy, in a wild desperation, my half-nerveless fingers fumbling to get my own gun from my hip, and—*Joe Dunphy was blown from his feet!*

It was as though he were kicked in the small of the back. He went up to his toes, arching, his stupid face contorting, his gun flying up in the air. Reeling, stumbling, I somehow caught myself against the wall, staggered aside as he crashed down—and tripped over his feet.

I landed on my face in the mouth of the cross-corridor. I saw the little man flying for the staircase at the other end—

saw him and recognized him. I don't know if I blurted, "Ben Almon," or if the dapper, dull-eyed, sharp-faced, little private detective's name just sounded in my mind.

I fought again to my feet, and everything spun round. I fell down again—but I could feel in my right side and I could almost have prayed with gratitude. I groped—and was certain I had only a flesh wound. The bullet must have bounced off a rib.

MEN WERE running, shouting. Two doctors appeared from somewhere, half the white-faced staff of the hotel. I was half giddy when the first of the police swooped down, the tormented face of Charlie Dumart over their shoulders—but I held two things rigidly in my mind. First, that I had not seen, could not guess, who had shot Joe Dunphy. Second, that I was not going to any hospital. Tearing urgency held my mind above water—above the bewildered questions of the police. From what they asked me as I lay on a bed in the hotel room, I knew that they were getting no satisfaction from the MacWhinney party. I wanted to get out. There was a swirl of bandages, antiseptics, a wild kaleidoscope of faces and uniforms. I went a little giddy—for no more than minutes. Then I was alone in the room with a short-sleeved interne who urged me to come to the hospital—I must have argued with him previously—the house doctor, and Bill Beauharnois. Someone had notified my office and the blond little Frenchman had come running.

I got the diminutive op's ear and whispered, "Go and find Ben Almon and collar him, like the wind. Phone me here," and he went out without a word.

I said, "Go away," to the interne, as the door opened a minute later and I saw the frightened faces of the little countryman, MacWhinney and the be-bearded, owlish-eyed lawyer in the opening.

Byron looked shocked almost sober and his eyes were bloodshot and frightened.

Then somehow I was alone with the house doctor, while he said, "I shouldn't be doing this," as he shot a long hypodermic into my arm, and then I was sitting on the edge of the bed, parrying the last of a series of questions from a witch-faced headquarters detective named Hallett.

"Is Joe Dunphy dead?" I asked him.

"Ha! So you know it was Joe Dunphy! What was he after you for?"

"I saw him when I fell—and when he fell. I don't know what he was after me for. I haven't seen him in months. Is he dead?"

"Just about. The bullet went clean through his left lung," the detective grumbled. "Damn it, how do you expect us to catch the guy who shot him if you give us nothing?"

Ten minutes later I was almost myself again, save for the stiffness in my right side, and Preeker was on the phone, squealing excited questions in my ear.

"There's a flatfoot outside my room," I told him. "Stay in your office. I may break this thing right away—only clear this wire."

Then—after what seemed eternity, the phone rang and Bill Beauharnois' soft voice was in my ear. "I've found your Ben Almon. I chased him all over town. You know where he is? Right back in the same hotel you are—one flight above you—Room Seventeen-thirty."

"Hold him," I blurted.

IT TOOK me twenty minutes, a pitiful tale to the dick guarding me, a lofty declaration that he could find me

when he wanted me and that I would not suffer persecu-
tion, a quick shoot around half a dozen blocks in a taxi—
before I could eel out of his fingers. Then a quick dive
back into the hotel and down into the basement, a modest
bribing of the hotel's engineer before I was shot upwards
again in the freight elevator—and at last I was being let
into Room 1730 by the placid, blond little Frenchman.

Ben Almon sat on the bed, strips of adhesive around
wrists and ankles, a welt along the side of his neck.

"He cut up a little when he heard me talk to you." Bill
Beauharnois nodded at the detective.

"What is this?" the dull-eyed, sharp-faced, little private
dick snarled. "I don't know what you guys are talking…"
He ducked wildly away and fell on the bed as I took a quick
stride and cuffed him with the flat of my gun.

I had to hit him twice, and promise to turn him in to the
cops if he clammed up, before he began to sing.

"All right," he gasped. "I'll spill if you guys will cover me.
You won't like it, but if you swear not to pop that I told you,
you can have it."

We told him to go ahead.

"I didn't even know you were there," he told me fretfully.
"I'm hired to guard this guy MacWhinney while he's in
New York—and see nothing happens to him till further
notice. I'm hanging around the corridor and I see this big
lug take a plant, watching his door. When he starts blast-
ing, I think he's shooting at MacWhinney and I have to
stop him. That's all."

"Who's your client?" I said. "The Federal Government?
You mean you hire out to go around potting people in hotel
corridors and running away? If you were caught, no pull
in the world would save your license. You're not damned
fool enough to—"

"My client is as good as the mint. He could—and would—cover me. But if the cops got me they might force me to expose him and—"

"Ah! J.P. Morgan, no doubt."

"Just about as good." He started to clam up. We jumped at him, yelled at him till he coughed it up. "P.L. Harland, of the Harland Oil Company, and he'll back me to the limit."

It was like a Roman candle popping alight in my head. I dashed out, headed for the office.

PREEKER'S BONY little face was almost bursting when I walked into his office. He was yammering into a telephone, "Well, how is he? Is he dead? I want to know every change," and hung up.

"Who?" I asked.

"Joe Dunphy," he moaned. "What in God's name is going on here? Why…?"

"Skip it. How is Dunphy?"

"He can't live through the night. He's conscious, but one lung is shot and he's had an internal hemorrhage. They're putting him in an oxygen tent. They won't let the cops near."

I sat down and reached for a phone.

It rang as I touched it. Preeker's bony claw snatched it away from me and he barked a peevish, "Hello," into it.

He snatched a pencil and pad, snarled: "Go ahead. What…? Oh, all right."

"There goes one of your bright ideas," he told me when he had hung up. "MacWhinney isn't putting over any real-estate deal. The only real estate he owns is a flock of swamp he inherited from his first wife."

My "What!" as I jumped to my feet nearly knocked him over. His mouth hung open and his glasses glittered.

"What's matter? What's…?" he gulped as I snatched up the phone book, grabbed a phone and dialed the Nightingale Club.

"You—you've got something? You know…?" he demanded excitedly.

"I think so—if you can find who Joe Dunphy is working… Hello. I want to speak to Gloria Lee, the singer. What?"

The voice told me: "Miss Lee is not in the club. She was called to Mercy Hospital—a relative, dying…."

For one second, I was confused again. Then light started to break. I clapped down the receiver, called the Hammond. When I got the frightened voice of the little countryman, MacWhinney, I threw at him: "May I speak to Mrs. MacWhinney a minute? It's most urg—"

"But she went out," he interrupted me worriedly. "She and Mr. Byron went out for something to ea…."

I stood there, after I had hung up, my face flaming, knowing I had the monstrous little puzzle almost in my hand—agonizing because I could not quite see the solution.

Then my eye fell on Joe Dunphy's record on the desk—and I exploded.

I did not have to read more than the first line of the mass of stuff they had dug up on him: …Joe Dunphy (alias Harry Mehr) *born in Grimsby, Maine, acquitted of murder 1934, came to New York….*

I said, "Oh, my God!" and dived for the door.

Preeker screamed: "Wait! Where are you…?"

"Mercy Hospital," I flung at him, "and you can pray I'm not too late."

WHEN I got to Mercy they told me: "Mr. Dunphy is in the isolation wing—Room Eight Seventy-six—but absolutely no one can see him. No one but the staff are even allowed in the wing. If you are the police...."

I opened my mouth to bellow at her—and bit my tongue. Instead I clipped: "Has a girl in a red evening gown come past this desk in the last little while?"

She frowned and tried to remember—while I sweated blood. When she said. "Yes, I believe so. She was with one of the nurses, I believe," I went cold.

I said, "Thanks," and the instant her back was turned, raced for an elevator, got in, and asked for the ninth floor. The operator had no objections to telling me which wing was the isolation wing as he swooped me up. I asked if it ran the full height of the hospital and he said: "Oh, no, only to the tenth floor."

I got off at nine, ran up to ten, found my way to the part of the hospital that was above the isolation wing, raced down the fire stairs. I had to pick the lock on the fire stairs door and then I whipped through, saw the back of the nurse at the desk that blocked off the corridor ahead of me—and dived down the cross-corridor.

The maddening realization was pounding in my mind that a nurse could have found a dozen different ways to circumvent all my roundabout scheming.

Then I was at the door of 876. For one second I tried to listen, damned myself as I realized the rooms must be utterly soundproof. I jerked my gun as I plunged in. I was too late.

That was the searing, agonizing stab that went into my heart as I saw the tableau. I had finally caught up—just a split second too late.

The blond singer, Gloria Lee, stood at the end of the bed, tied to the bedstead. Her face was frantic, her eyes white-rimmed as she writhed frantically.

The nurse's deep-blue eyes jerked to mine for a second as I plunged in—and maybe that was what gave me a chance. I did not need even the first instant to recognize her even, dark features, her white face. Even the vicious savagery of her expression did not disguise the fact that she was Valda MacWhinney.

The face behind the isinglass of the oxygen tent—Joe Dunphy—was white and strained. His hand was out through the slot in the tent and he was struggling with all his will power to summon the strength to raise a flat black automatic from the covers.

And in the second that I was there, the pseudo-nurse acted like lightning. She snatched at the gun herself, jerked it up and—while it was still in both their hands—flame and roar jumped from the muzzle.

I fired at the same instant. I don't know yet whether they were trying to hit me—or the roped girl at the end of the bed. My bullet was almost miraculously true. It hit the gun with a metallic whang, knocked it clear of their combined grip, sent their shot wild—and for the first time I saw the third person in the room. Byron, the drunken lawyer, was in one corner. Only the fact that he was really drunk saved me. I saw the motion as he went for his gun, flung myself aside. I had no time to aim for him. I just fired at his head.

The fantastic little payoff capped fittingly. My bullet caught him squarely in the bridge of the nose. His gun belched flame—and the bullet took the pseudo-nurse squarely in the side of the neck, knocked her choking and screaming, across the bed, blood spurting from mouth and wound, as the bearded lawyer tottered—and crashed down.

The girl in red sagged in her ropes, collapsed to the floor, and for one mad second I thought they had hit her—but she had only fainted.

I WAS holding her up when the first of the wild-eyed cops rushed in, Preeker at their heels. "Don't shoot," I yipped as half a dozen gun muzzles covered me. "I just prevented the murder of this girl."

"Prevented?" a red-faced cop bellowed. "You've knocked off two—"

"Two killers! Wait—it's simple—too simple. That's Valda MacWhinney, the second wife of a guy. This"—as the girl in red—Gloria Lee—stirred in my arms and moaned—"is his first wife. She was supposed to be running away, five years ago—meeting another girl on a bridge in a storm. They found a body which they thought was this one's—probably it was the other girl's and she never did meet her—thought she had failed to show up. They identified that as this girl's body."

"What of it?" the cop roared.

"Just a minute. There's an angle to it. This girl—the first wife—owned some supposedly waste marsh land. The husband fell heir to it. She shook the dust of the town from her feet, evidently didn't even read the papers or communicate with anyone. They thought she was dead—even tried a guy for murdering her and acquitted him. The husband got the waste land. Some oil scout must have found oil on it—because a big oil operator is buying it from him now and is anxious enough to have the deal go through to have him guarded by a private dick."

"What the hell are they doing here?"

"That's the neat part. The second wife—that one in the nurse's get-up—and the lawyer, must have heard from this one or something. That's why they came to New York—to silence her. If she showed up the fortune would be hers, not theirs. They brought along the stooge—MacWhinney—in case this one should make any further attempts to get in touch with anyone back there. They came here to kill her. His meandering into our office upset the apple cart, forced their hand, but that's what they came here to do. They located Joe Dunphy—"

"What the hell for? Why couldn't they kill her themselves?"

"That's the neat part," I said as the room filled with shouting medicos. "They had to get Joe Dunphy to do the killing—because he had already been tried for murdering this same girl and acquitted. There wasn't a thing could be done to him—ever. Unfortunately, he got in the way of a bullet."

It went over big with everybody except—guess who? Ames, our ascetic, high-powered salesman. He still claims Preeker and I deliberately knocked off Valda MacWhinney to dynamite the sale of the joint coverage policy.

ONE VOTE FOR MURDER

POLITICS IN MIDDLEPORT
WERE SO CROOKED THAT
THE VOTERS EVEN DOUBLE-
CROSSED THE CANDIDATES—
AS WELL AS VICE-VERSA.
BUT THAT HARDBOILED
INSURANCE OP HELD THE
DECIDING BALLOT. ONE
VOTE CAST FOR MURDER BY
HIM WOULD CLEAN UP THE
COUNTY—IF HE COULD ONLY
GET TO THE POLL ON TIME.

CHAPTER ONE
THE STUDIOUS THUG

IT WAS only the second time in my life that I had been in Acme's Records library. It occupied approximately the rear quarter of the twenty-first floor of the vast Acme Building. I was piloting Captain Ferrara through—on one of his interminable missing persons hunts—to wish him off on Miss Griver, the records' custodian. Her office was at the rear of the library.

I saw Eddie Albright as we stepped in from the hall and I almost missed a step.

He was sitting, not thirty feet away, at the first of the long reading desks, a volume open in front of him, a pad and pencil beside it. He had his back to the door, but he half squirmed sideways, to let his eyes crawl over his shoulder at us. Ferrara was in uniform and Eddie seemed to shrink. Hastily, he bent closely over the table, propped up his elbow and shielded his face with his hand.

Ferrara didn't see him. I barely did—but I couldn't miss his chunky shoulders, his crisp, wiry, dark-brown hair, his close, mild little green eyes, nor his rocky football-player's face with its odd air of general weakness. Matter of fact, I think he did play football for some Midwestern team, his vague, baby-faced stare providing the Conference with some of its most unpleasant shocks. It had been providing, ever since, similar unpleasant shocks to police, holdup

I spun in time to see him swing himself
desperately around and try to fire.

victims, loft-watchmen—even the wardens of two or three
prisons. He wasn't an especially big-time thug but he was
tough and vicious, and educated.

I was sure he hadn't seen me spotting him. The library was a dim, vast place of shadows and green gloom. It was almost dark outside and the regularly spaced reading lamps all over the somber room only made isolated little pools of glow between stretches of murkiness.

I ushered Ferrara down the long center aisle, through into Miss driver's office, performed introductions, patted him on the back, excused myself and slipped back out, acutely curious as to Eddie Albright's interest in Acme's records.

FROM THE heavier shadows of the doorway, I could just see the top of his head, but I knew I had made no mistake. Twelve years of sleuthing for Acme had given me a pretty fair mental rogues' gallery. There was only one stickler. I had thought that Eddie was well set in the big house, doing ten years for hi-jacking an interstate truck shipment of orange bitters. Wearily, I damned the wooden-headed parole board that must have turned him loose to add to my official worries.

I slid my hands in my pockets and strolled quietly back down the aisle. The twenty-odd reading desks that filled the dim room were heavy, thick, sixty-foot tables. Thin upright partitions divided them down the center, supporting the regularly dotted emerald reading lamps. They had been designed by the efficiency engineer who had dug the hundred years' accumulation of dirt out of Acme's ears, some two years back—no small feat, Acme ranking as one of the three largest insurance companies in the country. The whole layout was his conception—this gag of assembling all the open records of the company.

It was not a bad scheme, I guess. I understand we once had a hundred girls who did nothing but answer inquiries from lawyers, doctors, students, executors, court officers, statisticians, newspapermen, authors, and God knows who else. Now all available information was assembled, bound into snappy-looking volumes, catalogued, and filed down here for the public to help themselves. I had heard that they did so—in droves—but this was apparently an off day, or hour, or something. There were not more than a dozen people in the room, exclusive of Eddie and myself.

It was painfully quiet in the semidarkness. The customers took seriously the *Silence* signs that sprouted at intervals along the tables. I loitered to a stop at the end of the table next to Eddie's, stood there pulling my ear. I guess I was toying with the idea of getting a quick peek at what he was studying.

Don't mistake me. I was deadly serious. It wasn't that I had any idea of what he was doing, or planning, but I couldn't afford to expect anything but trouble of some kind. Not with Eddie Albright. I decided to try and ease around behind him, still believing that he hadn't noticed me, either in the first place, or now.

I found out my mistake before I could take a step.

His legs, of course, were vaguely visible under the table, if I cared to stoop down. I didn't, but I glanced down as I heard a soft thud on the linoleum floor, just in time to see his toe send a short-barreled, silencer-equipped pistol skidding quietly across the space between the two tables. It disappeared in the darkness beneath the one I was leaning against.

I felt like a raw fool. He had evidently been coolly watching my every movement and now, fearing I was about to brace him, he had brazenly ditched his gun. He did not even bother to look up as I stared, red-faced, at the top of his head. I swore under my breath. If I could have caught the gun on him, I could have jerked his parole from under him, and....

I saw the girl then in the instant when I was bending over to pick up the gun—saw her standing behind Eddie, raising her tiny body on tiptoe to peer over his shoulder. He was evidently quite unaware of her. She must have slipped in, slipped up behind him while his mind was focussed on me.

I caught just a flash of her frightened, heart-shaped little face, framed by shining mahogany hair. Her starry, long-lashed blue eyes were almost black with desperate intentness as she tried to see what he was reading. Apparently she didn't even know I was alive.

I SAW all this in the instant that I went down for the gun. It made me speed up my grab for it, brought me almost jerking up again—till caution checked me. From halfway up I straightened by inches, my eyes jumping incredulously to see if it were possible that my first impression of her were true.

It was.

God knows, I've passed the age of susceptibility, but there was a split second when I forgot everything in just staring at her. She was unbelievably young, radiant. Her skin was like fresh cream, her mouth a moist, warm, scarlet flower. Her eyes were soft, shining. She belonged in old-fashioned hoop skirts and pantaloons, blushing and curtseying. She looked barely out of her teens. Her slender, rounded little body was in some sort of red silk dress. She was the essence of freshness, of loveliness, of daintiness. It just wasn't possible that she could have any contact whatever with a grifter like Eddie Albright.

I didn't know what to say or do so I just stood motionless, startled, bewitched, while a crazy sort of paternal feeling for her welled up in my chest.

There must have been two full seconds when we were frozen like a tableau. As far as I was concerned, there was no one else in the room. Actually, there was some earnest little dark-haired girl almost across the partition from Eddie and I don't doubt there were others close by.

Then Eddie became conscious of the girl in red—and the picture exploded in sickening ugliness.

It could have been my burning stare that warned Eddie of the girl. Or maybe she had made some movement. Anyway, he suddenly straightened, whipped his head over one shoulder, then the other, anger thickening his features. She was exactly behind him and the arms of his chair bound him. She backed away, the back of one hand to her mouth. Eddie furiously kicked back his chair and sprang up.

I faced him across the partition. "Just a minute, Eddie," I said softly.

He whirled to face me—and his mild little green eyes suddenly veiled. He opened his mouth, but instead of speaking, gave a funny little sneering grunt. And then made faces at me.

At least that was what I thought. He seemed to crouch a little suddenly and the pads of flesh around his eyes winced, squeezed up in a grimace. He began to move his head from side to side and I saw, amazedly, the red hell of pain and fear in his squeezed-up eyes. He swayed forward, put out a hand hastily to prop himself on the table. I glanced down, saw his knuckles whiten as he unconsciously wrenched and crumpled the loose sheets of scratchpad he had been working on. Even then I didn't get it. Bug-eyed, I started round the end of the table.

"What the hell's the ma—?"

He collapsed like a sack of meal. He just gave way at all joints, pounded his face down on the open volume on the table, bounced off, crashed down to the floor, half on his face, half on his side, twitched once and lay still.

My mouth was open as I jumped to his side—and then I saw the thick handle of the heavy throwing knife that stuck out of his back. It didn't stick out far—the whole blade was practically buried. I didn't even have to debate whether he was dead. He had to be with an inch or more of cold steel in his heart.

ALL RIGHT. I fumbled it—if you say so. True enough, the whole thing slipped out of my hands there and getting it back was what threw me into the gruelling little drama—but I maintain I was ruined by the time the hall door snicked closed.

It had one of these self-closing gadgets that draw a door to with extreme slowness. Its soft, authoritive latching was what jerked my hot eyes up—and made everything clear as day. I choked, jumped around Eddie, and ran for the door, unconsciously picking up Eddie's crumpled worksheets. I jammed them in my pocket as I yanked open the door, dived out, and—faced an empty corridor.

I cocked my head for a split second, but I could not even hear footsteps. I ran for the nearest corner, swung round, saw no one. I sprinted straight up the corridor toward the front of the building, damning wildly the immense skyscraper, with its four separate banks of elevators and four separate stairways, any one of which the escaping killer could have chosen.

I saw no one in any of the cross-corridors as I ran past them, no one in the corridor that crossed the front of the building, as I finally swung across it.

I came to a feverish halt, looking back down along the opposite front-to-rear hallway, having seen nobody.

Then to top it off, I did see somebody—just too far away. I saw the girl in the red dress, close against the most distant bank of elevators, jabbing at the bell, struggling to wrap her dark coat around her and, even as I saw her, the light above the elevator door glowed red.

I yelled, "Hey—wait a min—" and the car door slid open. She flung me one glance as I sprinted toward her, bawling, "Come back here…" and waving the silenced gun at her. "Hey—elevator…"

But my voice didn't reach the operator of the car. The door clanked shut long before I was even well started toward it, and its red light went out as it dropped.

I cursed crazily, dived for the nearest office door beside me. It was some distant branch of the auditor's department—Acme, besides nine solid floors in its own building has these little broken suites scattered all over forty floors—burst in and snatched the phone from under the bespectacled eyes of an old-maid typist, rattled the hook. When I got an answer, I snapped: "The elevator starter in front of 'B' Bank—fast!"

When I got him I clipped: "Car number three—don't let it open on the ground floor. Send it back to twenty-one—let no one off!"

I could have saved myself the mental gymnastics. When the elevator door again slid open and I stared at its five round-eyed passengers, there was absolutely no sign of the lovely, blue-eyed girl.

"Girl in red dress—black coat—pretty—young—" I snarled at the operator. "You just got her here…"

"Oh, her?" He was a fawn-colored youth with a high tenor voice. "Why, she got off at nineteen—two floors down…"

I ground my teeth, half threw myself at another office door—and realized I was licked. For all her panic, and all her wide-eyed childishness, she had outthought me. Obviously, she had divined that I might have the car stopped, had coolly shifted to another one. By now, she would be nicely out of the building and away....

I was so furious and galled that I had to bite down hard. Even before I pushed open the door of the library again, I heard the shrill yapping of Preeker, my sharp-nosed, bony, excitable little boss.

When he saw me come in, he broke away from the knot of stunned people around the body, came toward me, waving his hands shrilling: "Well, where is he? Where is this killer that slaughters people on our own premises? Where is—?"

"He got away." My eyes were hot and I knew my face was brick-red. I expected him to crack about the girl next but evidently he hadn't heard of her. My eyes shuttled swiftly around the room. Far down at the other end I could see Ferrara, through the open door of the custodian's office, speaking into a telephone. I looked at Eddie's body. Some damned fool had pulled the wide, eight-inch, blue blade out of him and he was bleeding like all hell, dead or not.

I estimated swiftly—and knew I would have no chance to see if he had anything on him now. My eye went suddenly to the open volume on the table in front of him and I was suddenly conscious of the sheets of paper in my pocket.

Preeker was jumping up and down almost screaming at me: "...under your own nose...walks calmly away...laughing stock of the business...call yourself a detective...."

"Shut up," I snarled at him. "Get that book on the table there down to your office—substitute another one—fast, before Ferrara spots it. I'll clean this thing up or choke."

I GUESS I had some idea that the sheets of paper and the volume would show up the whole background of the murder, point me straight to the killer. Forty minutes later when we got down to it—it was that long before we could make a break from the police circus—it turned out to be a wispy, faint little dot of information and nothing more. All that Eddie had written was one line on the top sheet of paper: *Pd. 150 Gs. June 11, 1934, Jt.L.* By means of a thumbnail indentation we identified, in the book, the item that had interested him.

A partnership of one George Fowler and one P.K. Gillies, of Middleport, Long Island, had taken out a seventy-five thousand-dollar partnership policy, on the lives of the two partners in 1933. Evidently it contained provision for double indemnity in case of accidental death, for P.K. Gillies had been accidentally killed in 1934 and one hundred and fifty thousand dollars had been paid to the survivor, George Fowler.

It was open, straightforward and aboveboard. There was not the slightest question of anything phony about the death of P.K. Gillies, no question but that it had been a pure accident. We got it from the lips of Harry Behre, Acme's shrewdest and sanest adjustor, who had settled the policy and who remembered the details perfectly.

"They were a couple of struggling lawyers who wanted to take a flyer into a side business. Some old coot out there owned half a dozen acres of abandoned canning factories, full of old machinery. They wanted to tear it out and sell it for scrap iron. The old gent insisted they form a regular little partnership, take out that insurance and so forth.

I guess he was afraid he wouldn't get his dough, because evidently he hooked them into a bad deal. That is, they didn't lose much on it, but they had visions of making a fortune and it just sort of petered out.

"Gillies was a member of the volunteer fire department and the wall of a burning house caved in on him a few months later, killed him and two others. Half the town was right there and saw it. It's perfectly absurd to think there was anything phony about it. If ever I saw a perfectly clean, clear payoff, that policy is it."

That was what my promising clue boiled down to— that Eddie Albright seemed to have some interest in Mr. George Fowler of Middleport, Long Island, who had collected a perfectly legitimate insurance payment some six years ago.

I said, after I had sat there numbly for minutes: "All right. I'll go out to Middleport then. I know that town. I might be able to find a situation—"

The phone interrupted, and Preeker answered it. It was a summons for us to come back up to the library.

It seemed that I had erred in ignoring the earnest little girl in blue who had been sitting over and across from Eddie at the reading table. She, it seemed, had now informed the police about the girl in the red dress.

I don't know why I got obstinate, why I was impelled to play dog-in-the-manger, but I was. I said bluntly, to the barrage of police questions, "I didn't see her," and stuck to it. God knows it was irrational. Her running away was practically responsible for my being in the grease—but somehow it drove me silly to think of her being third-degreed by cops. Myself, I would take care of her, plenty—if I found her again. But her spell was still bearing down on me, giving me an unreasonable urge to shield her, to fend trouble away from her. There was no sense to it, but I was as certain as I was of my own name that whatever her involvement here, she was clean and sweet and innocent.

Not till then did the galvanizing possibility burn into my brain.

The earnest little girl in blue was acting out what had happened, was standing exactly where the girl in red had stood—they had removed the body now—and was saying in a flute-like, breathless voice: "She was right here—looking over his shoulder—right behind him...."

I felt a shrinking in my stomach as the overlooked question dawned on me. Was Eddie Albright's death what had been intended here? Perhaps not Eddie, but the exquisite, childlike little girl in red had been the target of the murderer's knife. The chances of one were exactly as reasonable as of the other! If it was the girl whom the skulking killer had tracked here, her life he sought....

That possibility electrified the whole picture instantly. Somehow thought of murder stalking the dainty, luscious little redhead was intolerable to me. Catching the killer grew to pressing urgency.

I faced my thin thread of information—and my heart sank. Strictly speaking, I knew nothing except that there was a wild chance that this thing had its roots in Middleport, that a respectable lawyer named George Fowler might have some connection with it. And that was the sum total.

Eddie Albright had had some interest in the lawyer. The girl had had some interest in Eddie Albright's interest. The killer had had some interest in—which of them? I had no idea. I had no idea what Eddie's interest was, nor the girl's. I did not know yet who the girl was. I did not, in spite of Harry Behre, know who this George Fowler was, apart from his name.

All I could do was hope I would stumble on the answers to all of them, in Middleport.

CHAPTER TWO
THE DOCTOR DIED IN JAIL

I DIDN'T have to wait till Middleport for some of them. They started breaking amazingly, the minute I crossed the county line next morning.

I stopped at Greenwater, just over the line, for gas and oil, got out to stretch my legs—and was staring at George Fowler. His face was a yard from my own, tacked against the service station shack—a picture, surrounded with heavy black type: *George Fowler for County Judge. Able—Fearless—Honest.*

The picture showed a man of fifty, with crisp iron-gray hair and a square sort of bulldog face, trying to look able, fearless, and honest.

I sat in the old convertible a few minutes, digesting this. The panic all died out of me, but not the urgency. I began to see light.

I had brought along the name and address of the county coroner who had signed the death certificate of Gillies, Fowler's former partner. He was, according to my notes, Middleport's only doctor. It seemed about the only starting point I had. I asked the gas station attendant where it was and he gave me explicit directions.

"You can't miss it. It's the prettiest house on Oak Street—all white, kind of broken up into peaks and gables. There's a little vestibule, sort of, on the Francis Street side. He's got a big piece of ground around it, keeps it nice. Willow trees and like that."

Ten minutes later, as I parked the convertible at the curb near the graceful, pleasant house, I endorsed the grease monkey's opinion. It was a charming place. The noon sun lit up the grounds like a stage setting. I gathered that Doctor Middleton, the county coroner, had a profitable practise.

There was a modest little black glass sign by the front door, not containing his name, but an invitation to walk in, so I did so and was in a little ivory-painted anteroom. Evidently, there should have been a receptionist at a neat little ivory desk which held a telephone and an appointment book. A table of magazines, half a dozen comfortable-looking club chairs, a settee and a fireplace, with a neat log fire laid and kindled, completed the picture.

A door behind and to the left of the desk opened and a little man with a discouraged, very small, round, weathered-red face and bald head came out, wearing a short white surgical coat. He looked at me with fever-bright tired blue eyes, wiping his hands on a towel.

I said, "I'm from Acme Insurance, Doctor," and gave him a card.

He looked at it without much interest. "What can I do for you?"

I groped for a gag. "We had a little fire in our warehouse and we lost a few records. I'm trying to reconstruct them, for the files. One of them was a partnership policy that we settled on the death of a Mr. Gillies of this town five years ago. The beneficiary—his partner—was Mr. George Fowler, who's running for county judge here now, I understand."

"And?"

"I was wondering if you recalled the details when Mr. Gillies was killed. It was in 1934."

He rubbed the side of his nose with a forefinger and said wearily: "I'm afraid I don't. I was in South America then."

"But you signed the death certificate."

"No, mister. I've signed death certificates for soldiers in South America, in Alaska, in Central America and in China, but never a civilian. Pity, isn't it?"

"What is this?" I asked. "Am I crazy or are you? Aren't you Doctor Middleton?"

"No. I am Doctor Talmadge—the sap that paid eighteen years' savings and gave up a snug army berth, for Doctor Middleton's practise."

I digested that.

"What's wrong with the practise?" I asked curiously.

"There isn't any. It was a phony. And now, of course, the natives act as though there were a pox on the place."

"Now?" I pressed. "How do you mean, now?"

"Since Middleton took his little trip."

"Trip to where?"

"Leavenworth, I believe. My esteemed colleague was operating a wholesale narcotic business from these premises."

"He's in Leavenworth now?"

"No. He died, some six weeks back, owing nineteen years of a twenty-year hitch—a chiseler to the end."

I absorbed the surprising information. If....

I cursed myself for having picked the burnt-file conversational gambit. The questions I now wanted to ask the bitter, tired-eyed little doctor wouldn't fit it. However, I needed a native anyway, not a Johnny-come-lately, so I got up to go.

THE DOOR opened and an imposing figure of a man in a long black coat—a vague modernization of a Prince Albert—and with a magnificent pure white mane of thick waving hair came in. That is, he was impressive at first sight. Not at close scrutiny.

His swarthy face was too sharply carved, too thin, his black eyes too shiny. He carried a broad-brimmed black felt hat in one hand. "Ah, Doctor." He beamed cordially and a little questioningly at me. I got the impression that he was about forty and that his old-fashioned-politico pose was a hard one to maintain. "Just in the neighborhood and thought I'd drop by and see if that analysis had come back yet."

He kept on beaming at me, till the doctor's tired voice said: "Yes, it's here." Then to me, "Probably Judge Anstey can help you on anything you want to know about George Fowler. This is"—he had to locate my card to read off my name—"of Acme Insurance. This is Judge Anstey."

Anstey beamed cordially, pumped my hand vigorously, but some of the interest had gone out of his eyes— evidently on finding that I was not a voter. "Glad to know you, sir. Proud to know you."

I was forced to repeat the now one-legged gag about a fire in the records department, trying to reconstruct, etc.

"Why, yes," he said. "I knew Paul Gillies—knew him well. And"—he laughed merrily—"of course I know my worthy opponent, George Fowler."

The doctor said, "I'll get that for you, Judge," and wandered through the open door of the surgery.

Anstey bunched his eyebrows and assured the floor: "A tragic thing, Paul's death—very tragic—"

He broke off, staring at the desk obliquely. I looked to see what had caught his eye and found that it was my card. He looked at me suddenly, sharply. "Aren't you—that is, you must be the detective present when Eddie—when that chap was murdered in your building yesterday."

I said: "Yeah."

"H'mmm," he said and threw a lightning glance at the surgery door. *"H'mmm."*

I decided to take a wild flyer. "Matter of fact, he died in my arms."

"Oh. Then you know who killed him?" He laughed heartily. "Listen to me. You'd think I was trying the case."

"Not yet—but I will very soon," I assured him matter-of-factly. "The killer was seen, though he doesn't know it. We're in touch with the witness?"

His eyes searched mine, dropped to my tie. "Yes. Well—" as the red-faced little doctor came back in looking over a hieroglyphic-covered document. "I—" He looked quickly at the turnip of a watch that was cabled across his middle. "I shall have to run along. You'll send me the bill for this, eh Doctor?" And to me, "Drop in and see me at my chambers—on Main Street. Anytime."

I asked the doctor, when the door had closed behind the judge: "He's running against George Fowler?"

"Trying to. But I think he's had his day. People are beginning to wake up to how rotten politics really are in this county. Those dog-track scandals opened everybody's eyes."

"You think George Fowler will beat him?"

"Well, he thinks so at any rate. He's pretty desperate. He didn't need that urinalysis. He was just after my vote."

Another bug popped into my mind—a question, but a question to which I knew the answer the minute I thought of it. I asked the doctor to let me make some long-distance calls from his phone, settling the tolls with him and he agreed disinterestedly, left me alone while I put through four calls. The last one brought me confirmation of my sudden suspicion.

The principal keeper at Leavenworth broke down and told me: "Yeah. Doc Middleton and Eddie Albright were here together. They weren't cellmates, but they palled around a lot together."

I sat staring at the mouthpiece after I had hung up, trying to piece my little bits together, but I didn't seem to have enough of them.

I settled with the bitter little medico, thanked him and let myself out.

I HAD walked down the doctor's pathway and almost to my convertible, before I saw Anstey. He stepped out from under the shadow of a fat willow tree and waited for me to come up, his hands clasped behind him.

His face was no longer professionally amiable. It was hard and bitter and his coal-black eyes were strained. He said plainly: "I think you're a young man who has his head screwed on right. I want to talk to you—and maybe put something in your pocket."

"Go ahead."

His strained eyes searched mine. "Maybe you can guess what I want to know."

"I'm no good at guessing."

He hesitated, still trying to get something out of my eyes. "All right. Have you found any connection between Eddie Albright and George Fowler?"

"Do you know Eddie Albright?"

"I only know that he phoned me three days ago and made some wild claims about what he could do for me in this election."

"What did he say when you saw him?"

"He—" His face flushed darkly. "I didn't see him, of course. I don't consort with paroled convicts."

"All right. Why do you think he's connected with George Fowler?"

His face was maroon and his breathing came heavily. "Look, young man—don't fancy-dan me. If you've got the information I'm the man to bring it to. I'll take care of you."

"But I haven't," I said innocently. "I'm hoping to pick it up around here."

"How?"

"Oh, I don't know. Just nosing around."

I had him nearly out of his mind. I didn't know why.

For five full seconds he glared at me and I could see the frenzy of indecision in his hot eyes. Then he blurted: "If you're sticking your nose into something you know nothing about, you'll wish you hadn't been born. Believe me."

He turned on his heel, tramped a few rods and climbed into a brand-new Buick coupé, sent it whirling round in a U-turn and disappeared over a hill.

I drove down into Middleport's business section—two long blocks of stores lining Main Street just above the harbor.

My brain was beginning to pump.

I parked on the street before a hardware shop, needling my brain. I finally drove on up the street to the combination firehouse and police department, spent an hour with the grizzled police sergeant.

He recalled and had officiated at the fire in which Fowler's partner, Gillies, had lost his life, but he could tell me nothing new. I spent another hour or two with the present county coroner, who dug out what records there were for my examination. I didn't really expect to find anything in all this, but it had to be done and it was the only activity I could cook up. Despite what I had learned, I still could not conceive a plan. I had to plow on, praying, hoping desperately for one more break. It was maddening. I knew now that I was not shooting at the moon, that my picture was here—but for all I understood of it, I still might as well have been a million miles away.

Eddie Albright. The girl in red. George Fowler. Judge Anstey—and the renegade Doctor Middleton. I ran them over and over through my head, vainly.

A lot of people going into and coming out of one of the stores in the business block, brought me to a stop opposite—and I was looking into George Fowler's campaign headquarters.

I EASED in, stood in a corner, watched him glad-handing his supporters, answering a stream of questions, handing out pamphlets. His poster-pictures had done him more than justice. The strain he was under and weariness had harshened his lined bulldog face, gave him a crafty, sly look. He was a big, square-bodied man, with a lawyer's erect carriage. The place was a beehive. I had already learned—from posters—that election day was less than a week away.

I couldn't resist the gnawing itch to do something, to make some move. I didn't think it through. All I was certain of was that something evil was definitely going forward here and I racked my brain for a monkey wrench to toss into the machinery. If I could break it open somewhere, maybe I could spot what was inside.

I worked my way over to stand a little behind and to the right of the politician.

When, presently, he became aware of me and wheeled on me with a tired mechanical smile and a psuedo-hearty, "Yes, my friend. What can I do for you?" I said in an undertone: "I'm an insurance detective. I'm waiting to talk to you about the murder of Eddie Albright." I said it with my back turned to the room, confidentially, so no one else could hear it.

His bulldog face and gray eyes became a sick mask. The smile was fixed on his face. For a second he could not get words past his bobbing Adam's apple.

"What time are you through here?" I pressed.

His eyes shifted frightenedly at the crowd and he choked, half under his breath, "See me at my home at ten o'clock," and I nodded promptly, and went out.

I stood across the street for a while, alternately on fire with certainty that I had, and hadn't, stirred something up.

I saw a drugstore sign and walked down towards it, to inspect a phone directory for George Fowler's address. The sun had gone down by now and it was dark. As dark, I told myself uneasily, as the politics of this shoddy little county.

Then I saw the girl.

CHAPTER THREE
VANISHING VENUS

THERE WERE two wide stone steps leading up from the street to the brilliantly neon-lit front of the drugstore. I saw the girl's back as I reached for the door. That is, I saw her cluster of dark-red hair and it stopped me in my tracks. She had on a blue jersey suit, no hat, and she held a blue patent-leather handbag in one hand. She was drinking something at the soda fountain.

I held my breath—and then she turned her head. I felt the same shot of weakness that I had felt the first minute I laid eyes on her in the library. She was an exquisite, dainty child. She was talking to no one and there was a tenseness to her slim, lovely figure. I couldn't see her blue eyes.

I backed away from the door a step—almost into two loitering conversationalists on the steps. I got a break. One of them was my lone cordial acquaintance in the town— the weary little red-faced doctor, Talmadge.

I excused myself, nodded through the screen door at the girl's back and said: "That girl has the prettiest hair I ever saw."

He stared disinterestedly in—and rose nicely. "Miss Fowler? Yes, very nice."

He started down the steps with his friend and I had to frame my casual question hastily: "Is she George Fowler's only daughter?"

"I believe so, yes. And his campaign manager. Goodnight."

"Goodnight," I said.

I stood there waiting, my head buzzing. She took an unconscionable time with her drink. I hastily cooked up, and discarded, a dozen things to say to her.

Finally she finished her drink, set down the glass—and at that moment the white-coated clerk came out of the phone booth at the back and called: "Oh, Miss Fowler—I think your father's calling."

My impatience nearly got the better of me after she emerged from the phone booth. It was as though she deliberately loitered, talking to the clerk. I could see now that her face was a little pinched, her smile a little shaky.

Even so, I could not make up my mind whether to brace her publicly, or wait till she got to some more secluded place. Not having decided, I was back in the shadows when she finally did come out. She stood poised on the steps a minute, looking up the street toward the lighted store front that marked her father's headquarters. Then she walked rapidly up the street toward it.

I sifted along after her, still struggling to make up my mind. Half the stores were dark now, and concealment was a cinch. She crossed to the other side of the street and I just settled my debate—decided to step up beside her and stop her here—when she halted abruptly at the entrance to an alley.

She stood, trying to peer into its blackness. She asked softly, "Dad?" and then turned and stared up the street toward the campaign headquarters. There was light enough to see her frown. I was directly across the street. I checked myself in the instant that I swayed forward.

And the whole deadly little drama exploded.

MADMAN THAT I was, I felt a thrill of relief—exultation as I finally knew I had succeeded in touching off something, at least. For if my visit had caused George Fowler to hastily locate the girl and arrange for a back-alley conference....

I looked swiftly up and down the street, along the black alley. The alley was about midway the interminably long block. The street beyond it was black. From here, I could be instantly seen if I attempted to listen at the mouth of the alley but from the blackness of the street behind....

One moment I hesitated, but knowing that the politician hadn't arrived, that he still had to make his way from headquarters, I gambled. I turned and went up the street as fast as my legs would move me without attracting notice. I shot across at the corner above, and ran, once I was in the blackness, on noiseless feet till I was practically back at the alley's rear. Then I slowed and drifted up to the little slot from that side.

There was not a street light on this narrow little thoroughfare. The few lighted windows that looked out on it did not light it up. I was safe in the murk. I stood at the corner, bent down, listened and, hearing nothing, moved my head backwards and forwards cautiously to try and spot her against the lighted street beyond.

It must have been two minutes before it finally dawned on me that she was not there. I didn't get it. There had been less than two minutes—or three at the outside—that I was out of touch with the alley. Certainly there had not been time for a conference and....

I pressed the button of my flashlight without thinking, as I moved into the alley. Something blue, crushed against the brick wall at the left, caught my eye and I stepped over—and my heart went cold.

It was the blue patent-leather handbag the girl had been carrying. It was broken, crushed in the middle where a heel had tramped down on it—a big heel. It had burst open and its contents of money, keys, cosmetics were visible, even though they had not spilled.

I whipped my flash further up the alley and I saw her handkerchief, lying in a gutter, snatched it up—and my heart climbed up into my throat as I saw the spot of wet blood in the corner.

I ran out of the alley, sprinted up the street to the campaign headquarters, drove through the loungers as though they weren't there. George Fowler was sitting behind the table now as I burst through to him. I saw a door in the back of the room, from the corner of my eye and I grabbed him by the bunched-up lapel, hopped around the table and whipped at him: "Come here—quick!"

I fairly dragged him into the storeroom beyond, shook him and put my hot face to his. "Come clean," I shouted at him. "Did you phone your daughter in Jones' Drugstore a few minutes ago?"

He was flabbergasted, aghast. "No—no, of course not," he stammered. "I—I didn't know she was back from the city."

HE COULD have been lying, but I knew sickly in my heart he wasn't. Instantly, it became apparent that the killer himself must have made the call, imitating Fowler's voice, and had spirited the girl away the minute she reached town. It was the killer I was after—and I nearly went nuts as I realized what must have happened, what must have scared him into it. This was the ghastly, ironic fruition of my bland threat of the morning, of my feckless, mad bluff of being about to be informed as to the identity of the killer. Scared witless, he had jumped to the conclusion that the girl must be the witness, that she must have seen him....

I knew it—knew it in my crawling veins, as certainly as I knew that the girl's chances for living another hour now were so slim as to be negligible. I had frightened the killer. My blind prodding had built a fire under him. To think that, after trapping the girl, spiriting her away, he would let her return unharmed was insanity. He would not have disclosed himself, convicted himself, by the very act—if he had not determined to put her out of the way permanently.

I was stung—damned near to frenzy, as I realized that I had unwittingly flung the whole thing to a mad, terrible climax. That unless I could do something, literally within minutes, it would end with her lovely, breath-taking body lying stiff and cold in some ditch... And her death would be on my head! I had sent her to it, by my blatant blundering around.

I almost threw the stammering, gasping Fowler back out into the outside room. I could think of nothing but to snarl out as loudly as I could: "You can announce that I know the murderer of Eddie Albright—that I have enough evidence to convict him now, that I have already contacted the witness I came here to see. I am just waiting for one more thing before I expose him."

Of course it was mad, but the icy fear was at my heart that I would never be able to catch up with him myself in time. Maybe some wild miracle would let my words reach him...

A bespectacled old maid scurried into my path, ran along beside me, chattering excitedly. "I'm Miss Moore—of the *Middleport News*. What was that you…?"

"I'm an Acme Insurance detective," I tossed at her. "A crook named Eddie Albright was murdered last night in New York. I'm going to turn up his killer here tonight and blow your county election sky-high. You can tell that to the police—and anybody else you want to. Where is Judge Anstey's home?"

"Why, why, it's in Bethville, but I imagine he'd be at his campaign headquarters. See? Right there—up the street."

She pointed to a store two hundred yards north—a little nearer that way than my parked car was the other. I walked as fast as though I'd been running, crossed over and strode in the store. It was a ringer for Fowler's cubicle—except that it contained only one lone, sullen-looking Latin youth behind a table—silent tribute to the desperateness of Anstey's case.

"Where's Anstey?" I snapped.

He shrugged wearily. "Don't know. He went out maybe half an hour ago, didn't say where he was going. He oughta be back some time."

"Call his home and see if he's there! Go on! Hurry up!" I flashed the little badge they make us carry and his eyes popped. He hastily grabbed the phone, made the call, asked some one if the judge were there and identified himself as Murray. He said into the mouthpiece: "Not there, eh? Any idea when he'll be back? No, eh? O.K."

"Where else might I find him?" I drove at him when he hung up.

"God knows."

I went outside and squeezed my head. I strode back toward my car. Passing in the deep shadow of a clump of trees, I took the flat gun from my hip, unbuttoned my shirt and put it between my Adam's apple and my chest, buttoned the shirt over the slight bulge. In the darkness it would get by. My teeth were clenched so hard they hurt.

My car was in front of a darkened store. I angled out into the road to climb in the driver's side—and my heart went off like a machine gun as I saw the shadow move in the well of the store. I slid in quickly behind the wheel, slammed my door and pulled down the glove compartment lid. I had my spare gun half out of it, when Anstey whipped open the other door and was in the seat beside me like a cat, his pistol nose tight against my ribs.

"Let it go," he said through chattering teeth.

I dropped it on the lip of the compartment. "Get this car going," he said as he snatched it into his pocket. "If you take your hands from the wheel, I'll shoot you."

"And kill us both?" I sneered.

"No," he said gulpingly. "I won't kill you. Not till you've done some talking."

CHAPTER FOUR
ONE VOTE FOR MURDER

I GUESS he was senseless with desperation. Maybe the organization he belonged to was used to dirty work, but certainly he had never handled this sort of thing in person before. If it weren't that I didn't trust his nerves as regards his trigger finger, and that I wasn't frantically praying that he would lead me to the girl and I would find her still alive, I could have taken him easily.

"Where to?" I asked.

"Straight on."

Presently Main Street became the highway. "Stop here," he gritted.

I stopped. "Get out," he said. "Keep your hands up." He followed me out, searched me, took my handcuffs. "Get in again," he said, "and take the wheel." He crowded against me. "Drive on," he said. "Take the next turning but one to the right. Go slow. It runs into the woods."

"Where are we going?" I asked.

"To the one spot where we can have a little talk in peace," he said huskily. "This time, my friend, you're not going to fancy-dan me. You're going to talk—including all you know about this murder you're going to solve here tonight."

"Fair enough," I said quickly. "I'll tell you all I've got—if you'll let the girl loose. She doesn't know anything."

"The g—" He choked himself off queerly. My heart squeezed again. Had he already killed her? Had…?

I warned savagely: "You'll get nothing out of me unless I get the girl, unharmed."

"Drive on," he said. "Here—turn here."

We swung into an almost overgrown dirt road. Woods closed it in overhead and the headlights danced on a solid wall of greenery on either side. Presently, the road slanted downwards, and presently we came out into a clearing at the bottom of a round valley. There was a huddled, black building in the very center of the valley. I could see no more than that—and that the road came to an abrupt halt at the foot of the hill we were on.

He told me, "Stop here," and I stopped, cut off the ignition. "This is the spot our county police bring dumb prisoners to when they don't want to talk," he told me through tight teeth. "It's the one spot in the county where you could set off a dynamite blast and it wouldn't be heard a half mile away. We're in a valley, surrounded by woods. It's up to you whether there's any noise or not."

"I'm not making any noise."

"You're going to. Mouth-noise. You might as well understand this, before we start. I've got to win that election. I'm a desperate man. I need one more term to—well, fix certain things up. If I'm booted out, I'm done for. I don't care what I do to lick Fowler. You understand?"

"I understand."

"All right. We'll go inside and talk. You can make up your mind to it that you're going to spill everything you know. How painful you make it for yourself, is up to you. Get out."

I got out. He flashed a powerful torch beam, and it fell on a crumbling, old stone mill. It was long deserted, its windows boarded up. He prodded me in the back.

"Go on."

Anstey pushed me up to the sagging wooden door. It had an ancient wooden latch on it. He reached over my shoulder and lifted it, sent the creaking door inwards and his torch showed a dust-laden room. He pushed me forward, followed me in, his torch beam holding me steady while he closed the door behind me.

He said, "All right, now—" and the words died in his throat.

My heart jumped, skipped a beat—and then went off again crazily.

His torch beam had picked out the bound and gagged figure of the girl, sitting on the floor with her back against a mammoth stone fireplace. Her eyes were wide open, terrified—but they were very much alive.

After a moment of strange, dead silence that seemed to stretch forever, Anstey said huskily behind me: "So now we have two people to answer questions, instead of just one."

I think it was at that minute that it dawned on me that Anstey was not the murderer.

And in the same instant, I knew that this was trail's end. As the deadly little jigsaw suddenly settled into place, the wild hope that had buoyed me up a second past was gone— and I knew we were in an infinitely worse case than I had begun to imagine. And Anstey, his thinking muddled by desperation, did not seem to see it!

He said behind me hoarsely: "All right. Go on—talk."

I jumped at the chance. My eyes were already on the half-open door at the other side of the fireplace.

I fairly poured out the words, as I let my hands creep up toward my vest top.

"It stacks up like this," I said, as light broke in waves on my brain. "Eddie Albright was a cellmate, or a friend, rather, of Doc Middleton in the federal pen. Middleton, when he was dying probably, passed on a little secret he had, to Eddie Albright."

"What secret?" Anstey blurted. "That's what I want to know..."

"I know you do. You've been going nearly crazy—ever since Eddie came to town and called you up with an offer to sell it to you. What did he say—that it would dynamite George Fowler completely out of the election?"

"Yes, yes. I don't know why he didn't come back. I offered him anything in reason for—"

"He didn't come back, because he had a better offer from George Fowler himself. He was playing one of you against the other and Fowler was just as desperate to buy it as you were. Because he knew—"

Then it blew open.

IT DIDN'T come from the open door on which I had my eyes fixed like a cat. It came from the door behind me—the door through which we had come. Like a fool, Anstey had been too eager to hear what I had to say and had not gotten far enough away from it.

It suddenly whined inwards. A second, brighter torch lit up the scene from behind Anstey and in the glow I saw George Fowler's bulldog face. His hoarse voice blurted: "Don't move. Put up your hands! I thought that this was where you'd bring her, you— *Don't!*"

I heard the desperate moan in Anstey's throat, and I spun around—just in time to see him fling himself desperately around and try to fire.

His gun went off—but the bullet hit the ceiling. George Fowler had leaped forward, slashed down with his heavy automatic pistol, laid open the other's scalp with all his force. Anstey was fairly hammered to the floor, his flashlight rolling crazily, its beam threshing wildly over the ceiling—and finally going out. The other beam centered me squarely.

"Don't you move, either," George Fowler warned me hoarsely. He jumped over to the girl's side, his beam following me around. He had an open knife in his hand. He slashed the girl's bonds, slashed the cord that held the gag in her mouth and she cried out, sobbing, "Oh, Dad—Dad—"

"Stop it!" he croaked at her. "Tell me everything—fast! What happened to you—tell me the truth—the absolute truth—quickly! It—doesn't matter if he hears it! Tell Dad, Anna—quickly."

She tried to get up, sobbed with pain as her limbs wouldn't support her.

"Quickly," the old man almost sobbed. "Tell me—did you stab that man in New York?"

It jerked her head up. "No! Oh, my God, no!" she cried. "I—I thought you... No, I swear I didn't. I—I heard him insist on seeing you last night—heard him threaten you. And then—when you came out from seeing him, you were white as a sheet. I knew you were lying when you said he was just a gunman—that he was someone Anstey had sent to threaten you—to scare you out of the race. I—I followed him to New York, trying to find out what he was doing to you. I—I don't know who killed him— I didn't see...

When I saw he was dead, I knew if they found who I was that it would ruin your chances; I knew how you'd been hoping for years to get elected—how badly you wanted…" She swallowed, tried again to struggle up. "Then—then it *wasn't* you that killed—you didn't—oh, I didn't see how it could be, but I was afraid…."

AND THEN it came—from the half-open door. I was just ahead of it—divined the only logical consequence, a half heartbeat ahead of it.

The drawling voice said from the blackness: "No, he didn't do it, my dear. I'll tell you who did in a minute. Drop that gun, Fowler. Don't worry. You can't hit me from there, but I can put a bullet in your heart without trouble if you force me. Not that I want to, God knows. Because I've got the little item you want so badly."

There was a second of crawling silence. Fowler stood rigid, his bulldog face gaunt and doughy. The girl was huddled, shrinking, on the hearth. I had my hands at my shirt button.

Fowler's gun dropped. "You—you have it?"

"Yes, my friend, I have it. Maybe you don't know exactly what it is, so I'll tell you. When our dear crooked friend, Dr. Middleton, examined you in '33 for that joint life policy, he wrote out a true report—at first. A report that contained the fact that you had such a bad aneurism in your heart that you were absolutely uninsurable at any price. That was before you reached him, bribed him to make a phony report, covering up your disability."

Fowler swallowed, gulped hoarsely: "I swear…"

"Don't swear to me, my friend. I'm only too pleased you did it. Because now, having obtained the joint policy by pure fraud—which would make it null and void of course—and having coolly collected one hundred and fifty thousand dollars on the policy later on—you will go to prison the minute the insurance company finds it out. And that suits me down to the ground."

Fowler licked his lips. "Please—you don't understand. I didn't mean to—"

"I understand, friend. Not you. It's you that doesn't understand. Think it over. There is absolutely no evidence, no nothing in the whole world that can convict you— except that first written report drawn up by Middleton before he went to the penitentiary. He was a slick article himself and he carefully hid it away—no doubt with the idea of using it later on to shake you down if he felt like it. He hid it in a secret cupboard in his office."

The girl's whisper was almost inaudible. "Dad—you—"

"Let me finish," the drawling voice continued from the blackness. "Middleton, having hidden the choice little item away, was sent up. In prison, he became pals with Eddie Albright and, on his deathbed, passed along the secret to Eddie as a favor. When Eddie got out, he came directly here.

"Like a fool, he started dickering with both you and that specimen on the floor there—Anstey—before he'd got his hands on the report. He saw he had a sweet market for it—so he tried to get it.

"Tried—only. He burgled Middleton's own house the night before last, got just far enough to expose where the secret cupboard was—and then I chased him. Naturally, I finished his little job and got the paper myself. It's right here in my pocket now. I need hardly add that the minute I read it, I knew that the Gods had been good to me. For quite some time now, I have been very anxious to lay my hands on seventy-five thousand dollars, shall we say—so that I could light out of the country. Of course, I realized that having Eddie in the picture would complicate it to an enormous extent, so I quickly caught up with him and liquidated him.

"Partly for my sake, my dear Fowler, and partly for your sake. However, that is neither here nor there. The point is—I have the item."

I COULD not see him, none of us could see him, but somehow I knew instinctively, the minute he turned his eyes on me. "I regret very much," he said softly, "that I had to trouble your daughter. You can lay the blame to this loudmouth here who led me to think that your daughter—ignorant as she was of the true state of affairs—had seen me throwing the South American knife in the office in New York and might expose me to this sleuth prematurely. However, it come to a happy conclusion after all, thanks to the fact that this particular mill is about the only nearby place where one can—question people, in privacy, and we all wound up here.

"I presume you are ready to hand over seventy-five thousand dollars and receive my little paper?"

Fowler's bulldog face was ghastly. The girl, from the floor could not contain her blurted whisper: "Oh, Dad, no…"

Fowler did not speak. The veins were standing out on his forehead.

Suddenly the voice in the blackness chuckled. "Why— of course! I see what's the matter! You are worried about our young friend here. Well—"

As I say, I got it just a half-moment ahead of time. He fired as he drew out the "Well…" but I fired on the middle of the word. His slug hit stone somewhere, ricocheted whiningly all over the place. The slug got just a gentle cough from him.

Then I was halfway across the room, behind a dust-laden packing box—but it was unnecessary.

He fell slowly, deliberately out of the blackness, crashed down on his face.

The girl whispered, "Doctor Talmadge," as I sprang to his side and kicked his pistol far across the room. I went hastily down on one knee, flung him over on his back. The bullet had gone straight into his heart. A corner of a document stuck out from inside his coat. I snaked it out, took one swift glance and sprang up, pocketing it myself.

Fowler's bulldog face was dead, his eyes glassy. The girl had finally regained the use of her legs and was backing over toward him. Anstey, on the floor, moaned.

Fowler's hollow, husky voice said desperately: "All right. I won't make any trouble."

I snarled at him angrily—angrily because the girl's blue eyes were on me, melting the starch in me like hot water: "Think up a good story to explain this killing and pay back the one fifty to my company and I'll see it's kept mum. In fact, I'll keep this document myself. The company will never see it."

"Ah, God," he gasped. "You—you—I swear to you, I never meant to defraud—but I had to get the insurance or a—a deal that we thought would make us both rich would fall through. Then, when Gillies was killed and they offered me the money, I was afraid to—to confess the fraud...."

"I know, I know," I growled. "You certainly must be crazy to be a judge—and crazy is the word. However, don't ever expect that this will be forgotten. I'll hang right on to it—just to see that you keep in line, the rest of your natural life."

The girl's eyes widened blankly, uncomprehendingly. "You—you mean—" she whispered, "that you—you are going to blackmail my father…"

I looked at her for a solid minute. Her eyes dropped. She whispered. "Oh—I—I'm sorry."

"Any blackmail I collect," I told her finally, "I'll get from his campaign manager."

You should have seen her blush.

THE MURDER WAS A PLEASURE

IT WAS ONLY A SMALL POLICY THE COMPANY HAD ON YOUNG MARSHALL—$10,000—BUT WE WEREN'T ANXIOUS TO PAY OFF ON IT WITH ONLY A YEAR'S PREMIUMS IN THE ACME TILL, TO DATE. WHICH STATE OF AFFAIRS IMPELLED MY BOSS, PREEKER, TO SEND ME OUT TO STAND BY THE KID WHEN HE GOT HIMSELF CAUGHT BETWEEN THE SLASHING BLACKJACKS OF ALEC HUDSON'S PLUG-UGLIES AND THE BLASTING RODS OF THE COPS.

CHAPTER ONE
"I WOULDN'T KILL
HIM—QUITE"

THE CHERUBIC, pink-faced pansy from the records department was in Preeker's office when I came in. He was crushing some slips of paper to his chest and saying: "… most dreadful person at his place of business snarled at me and declared Mr. Marshall would *need* his life insurance if he, this monster, could catch up with him. I tell you, I was terrified—terrified. I thought, at once of reporting it to you…"

Preeker's fretful voice said wearily: "You did fine." He twisted round in his swivel chair, thumbing the slab of salt-and-pepper hair back off his bony little forehead. "You! Hey, you! Don't take your coat off. Are you doing anything? Of course you're not. Come here."

I scowled. "Behave. It's after five o'clock. Quitting time. I've got a report to write…"

"Quitting time? Oh, I suppose there's an Insurance Investigator's Union now? Eight hours a day, five days a week, time-and-a-half for overtime? Bah! Listen to this…

"Acme has a ten-thousand-dollar life policy on one Daniel Marshall, twenty-four years old, beneficiary wife. He was employed as accountant in the offices of the Chesterfield Sporting Club. He was fired three months ago and, simultaneously, disappeared from his rooms—his wife, too.

"Their landlady hasn't heard a word from them, although they left a lot of stuff there. At the Chesterfield Club— that's the outfit that operates the West Side Arena—runs fights and roller-skating—they refuse all information and act as though he's done something criminal. The accounting department got their notice returned—his second premium's due now—and turned it over to the records department and Mr.—uh—"

"Leroy. Arthur Leroy."

"—Leroy here was sent over to investigate. He got no satisfaction. It sounds as though there was something fishy about it. This Arena—the club's offices are on the second floor—is on Broadway, around Eighty-fifth Street. This Marshall and his wife lived only a few blocks away. Here—" He threw a slip of paper at me. "Here's their address on Eighty-second. See what you can find out."

"So the investigation department now piddles around running down changes of address."

"The investigation department runs down anything peculiar in connection with our policies," his bitter, fretful voice assured me.

"He kicked me downstairs—actually kicked me," Leroy shrilled.

"What's peculiar about that?" I growled.

MAYBE I could have wriggled out of the silly-sounding assignment—after twelve years I have some privileges around the joint—but I was curious. One Alec Hudson ran the Chesterfield Club and I was interested to see what he looked like. If half what was said about him was true, he was as wily a little chiseler as ever slicked his way into the New York fight scene, which is one closed corporation. On the strength of one good heavyweight fighter—and there

"I said, "McDerm..." and the
room caved in on my head.

was some question as to how he acquired *his* contract from
a pair of Chicago businessmen—he had built himself up
to importance.

Trading on a temporary crying need for a good challenger to face the downtown-controlled champion, he had turned over the boy for a series of ententes and little agreements that gave him undisputed control of the second-rate club-fights in town, plus a nice, steady run of business for his stable of "guaranteed" fighters. That is, they were "guaranteed" not to interfere with the budding career of any fighter undergoing a build-up by the moguls from Fiftieth Street. He shunned top-notch, and even coming fighters, like the plague, ignoring the thousands that were carved up around the fight banquet, but snatching for the drippings—the fifties and the hundreds. He must have had the right slant, for he had wound up by taking over the Arena on upper Broadway, to the surprise of a lot of people who had thought he was starving. Not that all this was in the public prints, naturally.

I got up to the looming, gray-cement building about eight o'clock.

The marquee, of course, was on Broadway. There were fights tonight and it was brilliantly lit, with crowds moving in. The business offices were on the side of the building. I walked down the side street, looking up at the almost solid block of dark masonry that stretched back three-quarters of the way to the next corner. There were little niches of masonry spaced regularly along it at the height of first, second, and third stories, looking as though they were intended to be windows, but faced with solid brick. The only openings in the side of the vast structure were fire-doors far at the rear, and the doorless little arch that let out a dim glow halfway back. When I got opposite it, I could see a flight of iron-and-stone stairs inside and that was all.

I stood in the black little side street a few minutes, deciding that this poke-away little door was probably designed because a lot of Alec Hudson's callers preferred the dark to the light, and that now ought to be a good time to catch him in.

I went in and found that, beside the flight of stairs, there was a single metal elevator cage in the tiny hall. I also found that the flight of steps was extremely short—only eight shallow steps before there was a landing. Facing me on the landing was a heavy, blank, metal door. The stairs curled round and went on up into the building. I couldn't figure whether this was the "second" floor, as specified by Preeker or not, so I tried the handle of the door—it was thick enough so it didn't seem that knocking would do any good—and it was unlocked.

I went into a wide office and found myself in front of a little mahogany railing and behind it were spaced six mahogany flat-topped desks, cleared and deserted for the night. Straight ahead of me, the ground-glass panel of an unlettered door gave out light.

A bruiser about six feet tall, with a broken, lumpy face, wearing no hat, no tie, a sport jacket, and slacks that seemed to fit him nowhere, sat on one of the closed desks, picking his teeth. He gave me a blank look from stupid gray-brown eyes and said, "Yeah?"

"I want to see Alec," I told him.

"What about?"

"Not anything that I'd be likely to talk to you about!"

He thought that over for a minute and evidently decided it was the right answer. He took his feet off the swivel-chair and threw away his toothpick. "What's yer name?"

I told him and he lumbered over and went through the door. He went through slowly enough so I had a chance to see the two men inside. One was a dumpy little man with plum-colored red-brown hair and tired brown eyes.

He was attired in a tan-linen approximation of a surgeon's coat. The other was undoubtedly Alec Hudson.

He sat at an oversize flat mahogany desk. He was as repulsive a human as I hope to see anywhere with his undersize head and liver-colored skin. His face looked as though it had been squeezed up, then flattened out again giving the effect of successive flaps of flesh piled on one another. His little gray eyes peered out from between flaps and there was a black shiny dot in the middle of each pupil. His head was bald, save for two borders of black hair over his ears. In the glimpse I had of him, he was urging a pack of cards across the desktop toward the other man and saying nastily: "Come on for God's sake—cut one! Don't be a cheap-skate. Ten bucks ain't going to kill...."

The door closed.

Presently it opened again. I heard the guy in the doctor's jacket say wearily, "I guess I better be getting down to look after your so-called fighters," and he strolled out on the heels of the slab-faced plug-ugly. His tired brown eyes gave me an uninterested glance, as the bruiser snarled, "Awright," and I went in.

YOU COULDN'T avoid thinking of half a dozen nicknames for Hudson—Liverlips, Baldy, Pinhead—and it was a cinch bet that Hudson was not his own original handle. Yet I didn't recall anybody ever calling him anything else. He sat with his hands below the level of his desk, his black-centered eyes suspicious on me. The pack of cards was on one corner of the desk.

"What you want?... Stay here, stupid!"

The thug closed the door, wandered around and stood over Hudson.

I made my voice tough enough so that I could hope to get an answer out of him and told him: "I'm an insurance cop. One of your former employees—Daniel Marshall— seems to have disappeared. We're taking a quick look for him ourselves before we throw it to Missing Persons."

His thick lip curled. "Disappeared, has he? Well, he knows what's good for him, that's all I got to say."

"What'd you fire him for? I heard he was fired."

He leaned back in the chair and carried a half-smoked, fat cigar to his gray mouth. "I'll tell you what I fired him for. I fired him because he was married and there's a rule in this office I don't want no married people. He knew it and so did she."

"She?"

"Yeah, she—the liddle typist. They went and done it on the sly and was workin' here six months before I found out. So I bounced him—and her, too—on the spot. So he takes a pass at me."

"He what?"

"He socks me, gives me a goog I just now got rid of. He would of beat the life out of me only he heard Ike there and the others comin'. As it was, he knocks me cold and the two of them light out."

"You don't know where they went, eh?"

"I'd *like* to know where they went," he assured me viciously. "I sent a couple the boys around to try and find out but nobody seems to know. If you find them, it's worth something to me to be tipped off. What kind insurance is he got?"

"Life."

"Well, I wouldn't kill him—quite. I'd just see he got something to remember me by, that's all."

Just out of curiosity, I had managed to get my hand on the pack of cards and fingered them idly. I let them slip through my fingers once, casually enough so that it didn't catch his eye. Once was enough. They were either strippers or there was a long card in the deck. The little chiseler apparently even clipped his own employees for fives and tens.

"I'll remember that," I said, "in case I do."

I WENT over to the rooming house on Eighty-second, just a few numbers this side of Columbus. It was a dark, quiet street of motley architecture—some brownstones, a very few ultramodern apartment houses, some old-fashioned ones.

The number I sought was a cramped, three-story brownstone that looked stunted and dark between two taller neighbors. Bay windows curved out at all three levels. I had to wait an interminable time for my ring to be answered. Then a woman with smooth Slavic face and gray hair drawn tight to a knot at the back of her head opened the door on a chain and regarded me with electric suspicion in a pair of jet-black eyes.

"I'm looking for Mr. Daniel Marshall," I told her. "I represent Acme Insurance..."

"Wait a minute," she told me and shut the door in my face. Through the glass panel of the door I could see her retreat into a room at the side of the hall. The door of that room closed.

I scratched my jaw and waited, maybe four minutes. Then I became conscious of a bulk moving in on me from the shadows of the street and turned quickly. Blue and brass twinkled in the distant streetlight and I recognized the beefy face of Hal McDermott. His friendly blue eyes were hard and stony till he recognized me, then startled.

"What the hell? Are *you* asking about Danny Marshall?"

I am not excessively dumb. I looked up at the house, then at him. "Sure. What's the idea? Did the old dame call you?"

"I told her to call the station house when anybody asked for them. The sarge relays it to me on the beat."

"Why?"

"That clay-faced louse Alec Hudson has got his gorillas looking for the kids. Two of them came around a few weeks ago and got very tough with the old dame, trying to find where they'd moved to. I aim to bounce this nightstick off their skulls if they show up again."

"You were pals with this Marshall?"

"Just by seeing him around. They were good kids, both of them. It makes me boil to think of Hudson sending tough guys after them."

"He beat Hudson up, according to Hudson."

"Well, he probably had good cause."

I looked at him a minute in the dark. "You wouldn't know where I could find him, would you, Hal?"

He rubbed his ear vigorously and stared hard at me. "What do you want to know for?"

I told him.

He rubbed his ear some more and then grumbled: "They're on 168th Street, up in the Bronx." He gave me a number. "And God help you if you let it get to the ears of Alec Hudson and his gorillas. Can he raise any dough on that insurance policy?"

"I don't think so. He's just had it about a year."

"Geez, they need it. They ain't got a dime, and her going to have a kid. Mind you keep this to yourself."

I said, "Sure," and, "Thanks," and the subway took me up to 168th Street. It took about half an hour.

CHAPTER TWO
BLACK-OUT IN THE
BRONX

THIS PLACE was in the middle of a block of two-story stores. Half the stores were dark, at ten o'clock. The number McDermott had given me was just discernible in chipped enamel over a narrow doorway between a delicatessen store and a stationery shop. Looking up, I could see the gold lettering of a dentist's office on the front windows and when I went in and up a flight of narrow steps to the dreary, dimly lighted wooden hall above, there were only two doors to choose from. One had a rippled-glass panel bearing the same dentist's name—at the front. The other was a plain wooden door without lettering—at the back.

It took a full minute after my knock, before there was the slightest sound inside. Then a girl's voice, soft and velvety with fear, said desperately: "Who—who is it?"

I told her my name and added: "Acme Indemnity. It's about your husband's insurance."

This time I had a two-minute wait, while she tried to make up her mind about it. Then she said: "He—isn't here."

"Well, you can give me the information I need. All I want is about two minutes of your time." Then I added the telling argument. "Patrolman McDermott knows me. He gave me this address."

I thought even this wasn't going to get me in, for about ninety seconds—and then the door opened a little.

She was the essence of daintiness—a soft little wistful face, with a strawberry mouth so beautifully shaped that you wanted to run your finger over it, a softly molded little nose and skin like cream velvet. She was without make-up and fear had her cheeks colorless, her soft, long-lashed pansy-brown eyes driven and strained. Yet her round little chin was unflinching. Her dark-brown hair was drawn softly back around her head, to fall in curls at the nape of her neck, and she wore a black dress, perfectly plain save for a sort of pucker-string around her neck and a belt that caught it in at her trim little waist. She came about to my Adam's apple.

"My husband isn't in," her soft voice repeated breathlessly. "I could have him call you when he comes."

"I wish he would," I said, and gave her a card. Her eyes never left mine. They were as soft and luminous as purple amber, and the edge of fear in them suddenly seemed a maddening shame.

On the spur of the moment I let out—fatuously: "Mrs. Marshall, we've heard some unpleasant rumors as to your husband's—and your—troubles with Alec Hudson. Your insurance company is your friend, you know. If we knew all about it, maybe we could be of some help."

Her eyes swelled, dilated, for just a flash, but she showed no other emotion. She looked from one of my eyes to the other, almost desperately, for a full minute. Then her soft voice went a little lower. "What—what do you mean?" she asked.

"Well, I don't know. Suppose you tell me just what happened."

She searched my eyes again fearfully. Then she backed a step or two into the room.

I edged in, taking my hat off. It was a bare, rugless room, containing a rickety made-up bed, a kitchen table and chairs, a bureau, an open—and empty—clothes-closet. Through a half-open doorway I could see a dingy bathroom. Light came from a single bulb overhead, shaded with a ten-cent paper shade. There were three paper suitcases of graduated sizes on the floor in front of the closet. It looked as though they had just this moment moved in.

"Mr. Hudson says he discharged you and your husband because he has a rule against married people working there, and that your husband became enraged and attacked him," I said.

Her hand flew to her mouth, to smother the, "Oh!" that came involuntarily. Then she swallowed and told me desperately: "That—that isn't true. He—oh, believe me, that isn't true! He—he did discharge us for that, but it wasn't the real—"

"Suppose you tell me the—what actually did happen."

She looked down at her hands, and color flooded her face. "I—Mr. Hudson was dictating a letter to me and as I finished he—he grabbed at me and I—sort of half fell down on the desk and he—his hand—my dress—and then Danny was coming in with the statement and he ran over and knocked Mr. Hudson across the room."

I swear I felt the color burn in my face almost as richly as in hers. She was that kind of a precious little package.

"And then he fired you?" I said grimly.

She shook her head, nursed her hands. "No, he—he was unconscious. Danny just—just grabbed our hats and coats and walked me out. Then when—when we got home, he started being afraid that Hudson might send some of his—his men after us, so we—we moved up here without telling anybody but Mr. McDermott."

"I see," I growled. "What's your husband doing now, Mrs. Marshall?"

"He—isn't doing anything."

All right. Sure—my work was done and there was no reason why I didn't bow promptly out and go back and make my report. No reason except that I had a heart and that this whole proposition seemed a rotten damned shame to me. Don't get me wrong. It wasn't that I had developed a yen for the girl. But sometimes you run into—even in the insurance business—people who are really right. She was—clean and honest and sweet, with her chin up. That a scaly louse like Alec Hudson could kick her around made me sore. I don't get the urge to try and help people out very often but this pair of kids— I don't know.

"It's none of my business, of course," I said, "but something McDermott said—that is, if you've both been out of work these last three months—I don't guess Alec Hudson paid you any giant-size salaries and if you really need any money, maybe a small loan could be arranged on the policy."

Sure, I know it couldn't as well as you do, but whose business is it if I had a few bucks in the bank I wanted to play the sap with? Besides, these two were friends of Hal McDermott, who is one of the two straight cops I know in New York. A guy has to give way to his impulses sometimes.

Even that faint ray of hope opened her up, where no amount of punishment would have. There was a tear glistening in each eye as she told me stammeringly: "... both tried to save every penny... couldn't put away much... playing policy and betting on horse races... took so much every week—"

"Wait a minute," I said. "You were playing the numbers and the horses?"

"We—we tried to get out of it when we could. But when Mr. Hudson gave us our pay each week, he—he'd sort of take it for granted we were going to bet and if anybody didn't he'd call them cheapskates and—and things. He made it so—so difficult *not* to bet that everybody was—well, afraid of their jobs if they didn't put *something* up…"

Alec Hudson's quiet charm was growing on me every minute.

"… so hard to manage, and we—we've a baby coming. Danny—my husband hasn't been able to find work and he—he's nearly out of his head. We've—neither of us have any people we can turn to. Danny—Mr. Hudson has told all the other fight-clubs not to—to give Danny work, and—"

"Well"—I frowned and tried to make my voice businesslike—"of course the policy hasn't been in force much longer than a year. But if a hundred or two—of course, it's rather unusual. We don't usually do this, but if you'll leave it in my hands.…"

She almost sobbed: "Oh, if you could—if you only knew what two hundred would mean. Danny's been nearly frantic.…"

I frowned importantly and said, "Well, I think…" and then the act went blooey.

I HAD left the door open behind me. That is, I had not latched it. Hence it swept wide open with only the barest creak. Danny Marshall blurted: "Mary, I told you to keep the door lock—"

He caught his breath, almost in a choke as he saw me. "Ah, God!" He snatched the gun from his coat pocket, had it out, covering me, in the split second it took me to turn. His face was white and lumpy, his china-blue eyes seemed to swell to madness. He was a good-looking, redheaded youngster, with crisp, curly hair and a nice firm jaw. That is, he would have been ordinarily. Now his eyes were sunk, blood-streaked, the lines around his mouth pinched and twitching. He looked like a man in intolerable torment. All the venom and desperation inside him went into his vicious, almost shrill, "You dirty rat! I'll cut your heart—"

The girl cried out: "Oh, no, Danny, no—he's from the insurance company—going to lend us money on your policy…"

His teeth were chattering with the blazing fury inside him. "Get your hands away from your sides! Turn around! He's a liar, Mary. He's connected with Alec Hudson. I just saw him coming out of his office. There's no loan value to that policy. I've only had it a year…"

"If you'll calm down and let me—" I began.

"Shut your —— mouth," he lashed at me.

"Oh, Danny—wait—let him—"

"Has he laid a hand on you? Has he threatened you with anything?"

"Oh, no, no, he—listen to him, Danny—oh, please—"

"Listen hell! He can listen to me!" His voice was shaking, almost hysterical. "Get this, you stinking rat. If you—or any of the rest of your pals—come within a city block of us, you're going to get it. You're going to get exactly what your chiseling skunk of a boss got—"

She cried wildly: "Danny—no—he's a detective—"

"I wouldn't wonder. But no cop is going to lay a hand on me either." He grunted a little. I, trying to grab an opening to get a word in edgewise, didn't grasp what was doing.

I said, "McDerm—" and the room caved in on my head, followed by the blackout.

When I came to again, I was alone—all alone. Even the three suitcases were gone.

I struggled up eventually to sit in one of the kitchen chairs, nursing my throbbing head. There is something about a crack on the skull that makes you fiery mad and naturally I was a little put out. The half-hysterical youngster had not spared the rod—if it was a rod he hit me with. A couple of times I swore off, permanently, all charity, kindness, or any other form of extending a helping hand. From now on, the world could stew in its own juice without any sympathy or aid from little Sir Galahad here.

However, I have a pretty thick head and presently the sharp edge of the pain wore down to a dull ache. I went into the dingy bathroom and did things with cold water, found a cigarette—as far as I could make out he hadn't even searched me—and couldn't maintain my toughness. I got mellow again about the two desperate youngsters, regardless.

They hadn't left even a scrap of paper in the place. They were gone—and everything with them.

It wasn't till I was standing on the pavement down in front, debating how to go about tracing them further that the first startling little idea jolted into my mind. This exodus had not been because of my visit—it had been planned beforehand. The bags were standing packed when I arrived. "… *going to get exactly what your chiseling skunk of a bos got…*" Could it be that…?

I started for a cab, remembered that the subway would do a quicker job and changed direction.

CHAPTER THREE
FORTY AND TWENTY
TO ONE

I TURNED the corner and hurried down the side street that banked the West Side Arena, at exactly eleven o'clock. The fights were just over and the crowd was streaming out the front entrance. They did not, however, open the side doors at this establishment and there was not a soul on the street alongside the looming gray building.

That is, there wasn't till the minute I turned in to the arched side entrance. Then I almost collided with the giant figure of Ike, Alec Hudson's bodyguard. He gulped and stumbled out of my way, but there was enough light for me to see the scared, excited look on his rocky face. My heart did a flip-flop. I grabbed his vest. "What's up? Where are you going?"

He swallowed. "He—the kid killed him. I'm—I'm going for cops."

"I'll do for cops, till— Did you ever hear of a phone?"

"The phone don't work," he said hoarsely.

"Well, show me where he is. Where the hell were you when he was killed? Aren't you his bodyguard?"

"He told me I could go down and watch the fights. I—I just come back and found him and called Doc Church. I—I gotta get a cop."

I pushed him ahead of me. "I'll take care of the cops. How do you know the kid killed him? You mean Danny Marshall?"

"Yeah, yeah," he whined. "He left a kite sayin' he did."

He stumbled ahead of me, up the few steps, through the railing in the outer office and into Alec Hudson's private sanctum.

Hudson was in the swivel chair behind the desk, his clay-colored bald head sagging down on one shoulder. His eyes were frozen into a white-ringed oblique stare, as though he were watching for something to crawl out from under the edge of the carpet. His mouth was a little open and a little saliva had run out of his mouth, shone on his chin. His tongue was between his teeth, blue. The room was inordinately hot and his flat face and head shone. I didn't realize for a minute that they were bluer than they had been. There was a nutty smell in the air and a cheap bone-handled hunting knife was rammed to the hilt in his left breast. He looked as though he had shrunk a third in size in the chair.

The plum-haired doctor in the sloppy surgeon's coat was standing back, wiping his hands on a piece of gauze. He turned sick, chocolate-brown eyes on me, then on Ike. He looked as though even curiosity had been beaten out of him.

"He's dead?" I shot at him and put a hand on Hudson's clammy, cold forehead.

"Quite dead," he said in a dull voice. "I wouldn't touch anything if I were you, till the police—"

Ike blurted: "He caught me just goin' out the door and wouldn't let me get the cop…"

"I'll do for the cops for a minute," I said and flashed the little badge from my vest pocket. "That knife—it's too far over to get to his heart…"

"I think he smeared poison on it, to make doubly sure."

"Poison?"

He nodded vaguely toward an open cupboard door at the side of the room. I stepped quickly over and looked inside. There was a sink and a hanging droplight in the little cubbyhole, with racks lining one wall. I recognized it as a photographer's developing room, but it was bare of the usual paraphernalia. There was a black bottle, however, on the little ledge of the sink. It lay on its side, its cork nearby. The nutty odor was sharp enough here to be identified—cyanide.

"He fell for the camera fad a couple of years ago, but he got tired of it," the doctor's tired voice informed me. "When he sold his equipment, I guess this bottle was left over."

"Ike said there was a note. Where...?"

The doc nodded toward the desk and I went back and saw the plain piece of stationery held down by the blotter roller.

My heart sank as I read it.

Dear Doc:

I guess you didn't believe me when I promised I'd kill him. It took some thinking over, but now I've done it. I hope nobody will lose their job and I guess somebody else will take over the Club—somebody maybe that won't clip you all of your salaries. Don't worry about me. I'll never be taken alive by the police and the satisfaction of knowing the rat is dead will be worth anything else.

Yrs,

Danny Marshall

"You were a friend of his?" I asked the doc. "You know his handwriting?"

"Yes. It's his writing all right. You can compare it with his ledgers and half a dozen other files around here."

I STOOD there, seeing a soft-brown-eyed, courageous girl's face—and the frantic, wild-eyed, redhaired, desperate kid. I couldn't even high-pressure myself into trying to find a doubt to cast on his guilt. It was too heartbreakingly apparent that there *was* no doubt. There was nothing but brutal, ugly certainty—and stark tragedy ahead for the pair of them.

A sharp buzzing sounded under the desk.

I wrinkled my forehead. The tired-eyed doctor blinked. "That's the telephone. It must be working again."

I took out my handkerchief and picked up the handset and growled into it.

"Alec?" a dull voice said. "This is Jack Hoyle. Are you going to send down for that winter-book bet tonight or not? I can't stay here forever…"

I said: "Alec is dead, Jack." I told him who I was. I knew him—everybody did. He was Broadway's largest and most substantial betting commissioner. I divined that he would be Alec Hudson's betting hook-up—the channel through which he laid off the bets he took from his employees and, perhaps, others. "What was he doing? Ten-percenting for you?"

After a second, he said: "Yeah."

Just as he said it, quick, decisive footsteps—more than one pair—sounded sharply in the outer office. Two men were coming through. Then the door burst open and we had an audience of law.

If anything could have made me sicker, this was it.

I was plenty puzzled. The one in soft brown clothes was Lieutenant Greely. He was a detective on the eighteen-carat squad at headquarters, as was the sandy-haired Sergeant Briggs who was with him. Eighteen-carat squad means—among other things—past master of the clip. Only valuables that were nailed down were safe from him. He was a short, stocky man with two ovals of dark hair plastered on his head like a toupée—maybe it was—and green sloe-eyes that gave an Oriental touch to his shining, walnut face.

In one sweeping glance he had the room tabulated. "Have you reported this?" he snarled at me.

"Just got here and answered the phone," I said. His type don't tread on the toes of insurance company representatives openly so I didn't have to pretend I liked him. "How did you get here?"

"An anonymous tip," he said, and spied the note unerringly. He stepped over and read it.

He looked up, his eyes sharp. "Who is this Danny Marshall?" and when he was told, he snapped: "What's the story? Wait a minute—one of you at a time. You—" He chose me. To his partner he said, "Take those others into"— he looked round till he found a small filing room opening from the left-hand wall of the office—"there. That'll do."

While they were being herded inside, he stood with the phone in his hand, but not using it. "All right. Let's have it."

I TOLD him everything. Sure. What was the use in trying to cover up? He'd have it from the others in minutes anyway and all I would do would be to put myself on the wrong side of the fence in case it turned out that there was anything I could do for the kid.

He took it all in, his crafty little green eyes never leaving my face. Then he nodded briskly and went at the telephone.

I didn't quite realize what was brewing until he ended his conversation with the radio room downtown by saying: "This kid is wacky, I think. He's got a gun and he'll be free as hell with it, from the looks. The case against him is dead open-and-shut, so put a shoot-first trailer on the broadcast."

I suddenly remembered that I was working for Acme Insurance and that we carried a life policy on the redheaded youngster. "Hey—wait a minute!" I snarled at him. "You don't have to treat him like a mad-dog gangster. He's just a kid that went off his head when he got desperate. With the kicking around he took from this louse—"

"Easy on the names," Greely warned me. "Alec Hudson was a friend of mine."

"Nuts. Even you won't be admitting it, now that he's dead. He was a grade-A rat and chiseler and he got what was coming to him. This kid is a decent, hard-working—"

"Was. Was. He's a killer now and he's desperate. My God, man, he says he won't be taken alive. If I didn't put that out and he shot a cop or two, I'd be broken like that."

The hell of it was that he was perfectly right. In the frenzy young Marshall was in, it would be a miracle if he *didn't* try to shoot his way clear if they caught up to him. There wasn't a sane argument I could advance—and yet I kept seeing the girl's soft pansy-brown eyes and visualizing how they would look staring down at a bullet-riddled mass of blood and clothes in the city morgue, and being told that it was all that was left of her husband. I don't know when anything had gotten me the way that did. Yet there wasn't a word I could say.

I set my teeth. "All right. Let me use that phone, if you're through. I've got to call my boss."

He eyed me shrewdly, shrugged, and let me have it. When I got Preeker on the other end of the wire—he was at home by now—I told him grimly: "I found your Danny Marshall. He seems to have murdered his boss. The police are after him with orders practically to shoot him on sight. You better get hold of some of the bigwigs of the company and have them bear down on the cops to take it a little easier."

I hung up on his strangled howl.

Greely's dark lips smiled primly. He was very pleased with himself. "Even the commissioner wouldn't dare change my orders on this one."

He was too pleased with himself to notice, apparently, that the minutes were slipping away. His partner, the sandy-haired Briggs, came out of the filing room with a hot, irritated look in his red eyes. "Hey, listen—the Homicide boys and the M.E. will be here any minute. Hadn't we better take a look around…?"

Greely came back to earth with a jump. He said quickly, "Yeah, yeah." He scowled at me. "You—you better hang around outside or somewhere."

I took care that my growl didn't carry any sense, and went out to the outer office, closing the door behind me.

I had expected to be able to use one of phones in the outer office. Now I found that they were all dial instruments equipped with locking devices. The dead Hudson had not even taken chances on losing nickels. I had to go out.

Don't ask me what was in my burning mind. Some vague idea that I might somehow locate Danny Marshall myself, I guess, and somehow manage to take him in without killing him. Surely there was some chance that a court might give him a better break than the guns of the cops. Certainly, it could be no worse.

WHEN I got to the street, I started toward Broadway but the sound of sirens turned me back before I had taken a step. I looked quickly along the street toward the river— and saw the lights of a dining car restaurant on the corner ahead of me. I hugged the building shadows as I hurried for it. I reached it, just as the first sirening squad car swung round the corner from Broadway and squealed to a long stop before the side door of the Arena.

It was my good luck that the pay phone in the diner was in a booth. By dint of three quick calls I located Dick Holloway—one of the two other Acme operatives in New York City. I gave him the Bronx address at which I had caught up to Danny Marshall and his girl-wife earlier. I gave him quick descriptions of the two of them. "Around ten thirty those two left that address with three suitcases. Get up there as fast as you can and try to trace them from there. Keep calling Mott, the night man at the office, if you get anything. I'll keep in touch with him, too."

Mainly, I guess, to keep from facing the fact that it was senseless to even try to hope, I chased my brains around my skull feverishly, trying to think of something I could do. I stood on the sidewalk outside the diner and watched the three police cars unload, the little body of men march across the sidewalk and disappear into the arch.

I had not meant to run out on the investigation, but now that I was clear, I hesitated to go back and get caught up in it. If I did, I knew that I was stuck there for at least a solid hour—and somehow I had the agonizing feeling in my heart that I had to do something within that hour—or not at all. New York's police machine is a deadly and mercilessly efficient thing when turned loose on a murderer who has no "connections." Danny Marshall, an amateur, with thirty thousand bluecoats combing the town for him, with orders virtually to shoot him down on sight—yes, an hour was a good estimate of how long he could be expected to last.

I thought of Jack Hoyle, the betting commissioner and circled round to the subway station at Seventy-ninth, took a ten-minute ride down to Times Square. There was still light in the honey-comb of offices labeled: *Jack Hoyle: Real Estate and Investments,* on the third floor of the Broadway skyscraper, and I was told to go in as soon as the switchboard boy announced me. I found the gray-faced, gray-eyed fifty-year-old gambler sitting alone in his wooden cubbyhole office.

"So Alec Hudson got it, eh?" he greeted me gloomily. He had the torso of a wrestler, but he sat in a wheel chair behind his scarred desk. His legs were no bigger than a child's. "Who did it?"

"A kid that worked for him, apparently—Danny Marshall. Did you know him?"

Hoyle shook his massive head. "I didn't know anything about his outfit. He came down here and wanted to handle a line of small bets through me, so I said O.K. It was piker stuff—the largest bet I ever had from him wasn't over fifty dollars and mostly they were twos and fives. All our business was done on slips, too—I wouldn't trust him not to try and chisel. He had to send that ape of his down here to collect his slips before post time or the bets were off. The only way for him to collect was to present—or have his customers present—the slips at my cashier's window."

"And he was willing to do business that way?"

"Well, he did it. To tell you the truth, I was hoping he *would* take offense and go somewhere else, but he never did." He looked at me curiously. "How do you people get into this? Did you insure him?"

"No. We insure the kid that killed him."

"Oh-oh." He still looked at me expectantly, as though he thought I had something up my sleeve. Finally, he put it into words. "Well, just what did you think I could do for you? If there's any way I can help…"

"God knows," I blurted. "I guess I'm just going around waiting for a miracle to happen."

HIS PHONE rang as I got up. I said, "Well, so long," and wandered out as he answered. But I didn't get out of earshot before I heard him say: "Oh yeah… Yeah… Well, sure. Certainly… Did you know Alec was knocked off tonight?… Yeah, sure… No, that doesn't make any difference… Certainly."

I had turned back and was standing in the doorway. He hung up and told me: "That was one of your friend's customers—with a nice win, too. In fact as nice a one as I ever paid out through Alec. A twenty-dollar parlay in the winter book on the Windsor Stakes—Mangrum to win, Brother's Keeper to show. They ran one-two this afternoon on the Coast."

"They were the favorites weren't they?"

"They were at the post, but they weren't eight months ago, by damn, when I was making the winter prices. I gave him forty to one and twenty to one. As a matter of fact, those *would* have been post prices if somebody hadn't sprung a leak. A bunch of Detroit guys were running that Mangrum as a sleeper. It was supposed to be a good thing in the Windsor and run under wraps all the way up till then. Only somehow it leaked out and the racket was shot to hell months ago. Everybody and his brother seemed to get wise and so much dough came in that it knocked Mangrum into the favorite's spot. I guess I'm not the only bookie in town that took a drubbing on the winter odds, though. Thank God I only had a few bets."

"Who was the guy that just called you? The guy that made the win?"

He looked askance at me, rubbed his jaw vigorously. "Well now, I don't know whether it's ethical—"

"I give you my word nobody'll ever know you told me. Hell, it hasn't any bearing on anything, anyway."

"Well, it was a cop. Maybe you know him—Lieutenant Greely."

I guess I went through about the same feelings as a drowning man clutching at a straw. For a second, it seemed that this must mean something, must give me something. Greely, the cop who had mysteriously reached the murder scene before the police alarm was given—and who had set the machinery in motion so mercilessly to cut down the redheaded youngster....

For about two minutes I stood absorbing that, my mind hanging open, waiting for inspiration to arise.

It didn't. Nothing arose. I gradually sank down to the hollow feeling that the drowning guy must have got when he finally realized that the straw was only a straw after all and not worth a tinker's damn to him.

Nevertheless, without inducing any conscious train of thought, it did send me out and down into the subway again, heading uptown.

CHAPTER FOUR
COFFEE FOR A COP

WHEN I edged carefully around the corner this time and sent a hot-eyed glance at the side door of the Arena, only two of the black cars were parked slantwise to the curb. There did not appear to be anyone in them and evidently they had attracted no crowd.

I stepped into the diner and called Mott, the night man at the office, but no word had come in from Dick Holloway, who was trying to pick up Danny Marshall's trail for me in the Bronx. I stood outside again, reluctant to deliver myself into the cops' hands again, but also conscious that I could get into trouble if I didn't show up soon. I walked slowly back, undecided, in the darkness on the opposite side of the street from the Arena, and stood debating.

I guess the tormenting haze of anxiety in my head first started to give way to thought when, just as I had finally made up my mind to go over and say my piece to the Homicide cops, the broken-nosed Ike, Alec Hudson's bodyguard slipped out.

I can't say there was anything furtive about the thick-headed thug's manner of emergence. He just stepped silently out. But the moment he was on the sidewalk, a sort of feverish tenseness seemed to take hold of him.

He started toward Broadway, stopped, his gaunt eyes shooting up and down the deserted side street. He hugged one arm tight to his side. I got the impression his hand was inside his coat. I stood motionless where I was. I was sure the shadows covered me.

He ran a finger of his free hand hastily around the inside of his collar, reversed himself and started quickly down the street in the other direction.

He lengthened his stride—and then seemed to get into difficulties. He suddenly swerved in tight against the towering wall of the Arena and huddled quickly over, as though he had a stomachache.

I guess the intentness of my curiosity gave me away. I was straining my eyes so hard to try to make out what he was doing that I unconsciously edged forward a little. And in the same moment that I decided he was reaching down inside his trousers for something, he swung a shining face over his shoulder—and saw me.

There was no doubt of it. He looked squarely at where I was—and then shot forward again as though spurred.

It made absolutely no sense whatever to me, yet naturally, I started in his wake. He was twenty yards ahead of me when he flung another hasty glance back in my direction. I lengthened my stride, yelled, "Ike!"

He seemed to shrink a little—and scurried even faster away from me, not turning. Wondering what in madness' name it was all about, I took after him in earnest. I hurried out into the roadway and yelled: "Hey—you—wait a minute. Ike!"

We were within two buildings of the corner diner—or he was—by then. He threw me one more quick, frightened look over his shoulder. I broke into a run and called sharply: "Wait a minute, you lug—or I'll take a shot at you…"

He vanished.

Exactly that. One second he was a crouched, hurrying huddle on the sidewalk across from and ahead of me—the next he was gone. I broke into a run, my eyes popping.

The mystery was no mystery, when I reached his vanishing point. I was at the narrow mouth of a service alley that ran behind the rear wall of the Arena—between it and the dingy little apartment building that adjoined. I cursed and ran in, a hand on my gun.

It was dim, but not entirely dark. I ran to the end of the shallow alley—and found that it blossomed out into a courtyard that opened off to my left. The courtyard was evidently the back yard of both the building nearest me and another smaller one, of the same type, further along—the two buildings that stood between the doorless rear wall of the Arena and the small vacant lot on the corner below that accommodated the diner. I could see a high fence at the other end of the courtyard, and the glow of the diner's lights showed above it. There was no sign of the thick-brained thug.

FOR A moment I slowed, as I realized that he might have ducked into the rear of one of the two apartment buildings, but no light showed in either of them and I had to bank that he hadn't, that he had vaulted the fence and tried to duck me that way. I sailed over it myself, and was in the little gravel patch on which the diner stood.

Enough light came from the diner to show me at a glance that he was not lurking here. The diner was L-shaped, covering the small corner lot almost completely. There was a narrow strip of gravel separating it from the apartment building beside me, but the strip was blocked where the diner L'd out. There was no escape that way, and although the diner had no rear door, enough light came from it to show me this little cul-de-sac was empty. I ran for the ten-foot opening between the near end of the diner and the building facing on West End Avenue. I shot a glance through the open end door of the diner as I burst out, but it was empty.

So was West End Avenue. That is, it was empty of Ike. Thirty yards up the street, a figure in blue and brass was bent over a notebook trying to catch the light from a street-lamp above him, laboriously writing in the book. It was a second after I came to a halt before I recognized him as Hal McDermott. Evidently this was still part of his beat. I yelled at him quickly, "Mac!" and when he looked up, "Did a guy just run out of here—a big lug with a cap on?"

"Huh? Oh, you. No, not in the past three-four minutes. Why?"

I groaned, turned back and stared at the two apartment buildings beyond the fence.

"Why, what's the matter?" McDermott asked as he hurried up.

I said grimly, "Nothing. Forget it," and ran around the outside of the diner to peer down the side street. If he had just ducked *through* one of the buildings....

Evidently he hadn't. Or at least he didn't emerge. I stood there waiting tensely, for two or three minutes. McDermott wavered, finally came and stood beside me, demanding bewilderedly: "What's—who you after? What's...?"

I said: "Ike—that big bruiser that Alec Hudson had as his bodyguard."

"What's he done?"

"I don't know."

He looked at me blankly. Then he said: "Listen—did you find Danny...?"

Evidently he didn't even know what had happened on his own beat. I blurted feverishly: "Mac—I haven't time to tell you about it now. If you see that Ike, grab him for me."

He stared at me vaguely, finally shrugged and said, "O.K. I was just going in for my midnight coffee. I'll be here if you want me," and went up the diner's step and in.

I couldn't bring myself to give up—yet I was properly skunked. I went back and climbed the board fence, and from the top of it tried to stare back at the back doors of the apartments.

Nothing moved there. I went back and looked down the side street again, badgered and feverish. I finally went down and, ragingly certain that it was all futile by now, went through the ground floors of both the apartment houses, retraversed the alley and the courtyard, to bring myself back on top of the board fence.

I GAVE up, turned to drop back into the courtyard— and then saw just a flash of something through a rear window, high up in the back of the diner. I didn't know just what it was that I had seen, to tell the truth. I caught myself and dropped down hastily into the gravel lot. Fortunately, I found an empty beer case tight against the little diner and by hopping up on it, I brought my face to the level of the window.

I let out a soft growl. My man Ike had not escaped me. He was inside the lunchwagon, crouched down in one corner, a black gun in one hand. *And from his other wrist dangled a set of handcuffs.*

The short-order cook and the diner's blond waitress stood looking at him with terrified eyes. Beyond the partition which the row of coffee urns made, I could see

McDermott's blue-and-brass, as he sat on a stool at the counter.

I snatched the gun from my hip, hunched to get my elbow up so I could cover the face of the sweat-streaming, wild-eyed thug through the aperture.

Before I could get into position, McDermott's voice called, "Hey—lemme have another cup of coffee," and my wildest hopes could not have conceived anything as galvanizing as what happened inside.

The waitress looked fearfully at the huddled Ike. The big bruiser's face was sweat-streaked and desperate. I realized, of course, what must have happened. Rather, a part of what had happened. The handcuffs still baffled me. But it must be that in clamping on to his trail I had chased him almost into McDermott's arms. He had ducked into the diner and jumped the counter, hidden in here—and been trapped by McDermott's presence ever since. Maybe had even overheard me ask Mac to hold him for me if he saw him. My guess—from the crazy state of nerves in which he seemed to be—was that he wasn't used to hiding from cops, that this was his first foray into such business. It was also my guess that he was, now, as dangerous as dynamite. He must have been penned up in here for nearly fifteen minutes and whatever it was that caused him to run from me—yes, it was more than the handcuffs, I was positive—must be burning holes in him. There was a wild, white-ringed frantic look in his eyes that I didn't like a bit and the handcuffed hand that clutched the black gun was shaking. He gestured fiercely with it at the waitress and she hastened to draw a cup of coffee from the steaming urn. She swayed—still looking at him—toward the narrow opening that would have taken her out behind the counter—and the thug's gun gestured again slashingly. I looked back at his face—

and the guy was off his head with jitters. His teeth were bare and clenched. He jabbed the gun against her as she sidled fearfully over and, with his free hand he snatched something from inside his coat and thrust it into her hand.

My hair nearly stood on end as I realized what it was. It was a bottle and he snatched the cork out with his teeth, jerked a thumb toward the blue-clad figure beyond the counter, jabbed the gun again and again into the girl's side till she poured—spilled rather—a teaspoonful of colorless liquid—all that was left in the bottle—into the cup.

The electrifying part was that it was the same bottle I had seen in the little developing cupboard in Alec Hudson's office—the bottle of cyanide solution, the poison that had been smeared on the death knife, according to the doctor.

For one moment, burning questions roiled up so feverishly in my head that I was only half-conscious of the wildeyed thug's pushing the girl away, his making a jerking circular motion with the gun, and her stirring the coffee with a spoon. What in God's name was the idea? Why had Ike sneaked the bottle away from the death room—let alone how—and been so frantic to get away with it? The handcuffs…? What could—was there something behind this whole mess that…?

I came back to life, just as the girl stumbled out to set the cup of coffee in front of Mac. In sudden frenzy I jabbed my gun through the glassless window, fired, and yelled, "Mac—don't touch that coffee," all in the same breath.

And fate, at the last minute, having brought me to the very edge of the answer, suddenly yanked it out of my hands.

I HAD shot at Ike's gun hand. If there was one thing in the whole world I *didn't* want, it was to kill him. Not while he held answers to the blazing questions in my head.

The thunder of my gun was a boom, like hollering down a rain barrel, but there was a ringing, metallic whang on the end of it. Coffee suddenly spurted from the urn beside Ike in a brown geyser. A streak of red ran up his cheek and he slammed over against the wall, crashed down.

Even in the wild moment when I heard Mac fall off his stool, outside, with a crashing of crockery, heard him yell, "Hey, what the hell…?" I realized that my bullet had done the most maddening ricochet in history, going from Ike's gun, which I had spun out of his hand, to the coffee urn, and back to rip up the side of his face and head.

I shouted, "Take it easy, Mac. It's me. It's all right," and jumped down, raced round. My heart was in my mouth, for fear the big bruiser was dead. I flung at Mac as I dived in and scrambled over the counter: "Come on—he's in here. You can put your gun away. I dropped him, just as he was going to spike your cup with poison so he could get away."

I ran around and dropped to one knee, ducking the still spurting stream of steaming coffee, grabbed at the fallen man. Almost unconsciously, I snatched up the black bottle and jammed it in one pocket with one hand, while I picked up his thick hairy wrist with the other.

He wasn't dead. But there was a furrow in his skull I could almost lay my finger in. He would be out for hours. I groaned aloud as Mac charged in behind me.

"What's—my God, what is it…?" I stood up and swore in the bitterness of my soul. He was no use whatever to me, would not be any use—in time to do any good. The whole thing was a blind alley, except—except for that poison bottle. What possible bearing could it have—how had he gotten it out of the murder room...?

"Have you killed him?" Mac was blurting breathlessly. "What's the story? What...?"

I suddenly wanted to be back in the murder room. "I haven't time to tell you now. He's not dead. Get him to a hospital and put a guard over him. Don't argue—these people can tell you what happened. For God's sake, don't interfere with me now, Mac—I'm working for your friend Danny. I've got to go—fast."

He looked as though he were going to burst into tears. "But, hell—wait...."

But he didn't try to stop me as I vaulted the counter again, ran out and ran back down the side street to the Arena.

CHAPTER FIVE
THE MURDER WAS A
PLEASURE

EVIDENTLY THEY were making a half-hearted effort to avoid attracting a crowd, because the uniformed copper on guard at the archway was inside, not out. When I swung in, he jabbed a hand at my chest and brought me to an abrupt stop. "Where do you think you're—oh, it's you? Where the hell have you been?"

I didn't bother answering him. As I ran up the eight steps, the door opened and I saw the welcome dour Scotch face of Inspector Halloran of Homicide. At least I got that one break—to have a decent cop in charge of the job.

He didn't look particularly pleased with me. His face drew down into a scowl. "Just what the hell do you think you're doing—running out on…?"

"Never mind my running out. Where is Ike?"

"Right inside there—in that filing room, wise guy. What of it? I cuffed him to a steam pipe to hold him…"

"Next time be sure you cog the cuff, stupid, and don't be in such a hurry to loot the joint. Ike is on his way to the hospital with a slug in his nut…"

He gasped, swung on the sloe-eyed Greely. "Isn't that thug in…?"

Greely jumped for the closed door of the filing room, cursing a blue streak, jerked it open and swung back toward Halloran, his brown face suddenly utterly calm.

"He's not there?" Halloran raged. Then, without waiting for an answer he swung on me. "All right, Acme. I don't know how you sneaked him out, but—start talking."

"Don't be any sappier than you have to," I snarled at him. "I had nothing to do with him—except to stop his escape and clean up this case for you. Come on," I squeezed past him and stepped into the inner office.

"Clean up?" he babbled at my heels. "What do you mean? You've got the killer?"

"No, but I damn soon will have."

The dead man had been shifted a little and now his pouchy face was tilted up at the ceiling. His coat and vest and shirt had been cut away, exposing his flabby chest and stomach. The lips of the knife wound were blue and caked. Further down on his side was the corkscrew pucker of an old bullet wound.

I looked at the others in the room. The walnut-faced Greely was leaning in a far corner, smoking a cigarette and watching me steadily. The M.E.'s doctor was there, as well as Hudson's "house" doctor, Church, of the tired-eyes and plum-colored hair. Besides them, there were a blue-coat and a detective.

"Now, wait a minute…" Halloran snapped at me.

"Wait, hell. When you guys are so dumb you let that ape, Ike, walk out of here with the poison bottle—"

I stopped. I stopped because I was looking into the developing cupboard—and the black bottle was still lying on its side on the shelf within. It had not been moved.

I don't know how many seconds I stood there, my mouth open—before clear white light suddenly cascaded with a wild rush into my mind. I gasped, as I suddenly saw the incredible, nightmare picture, from first to last. I swung around—and the phone rang.

The sloe-eyed, dark-faced Lieutenant Greely moved quickly toward it, but Inspector Halloran snapped: "I'll take it."

He lifted the receiver to his ear and grumbled unintelligibly into it. Then he winced and held the receiver a little farther from his ear. "What?" he barked. "Don't yell, I—"

And then it was like an electric current striking the room to breathlessness as we all heard the voice that rattled in the receiver.

"Yell? Why shouldn't I yell? This is Danny Marshall. Who are you? A cop?"

The inspector said, "Yeah," and hastily covered the mouthpiece. To the detective by the door he snapped: "Trace it, fast!"

He opened his mouth to say more into the mouthpiece but the hysterical, screechy voice was already yelling again: "Well, how do you like what I did to Alec Hudson? I killed the ——, in case you don't know it. And I'll kill a dozen more of you cops before you lay a hand on me—that is, if any of you have the guts to try."

The inspector's lips were white with fury. He bit out: "We'll try all right, wise guy, when we find you."

"You don't have to find me, yellowbelly! I'm right across the street. Come and get me if you dare!"

The sound of the receiver being hung up was like a pistol shot.

HALLORAN'S FACE was starch-white as he flung down the instrument and dived for the door. His hand snatched a gun from his hip. I had just time to make a headlong leap and fling my arms wide to bar him on the threshold. "Wait—for the love of Judas, wait a minute, Inspector…!"

He roared: "Get out of my way, Acme. If that pup's where he says he is, I'm going to feed him a little lead…"

"That's just what he wants!" I yelled. "My God—don't you see? That's just what he wants! This whole set-up—the note—the call—everything—he's just asking to be shot down…"

He flung me aside with a hand like iron. "Then he's going to get just what he's asking for!"

I grabbed his coattails, was nearly jerked from my feet, but I almost sent Halloran reeling too. I grabbed his lapels, held him and railed at him: "You damn fool, this whole thing is a plant! You don't get any part of what's happened here. Listen, you lunkhead—don't grandstand! If he's hiding across the street and means what he says, he'll pick you off like shooting fish in a barrel. If you've got any brains in your head over and above those God gave oysters you'll stop acting like a raw rookie. Get on that phone and have the block surrounded. Use some sense!"

He was too seasoned a copper for that not to have its effect. The fury died out of his eyes, to be replaced by a cold, icy gleam. He said through tight teeth: "Yeah, I am acting like a sap." He turned toward the phone, dialed hastily, and barked rapid-fire orders.

When he hung up, he snatched out a watch and said: "We'll give them five minutes."

I was still with my back to the door. "You'll give them nothing," I said. "I'm going out and bring him in alive."

He went purple. "Why, you —— —— fool," he roared. "Have you lost your mind? Come back here!" as I turned and started out.

I swung back and rapped at him: "It's none of your responsibility if he knocks *me* off—but he won't."

I got as far as the door to the stairs before he got to me and swung me around. "You're not…!"

I said quietly: "Now, look, Inspector—I know exactly what I'm doing. If that kid dies, it means ten thousand dollars to Acme. If you stop me making my play to get him alive, there's going to be plenty stink raised. Acme swings a lot of weight with the commissioner. And I know what I'm doing."

His eyes were red-streaked. "Well, what in God's name *are* you doing? You stop me, and yet you—I'm not going to let you walk out there alone! There'll be twenty dolly cars here in a minute…"

"And that'll be too late. You've known me a long time, Inspector. I'm no lightbrain. That kid's a fine youngster—or he was until worry and desperation drove him a little crazy. But I can handle him. I give you my word I can handle him. I'll bring him in and give him to you—if you'll promise me one thing."

"What?"

"That you won't let any of your flatfeet here open up on him till I give the word. You can all wait right in this room—stand back so I can leave the door open and so it doesn't look from outside like there was anybody in the room. Leave the channel down the middle of the room clear, if you see what I mean. I give you my word. I know I can bring him in."

His face was a frenzied mask of indecision. "But…"

"Will you promise me that? No shooting till I say so? Believe me, I know all the answers."

He swallowed. "If you're sure…" He still couldn't quite believe me.

I nailed him down. "O.K. It's a promise. Now call that flatfoot in from outside. I want nobody in the corridor, or on the steps. Come on, man—or you'll be responsible for the most ghastly blunder ever made in this town."

I guess I hypnotized him with the driving intensity of my voice. Still looking frightened to death, he opened the door without taking his eyes from me, called the bluecoat in.

"Get back around the walls," I snapped at the others and, when everything was arranged, I added: "Remember—no shooting until I say so. Right, Inspector?"

He licked his lips, nodded.

"That goes," I said over my shoulder as I walked out, "even if he starts shooting at me—and don't forget it!"

I was down the stairs and crouched in the archway entrance before he could make any suitable answer to that one. My heart was hammering like a riveting machine—but I knew I was right. I had to be right.

I DIDN'T see him—and then I did. A dark little huddle on the sidewalk directly opposite. I caught the sheen of metal. I said: "Danny—this is the insurance dick that saw you earlier."

I heard the sharp catch of his breath. Then he spat at me: "So what? Dicks are all alike to me. I'll bump any of you…"

"Better hear what I have to say first," I told him. My gun was up my right sleeve. My hands hung empty. "The racket's flopped, Danny. It isn't going to work."

"Racket?" He raved. "Work? It worked, all right. I killed the rat, didn't I? What do you mean it isn't going to work? What's the matter? Haven't you the guts to come and get me. Then try this!"

Flame roared in his hand. The bullet whacked into the stone of the building behind me, went whining away in a ricochet. I was cold sweat from head to foot. I fought to keep my voice clear and steady. "Cut it out, Danny. You know you're not going to burn me down." I took a step backward and was again under the arch.

He shrilled: "—— —— you! I *will* burn you down!"

His gun exploded again. I heard Inspector Halloran moan behind me as a chip of stone flew from the archway.

"Behave, Danny. I know you're not a killer. You're a decent guy—or you were until you went off your head and decided to cash in on your insurance so your wife would have the money for the kid."

He almost choked. I heard him panting. "I dunno what you're talking about," he cried wildly. "I killed him—and you aren't going to take me alive. The —— had it coming to him and he got it…"

"You don't begin to know how *much* he had it coming to him, Danny," I said softly. "Listen to me, for just one minute. Did you, about eight months ago, make a twenty-dollar parlay bet on two horses in the Windsor Stakes?"

"Bet? Horses?" He started to laugh raucously. "Horses he talks about…"

"Answer me! Did you make that bet? The horses were Mangrum and Brother's Keeper."

"How do I know? I made a hundred bets with the louse. I bought policy numbers, too. He practically made us, so he could chisel out his cheap little graft…"

"I know all that. But you've got to remember—did you bet on those horses—in the winter book—eight months ago."

For just a second he hesitated, then the crazy hysterical note jumped back into his voice. "I don't know. Maybe I did. I bet on some horses in that race. What of it? I killed him—and I'm giving it to you—now!"

Again his gun thundered—just as sirens started into screaming life all around us, at a distance.

I let my gun slip into my hand, and I yelled, "All right, if you've got to have it," and fired three times. Each time I took a backward step, crouching over. He was sobbing, panting now, coming after me, his gun banging—and the bullets going wild. I kept yelling, "Damn you, I'll get you," and firing over his head.

And then I was backed up the steps and standing in the doorway, facing him over my gun as he stood in the arch. His face was a white, mad mask, his eyes a madman's eyes, streaming tears. He screamed, "Damn you, I *will*..." and I think he really would have given it to me if he could. But I had counted his bullets like a hawk and I was almost certain he was using a seven-shot automatic and they were all gone. As his hammer fell on a dead shell, I dived.

He screamed, clawed, tried to bite and gouge me as we went down, but I knocked most of the breath out of him, had him tied up in a full-nelson before he knew it and had jerked him to his feet.

EVEN AS sirens screamed to a halt around us, I rushed him up the steps and into the office. I let him go and he pitched on forward onto his face.

The plum-haired Doctor Church cried out wildly, "Oh, my God, he'll kill us all," and snatched Inspector Halloran's gun from his hand and tried to fire.

I had very carefully saved two of my bullets for this possible contingency. I aimed very carefully and pumped them both. The first broke the doctor's arm just above the wrist, and the second shot a foot from under him, crashing him down.

Halloran said: "My God—what...?"

"Listen to me," I flung at him, "and listen fast. I can twist this thing to make the police department a laughingstock and worse. You've fumbled every part of it. I'll tell you exactly what's happened here—and you can claim you worked it out yourself—on one condition.

"Danny Marshall here made a twenty-dollar bet in the winter books. It was a long shot, hopeless bet at that time. But it suddenly grew up about three or four months ago when one of the long shots turned out to be a good thing being run under cover by some smart Detroit bookies. If you don't get the importance of that, think of it this way. Danny had bet twenty dollars parlayed on two horses at twenty to one and forty to one. That adds up to eight hundred to one in case you're slow at mathematics. At the time the bet was made it was a sucker bet—hopeless. Four months ago it suddenly changed complexion and looked like a whale of a good bet.

"If you listened to me out there you know by now that Danny forgot he'd even made the bet. It's a cinch that Alec Hudson discovered that fact somehow. He discovered it—and his chiseling soul nearly went crazy. He went to work to muscle Danny out of it.

"There was no particular genius to the rotten, lousy way he took to do it—but it worked. He set up that scene with Danny's wife, took a lacing from the kid—simply and solely so he would have an excuse to scare the kid away—out of town or somewhere, or at least fix him so he wouldn't dare come back even if sometime he did remember the bet. He put the boots to the two of them, even kept them on the run by sending his strong-arm guys after them.

He figured to keep their minds so damned occupied that they wouldn't have time to get to mulling over old bets. The louse succeeded, beautifully. Too damned beautifully. Because he drove Danny here into a corner. No money, blacklisted at all the places he might have got work, a wife he was crazy about and a baby on the way. He went off his head.

"He had only one hope in the whole world of raising money—his life insurance. He couldn't suicide—the policy would be void if he did that under three years. So he took this insane way out. He came down here and tried to kill Alec Hudson— Shut up. I said *tried* to kill and that's what I mean. The idea was that he would deliberately kill, then make it clear that he had, and then taunt the cops into going after him with guns. He didn't want a trial. He didn't want to be hung up in jail. He had to get that money for his wife quicker than that. He deliberately planned to be shot down resisting arrest— Damn it, will you shut up!

"You saw what happened just now. He got his fury up enough to make him take an ineffectual stab at a heel like Alec Hudson, but it wasn't in him to shoot down a cop. He didn't even try to hit me."

"Wait—wait!" Halloran shouted. "What do you mean—ineffectual? He killed Hudson or—or did he? What…?"

"The hell he did. He stuck the knife in him, yes. But you aren't sap enough to believe he smeared poison all over it first. He didn't even know enough to stab straight at the heart and the wound he made wouldn't have done Alec much harm. But Alec's bodyguard Ike came up and found him and called that one"— I thumbed contemptuously at the cowering doctor— "and he saw his chance. Hudson was still plenty alive, then.

"Naturally, he had to frame something that wouldn't let any doubt in. He was wise enough not to take the knife out and make another wound. He thought of the cyanide in the darkroom—a thing that all the employees in the joint would be expected to know about, including Danny. He figured to run a little of that into the wound and thus make damn sure of killing him instantly."

THE DOCTOR burst out hoarsely: "Are you going to listen to this madman? He's trying to protect his wretched insurance company. Danny killed Hudson—this man is crazy…"

"I *was* crazy," I admitted. "I was crazy because I saw Danny uptown, after he thought he'd killed Hudson. I came down here, nearly an hour later. There was saliva on Hudson's chin and sweat on his forehead. He hadn't been dead any hour. But that's not what tripped you, wise guy. What tripped you was that that cyanide in the cupboard there was two years old and had about as much potency after this time as water. You had to get your own stuff, pour some of it in that bottle and some in the wound. Where you fell down was in being caught here by me, then by the wise cop over there—whom Danny himself, incidentally, tipped off by phone, knowing he was a friend of Alec's—and then by the Homicide Squad. You still had the extra bottle here—dynamite if you were caught with it. So when there was a chance of Ike getting out, you slipped it to him to dispose of. Unfortunately, he didn't get a chance, because I was right on his tail. He's in the hospital now with a bullet wound in his head, and here"—I produced the bottle— "is your property. I don't know what angle of this rat's crookedness made you want to kill him—but since seeing that old bullet wound in his side, I can make a shrewd guess. Am I right?"

His head went down and his "Yes," was scarcely audible. "The—the devil came to me two years ago and offered me a grand to get a slug out for him and keep quiet. As soon as it was done, he not only paid me nothing but made me work for him. It would cost me my license for not reporting it—and he could turn me up at any time. *He* had committed no crime. He—ever since then he's made me—do illegal things for his friends, and for him. I—God help me, I went crazy when I saw the chance to get out from under."

I swung on Halloran. "All right, Inspector. There's your story—and if you don't get a medal on the strength of the publicity this opium dream will get, I'm crazy. How about my condition?"

"What—what is your condition?"

I turned and looked across at the flushing Greely. "This larceny expert got here ahead of Homicide and frisked the joint. Among other things, he picked up that betting-slip—the one that belongs to Danny Marshall here. I want you to make him cough it up—because the rightful owner of it can use the dough right now."

The inspector's eyes were like pinpoints of steel as he looked over at Greely.

Greely did not even try to put up an argument. He fingered the slip from his pocket and laid it on the desk. "I wasn't pinching it. I just saw it and thought it might be evidence of some kind. Why, this is the first time I even realized what the figures and things on it meant. If it belongs to this youngster and is worth money—why, I'm only too glad to turn it over to him."

I damn near choked on that one.